RECOIL

Joanne Macgregor

OTHER YOUNG ADULT BOOKS BY THIS AUTHOR
Scarred (2015, KDP)
Fault Lines (2016, Protea)
Rock Steady (2013, Protea)
Turtle Walk (2011, Protea)

If you would like to receive my author's newsletter, with tips on great books, a behind-the-scenes look at my writing and publishing processes, and advance notice of new books, giveaways and special offers, then sign up at my website: www.joannemacgregor.com.

First published in 2016 by KDP

ISBN: 978-0-620-70289-8
ISBN: 978-0-620-70290-4 (ebook)

www.joannemacgregor.com

"If we let things terrify us, life will not be worth living."
Seneca (Roman philosopher, mid-1st century AD)

"The spirit of resistance to government is so valuable
on certain occasions that I wish it to be always kept alive.
It will often be exercised when wrong, but better so
than not to be exercised at all."
Thomas Jefferson

Part One

Chapter 1

The Kill Shot

Why is it that even when you get what you thought you wanted, it never works out the way you thought it would?

That Sunday, two days before the black van came for me, all I wanted was to kill Jakhil. Because pancakes for breakfast are good, Sunday morning reruns of *Supernatural* are good, finding the perfect jeans in my size and on sale at Hunter.com is really good, but finally killing Jakhil?

That would be better than good. It would be awesome.

So I waited, as still and quiet as death, for the perfect moment to take the shot. He was out there somewhere, the enemy who had invaded our world, and he had to be stopped.

I had been stalking my prey for hours, and preparing for years — honing my skill with drill after drill, target after target, shot after shot. My eyes burned with fatigue, my throat was parched and my stomach empty. Sweat trickled down behind my goggles, but I kept myself motionless and focused.

I'd tracked him over the course of days, and I was not about to get myself shot by giving away my position. Three times before, I'd had the chance to take him down, and each time I'd blown it with some stupid mistake. The first time, he'd pinpointed my position and sent a round into my thigh. The next time, I'd taken the shot and missed. And in our last encounter, he'd melted away into the background before I could line up a good angle. Today I was determined to get it right.

So no matter how loudly my hollow stomach growled, I was not going to reach for the pack of candy lying beside me. Tempting morsels of sweetness — creamy, melting milk chocolate and sticky, salty peanut-butter. No, I was not even going to think about that.

I was also not going to hand over the take-down to the other sniper that I knew was camped out somewhere to my right, near the platform. We might be on the same side in this war, but Jakhil was mine. A *whup-whup-whup* noise signaled the approach of a chopper. Was it from his army, or mine?

My enemy was hiding somewhere in the deserted railway yard ahead of me — about 700 meters away, I estimated. I had long since stopped thinking of distance in feet or yards. Modern snipers used meters. I studied the scene through the high magnification of my scope, trying to identify the spots I would have chosen to hide. Maybe there — at eleven o'clock, in the dark shadows behind the open sliding door of a freight car. Or perhaps to my right, at two o'clock, behind the crumbling walls of the deserted station's ticket booth, or in the shade cast by any of the sidelined passenger cars, standing empty and abandoned on the unused sidings. I scanned systematically, side to side and near to far, for the usual giveaways: shine, movement, contrast to background, or the distinctive head-and-shoulders outline of a target.

I forced myself not to look up at the chopper. It was a distraction I couldn't afford. Silently, I cursed the downdraft it pushed across my field of action. The wind whipped dust and old bits of paper and debris up into the air, obscuring my vision, and it would have unpredictable effects on my shot.

A movement down on the railway siding caught my eye. One

of Jakhil's small robotic reptiles scurried mechanically across the rails. Through the rifle's scope I could see the unblinking green lights of the repbot's twin "eyes". Was it merely reconnoitering the field of action, transmitting back the same information about conditions that I was trying to ascertain manually? Or had he sent it as a decoy, to tempt me into taking a shot? Either way, I should ignore it.

Just as I made the decision, the robot exploded into fragments of steel and wire and microchips as the loud shot of a rifle cracked the air, followed a split second later by another report and a grunt from nearby. Damn. I hadn't wanted Striker22 to get the shot, but I hadn't wanted him to be shot either. He'd fallen for the lure and Jakhil had spotted him in an instant. Now it was just the two of us left in this battle to the death.

I refocused my scope on the scene, searching the spot where, in my peripheral vision, I had caught sight of a muzzle flash. *There.* In the deep shadow of the freight car I had noted earlier, there was a contrasting patch of light and dark and the faintest glint of shine about one foot off the ground — right about where a rifle would be if the target was lying on his belly aiming out. At me.

Moving slower than the second-hand on my father's old wristwatch, I adjusted my rifle. I had studied my enemy and knew he was right-handed, so I aimed fractionally to the right of the glint, where his head and chest would be. I did the mental math — running through the calculations to account for the distance, bullet spin and drop, the fast cold air of this high altitude, and the wind kicked up by the circling chopper. Then I doped my scope, adjusting the windage dial to compensate for the air currents, and the elevation dial to offset the effect of gravity on the bullet over this distance, so that my aim would be true. Settling the rifle between my shoulder and cheek, I closed my left eye, squinted my right, and fine-tuned my aim. I pulled my attention away from everything but him and me, pushed away worries about my fellow soldier, and tuned out the noise of the helicopter. All of me was here. All there was, was now.

Deliberately relaxing my shoulders, I breathed in through my nose for a count of four, held the breath for four beats, breathed out through my mouth for four, and held for four. One more time. In … two … three … four … Hold … two … three … four … Slowly out … two … three … four … Hold … two … three …

In the pause between breaths, in the space between heartbeats, I squeezed the trigger.

I watched the faint vapor trail of the spinning round as it travelled through the air and disappeared into the shadows of the freight car.

A second later, all hell broke loose.

Bells, alarms, flashing lights and the message box spelling out in bold, red, 3D letters: *YOU WIN!*

What?

I yanked off the virtual reality goggles, stared at the message on the screen, which was a little fuzzy now without the special lenses.

YOU WIN!

I screamed and punched the air, snatched up the realistic-looking sniper rifle — my game console's wireless controller — and crowed, "I win! I win! I win!" into it as if it was a microphone, all the while victory-dancing a small circle between my bed and desk.

My mother came rushing through the door, her face pinched tight and as white as her floury hands.

"Are you alright? You screamed!"

"I won! I won The Game!"

"Jinxy Emma James! You nearly scared the life out of me. I thought for sure you must have seen a —"

"Mom, you don't get it. I killed Jakhil. Me, little old Jinxy-me!"

"You and that blessed game!" She wiped her hands on her apron. "If you need me, I'll be in the kitchen, having a stiff bourbon for shock. And counting my new gray hairs — for which I hold you responsible, young lady."

"I win, I win, I *win*!" I resumed my war dance. I needed music, applause, fireworks.

Robin ambled into my room, running a hand through his rumpled hair and looking, as always, as sleepy as if he had just woken up from a ten-hour nap.

"How is it possible that we're related?" he said.

He yawned, clearly unimpressed at my uncontrolled display of glee. We're twins, and although we both have blond hair and blue eyes, we're about as un-identical in our natures as it's possible to get.

"I won!" I yelled at him. "I killed Jakhil!"

"You won The Game?" He wasn't yawning now, no sir. He was staring at me in shock. And, if I do say so myself, awe. Robin might not be a sniper — he played the Game as a programmer when he played it at all — but he, unlike my mother, at least got what this meant.

"I did! I'm the first sniper to take the leader down in eighteen months! That's one and a half years, brother! Woohoo!" I sparred with the air, hugged Robin, and then started my war-dance again.

"You know what this means, Jinxy? You're going to PlayState!"

As he said the words, my screen flashed a new message to the accompaniment of a repetitive bleep.

Congratulations! Jinx E. James, you have killed Jakhil, won The Game, and qualified for the ultimate prize of a real-life simulated sniper mission at PlayState's Southern Sector Headquarters, along with three of your highest-ranking competitors. Please be ready for collection on April 3 at 09:15. Full details and a liability waiver have been forwarded to your registered guardian, Marion James (mother), but you are directly advised that the wearing of Personal Protective Equipment is mandatory.

I screamed again.

Chapter 2

Threes

Four years ago, when I was twelve, three things happened that changed everything.

The plague began.

My dad died from a heart attack. He went to work one day and just never came home.

And then my mom sort of sank inside herself for a long while.

They say bad things happen in threes.

Three: the number of (confirmed) ways in which *Mononegavirales* Zoonotic Viral Hemorrhagic Fever (aka rat fever) spreads: contact with bodily fluids, contact with airborne and surface contagion, and bites. The pathogen was a Biosafety Level 4 hot agent, a superbug combination of Ebola, Bolivian Hemorrhagic Fever (black typhus) and rabies, that had been engineered by our enemies to decimate our population. In the early days when the terrorist attacks were first launched and before the borders were sealed, infected agents entered the country as human suicide bombs, infecting as many people as they could. They even took civilian hostages in supermarkets and subway trains and once, horribly, kids in a school, injecting their victims with plague serum before turning them loose to become human virus bombs themselves. These days, the terrs mostly use rats.

Three: the average number of days after infection that it takes the virus to incubate. Once infection begins, with a relentless headache and high fever, it soon penetrates the brain's blood-barrier, sending the victims into an increasingly demented and uncontrolled state until they die from multi-organ failure and hemorrhage.

Three: the number of mega-sectors the US was divided into for better control and security: the Northeast, the Mid-and-West, and the South, where I live.

Three: the number of remote, ultra-high security prisons resurrected from their mothballed status: Guantanamo Bay, Alcatraz and Florence ADX. No facility was too remote or too severe for the terrorists who had infected our population and continued to try to do so.

Three hundred thousand and rising: the estimated number of plague-infected giant rats believed to be running around our sector, biting wildlife and pets. And, of course, people.

Three: the number of rat poisons against which the mutant rats already appeared to have developed an immunity.

The total number of people who have died from the plague in the US alone? 12.5 million.

I guess not all bad things come in threes, after all.

Chapter 3

Rabid

I was already waiting at the front window, Robin at my side and Mom checking the fit of my respirator, when at precisely 09:15, the transport pulled up in our driveway. It was a huge black Hummer with tinted windows and PlayState's distinctive yellow-and-red logo emblazoned on the side.

"Cool," said Robin, nodding his approval.

"Very," I said, still amazed that this was actually happening to me.

"Are you sure you won't wear your full-face respirator?" my mother asked for the umpteenth time. There were shadows under her eyes — she'd probably kept herself awake half the night worrying about all the things that could go wrong on my adventure today.

"Mo-om, we've talked about this. I'm going to play a game at PlayState's headquarters, I'm not going to a hospital or Q-bay. Besides, this thing is bad enough," I said, adjusting my half face-piece respirator over my nose and mouth. My series 7000E was ugly, even though I'd tried jazzing it up with stickers on the sides. I hated wearing the thing — it was stuffy and it muffled my voice. I made some Darth Vader breathing noises, trying to get a smile out of my mom, whose anxiety level today was hovering somewhere between *extreme nervous agitation* and *completely frantic.*

"May the force be with you, my child," Robin said.

"I still think you should consider safety glasses and booties," my mother said.

"Not going to happen." I pulled on my latex gloves and waved my protected hands at her. "See? Double thick. I'll be safe."

"She'll be fine," said Robin, slinging an arm around Mom's shoulders, perhaps to hold her back from tackling me by the ankles and trapping me inside the house.

I grabbed my backpack and the liability waiver forms my mother had reluctantly signed, and headed for the door, eager to be gone. Eager to be somewhere other than inside these four walls.

"Be careful!" Mom said as I turned the anti-microbial copper handle of the door to the decontamination unit and stepped inside.

"Be awesome!" Robin called.

I waved, closed the seal behind me, and waited until the airlock on the front door of the decon unit released. After suiting up in Personal Protection Equipment (mask, gloves, and one of the disposable PPE suits Mom insisted on), going out of the house was easy. Once you stepped outside the decon unit, its door sealed again and it automatically went hot-box, flooding the cubicle with sterilizing ozone and ultra-violet light. Coming back inside was always more of a mission. When I returned to the house this evening, I'd have to do a mini-strip inside the cramped cubicle. I'd shove my PPE suit and gloves into the disposal bin for later destruction in the household incinerator in the basement, place my shoes and respirator on the high mesh shelf directly below the lights, and I'd have to hold my breath and stand still, protective goggles over my eyes, for sixty seconds while I was sprayed with decon mist and then given a low intensity UV bath for fifteen seconds. When the door popped open, Mom would be waiting inside the house with hand sanitizer and disinfectant throat spray, while behind me the decon unit would seal and go hot again to sterilize my shoes and respirator.

Now, outside the house, I stood for a few moments allowing my eyes to adjust to the dazzling light, loving the feel of the early spring sunshine warming me through my PPE suit and the unfamiliar feel of the breeze on the skin of my forehead. Somewhere nearby, birds were singing. It was always a shock to the senses to be outside. On any other day, I would have slowed my walk and enjoyed the rare experience, but that day I was too excited. I hurried over to the Hummer. The side door of the vehicle slid open as I approached, and closed behind me as soon as I had swung myself inside.

There were already two people inside. The boy had dark-blond hair cut very short, and he was big, with broad shoulders, a wide chest and large hands. He looked maybe two years older than my sixteen, and the girl looked like she might be nineteen or even twenty. She was slim with short, spiky black hair and warm, deep-brown eyes. They were emphasized with purple eyeliner, and she had a tattoo that looked like a Chinese character at the outer corner of her left eye. Her latex gloves were in a trendy zebra-striped pattern; the double-thick gloves Mom insisted that we wore because they were more resistant to tearing and perforation didn't come in anything but sickly beige or surgical green.

Both of them were wearing only E97 respirators — the basic, form-fitted, particle-excluding gauze mask. I knew this would happen. My respirator was complete overkill, but Mom was so paranoid, she'd never have allowed me out wearing anything less.

"Hi," the girl said, "I'm Leya."

"Bruce," said the boy.

"Hi. I'm Jinx," I said, and bumped elbows with each of them in greeting.

"Welcome on board, Jinx," said the driver, who was also wearing an E97. "You excited?"

"Crazy excited!" I said. Then I felt a blush rising — maybe it wasn't cool to be so enthusiastic. "Are we going to be playing together?" I asked, waving a finger between the three of us in the back.

"That's right, today is just for snipers," the driver said, as he backed down our driveway.

There were different roles you could play in The Game. Most kids played as soldiers in the war against the Alien Axis Army. I'd only ever been interested in playing as a specialist soldier, a sniper, but you could also play as a spy — intercepting the calls, texts and mails of Jakhil's invaders; as a code-breaker; or as an intel agent — analyzing the data at a high level, looking for patterns and predicting skirmishes, attacks and the enemy's next move. You could even play Ops Management — planning and distributing troops, equipment, and food; building army bases; and overseeing all the operations that kept the war game going. It was rumored that if you were good at code-breaking or programming, you could apply for training at The Advanced Specialized Training Academy, and get a great job working for the government afterwards. We snipers just played for fun though. And bragging rights.

The Game had existed before the plague began, in a really simple version. But after kids stopped going out to clubs and movies and malls, home entertainment took off in a big way. Soon, an updated virtual reality version of The Game was released with awesome graphics, multiple roles to play and a new Big Bad — Jakhil and his invading Alien Axis Army. And within a year of the plague breaking out, it seemed like every kid in the US was playing.

It was a fantastic game — all the parts and roles intersected with each other and you could track how the overall war was going, and there was something for everyone. Recently, they had even brought out fun cartoon versions for really young players.

Robin had tried sniping and code-breaking before he'd settled into playing as a programmer, though I reckon he would have played as a poet if that was possible. He was excellent at writing code, but not as obsessed with playing as most kids were. I was pretty much addicted to The Game — I played it every spare moment I had, especially since Dad died. When I played, I didn't have to remember, or think, or even feel very much. Not about losing Dad, or worrying about Mom, or wondering whether I'd be stuck at home for the rest of my life.

"We've got one more stop to make across town," the driver said, "and then we'll head back to headquarters and it'll be game-time for all four of you. Strap yourself in."

I clicked my seatbelt closed. Not wanting to appear unfriendly by taking a seat further back, I had taken one of the front seats which faced backwards, directly opposite Leya and Bruce, but I regretted it now. Bruce was staring at me intently, scrutinizing the cobalt-blue streaks which striped my long blond hair, looking into my eyes, and assessing my height —about three inches shorter than his own — as if trying to place me.

"I've never met you," he said.

I shrugged. That didn't surprise me, I didn't meet many people.

"It's funny," he said. "I live only a few blocks away from you, but I've never met you at one of the socials."

"Yeah, well, my mom's not too keen on us leaving the house unless we absolutely have to."

We were obliged by Health and Wellbeing Regulation 223 to attend a mandated minimum number of socials — six per year — but Mom made sure that we didn't go to a dance or a game more. She was convinced that Robin and I would contract rat fever if we were out of her sight for more than a few minutes at a time. Today I'd be gone for hours, and that would be hard for her. Robin didn't much mind being stuck at home. He was too introverted to find the socials anything but an ordeal, and usually took a book along with him so he could find a quiet corner and read while the rest of us used the opportunity to "practice our interpersonal social skills" and tried to "meet others with a view to pursuing relationships with them", or whatever it was the regulation advocated.

"Anyway," I added, "you may well have met me. With these things," I tapped my respirator, "it's hard to tell."

"I'd have remembered," said Bruce with a smile that was almost a leer. He looked me up and down as if to emphasize his point.

His unwavering attention made me uncomfortable. I exchanged a glance with Leya, who raised her eyebrows and tilted her head at Bruce as if to say, *"Get him."*

"Are you going to the social next Saturday?" Bruce asked me. "It's a picnic in the city park. I'll be there."

"I don't know. Yeah, maybe," I said.

I stared out the window, hoping he would stop looking at me and drop the subject. Our westbound highway was largely empty. Six-lane traffic jams were a thing of the past — the upside of a pandemic which kept people inside. It wasn't a scenic drive, but still it was good to see something more than the unchanging sameness of home. As we drove under an overpass, I read graffiti sprayed in black paint on the passing pillars: *World-War-Rat-atat,* and directly beneath a security camera on the wall to our right as we emerged, someone had painted the message: *One Nation under Observation.*

"We could hang out together," Bruce persisted.

I looked an appeal at Leya. In the unwritten code of friendly behavior, girls were supposed to have each other's back at moments like this, weren't they?

"We —" Bruce began, but Leya interrupted.

"So, when did you qualify?"

"Day before yesterday. I must have been the last of the four," I said, relieved at the change of subject.

"You're not … You're not the one who killed Jakhil, are you?" she asked, sounding incredulous.

I nodded and shrugged. I was trying to act casual but beneath the respirator, I was grinning.

"Dude!" she said, leaning over to bump elbows with me again. "Props!"

"Thanks."

"You won? You?" said Bruce.

"Yeah," I said, trying not to take offense at the note of disbelief in his voice. "I got lucky, I guess."

"No way was that just good luck. You must be hot, girl!" said Leya.

I tried to look modest. "You guys must be really good too, to qualify."

"I took out my fair share of the invaders and repbots," said Leya.

"Oh, I'm good alright," said Bruce, nodding and smiling. "And I'm looking forward to getting my game on with you."

Was I imagining the double meaning? I could be. Being cooped up inside and kept away from others for the last four years hadn't given me much experience dealing with people face-to-face. I frowned at him.

"I like a challenge," he said to me. It sounded a bit like a threat.

I asked Leya about her Game history, and for a while we three chatted about our favorite hobby, trading war stories and comparing scores. I heard enough to know that while Leya was no slouch in the sniping department, Bruce, unless he was exaggerating, was an exceptional player. On another day he might well have been the one to take down Jakhil.

We were still talking about The Game and whether Jakhil's second-in-command would automatically become commander of the Alien Axis Army now that he was dead, or whether there might be a leadership challenge, when we pulled up in front of a huge two-story brick house in a subdivision of similar McMansions.

"Check it out," said Bruce, peering out the window, "it's a starter-castle."

The boy who came out the front door decon unit was tall with orange hair. When he got closer, I saw that his eyebrows and lashes were pale, and his skin was the color of milk — I reckoned this boy saw the sun even less than I did. He, too, looked to be a couple of years older than me, and he also wore only an E97 mask. I was beginning to feel like an idiot, like an overprotected little girl.

The new guy's name was Graham. He seemed friendly enough, but I soon grew irritated by his constant fidgeting. He tapped his feet, fiddled with the cuff of his gloves and worried at a loose thread in the seat upholstery. Bruce studied him for a few minutes, asked about his game scores, and then apparently lost interest and returned to looking at me. Graham told us in detail all about the formulas and calculations he used when playing.

"It's all mathematical," he kept saying. "It's a science."

He had just said it again when we stopped at a traffic light and Leya pointed out of the window and said, "Look."

We all turned to follow her gaze. At once, the driver checked the doors were locked, then reached for his phone to call in the sighting, relaying our exact GPS coordinates to the operator while we stared at the man clinging to the pole of a street light a few feet away from us. On the left side of his body, he was wearing exactly half of a stained, white PPE suit, which looked like it had been torn vertically down the middle seam. His right side was completely naked.

"Ugh, gagnasty," said Graham, swallowing hard. "Imagine what he smells like."

The man's lips were moving furiously. Was he literally talking to a lamp post? Then he banged his head against the pole. And again. Over and over he banged it, perhaps in time to the inner rhythm of some hallucinated music that only he could hear. The skin of his forehead split open, and blood ran down into his eyes and mouth and beard and dripped onto the remnants of the PPE suit and the skin of his chest.

Without warning, he turned and hurled himself at the van, banged on its sides and windows, and screamed loudly enough for us to hear it through the sealed windows and reinforced panels. His bulging eyes were wild, unseeing, and washed red with blood. His skin was stippled with the purple-red rash and blotched bruises of the disease. His swollen lips twisted and split open as he howled. Then he slammed his head against my window, and the driver cursed and pulled off at top speed. Immediately he called ahead for a decontamination and disinfectant squad to meet us at our destination.

"Effing rabid!" said Bruce, his face twisted with disgust.

I stared at the smear of blood on the window. It looked black against the tinted glass. My heart was thudding somewhere in the region of my throat, and I fought the urge to throw up.

"I've never seen a rabid before," said Graham who looked, if possible, even paler than before.

"Don't call him that. He's a human being," I said.

"Not anymore he isn't," said Bruce. "They should take them all out." He mimed aiming a rifle out the window and taking a shot, his lips popping a sound.

"How can you *say* that?"

"What?" Bruce held up his hands. "It's not like there's a cure for rat fever. Might as well put them down and save them the suffering. We do it for rabid animals, why not people?"

"*Put them down*, dude? Really?" said Leya. She turned to face Bruce, or maybe she was turning her back on the window so she didn't have to see the blood. "Talk about a mouth-fart."

"They're people. They have a right to compassion and proper treatment," I said.

Bruce made a dismissive noise. "What treatment?"

"President Hawke said they're making progress with developing a vaccine."

"As fast as they isolate and study the virus, it mutates. My aunt is an epidemiologist at the CDC, and she told me it evolves in two ways: gradually through random mutation, and very rapidly as different strains of the virus. It can even swap genes inside a single animal or person. Nature is always one step ahead," said Graham. He sounded almost smug.

"One day there'll be a cure," I said.

"One day in the next week?" Bruce mocked. "By then, that one will be dead."

"He might live," I said. It was extremely rare, but some survived the initial illness.

"You can't call that living. Going blind and lying like a dead vegetable with your skin peeling off. Just existing for a few more months until pneumonia or rotting bedsores take you out. There'll never be a cure for that kind of brain damage. Once they've gone rabid, there's no coming back. They're not human anymore, they're oxygen thieves."

"You're wrong. That man is someone's son, maybe someone's father or husband or brother."

"Not for long he isn't," said Bruce.

"For an average of thirteen days and two hours," said Graham. He was picking bits of lint off his PPE suit.

"You don't agree with him, do you?" I asked Leya.

"Mostly I just feel really sorry for them. And their families," she said.

"Me too, it's freaking tragic."

"Well, of course I feel *sorry* for them. Everyone does," said Bruce. "But I think we should rather use all the money we put into trying to treat them and keeping the survivors alive into research. You know, trying to find a cure, or come up with a vaccine or treatment that actually works. Or into fighting the terrs."

I was only half-listening. I'd heard all the arguments before — or, at least, read them on online forums and discussion boards aflame with the debate. We never spoke about the plague at home. Whenever conversation approached the topic, even tangentially, Mom would change the subject or leave the room, clearly upset, so Robin and I had learned not to mention it in front of her.

"Hey Jinx," Leya said to me, "you're really upset. Big hug." People didn't give hugs anymore, they only said them.

"It's just … It could be any one of us."

"Huh, not if I can help it," said Bruce.

"We're here," said Graham, and I turned to look out a window. One without a smear of deadly blood.

Chapter 4

The Weapons

PlayState's headquarters were located on a large, wooded area of land a couple of miles down a private road. As the Hummer paused for the security check at the gate, we all craned our necks to get a better view. Bruce gave a low whistle, and Graham said what I was thinking.

"It looks more like a military base than a gaming company."

The perimeter fence was at least four meters high, topped with a double layer of razor wire, and then a six-strand crown of electrical fencing above that. I could see ground-level and elevated guard huts at regular intervals, pole-mounted LED floodlights and surveillance cameras everywhere — fixed on the poles beneath the lights, attached under roof eaves and on the corners of buildings. I smiled, pleased that my trained sniper's eye apparently observed details in real life too.

"Can't be too careful these days, what with industrial espionage and piracy. The Game is big business. We've even had gamers trying to break in to get their hands on new versions not yet released," the driver said over his shoulder.

We were directed to an external decontamination bay, where cleaners in full suits with integrated hoods and full-face respirators hosed down the van with kill-juice — a mixture of chemical foam and decontaminant spray. The blood was soon washed away, but the image of the man at the window remained, seared onto my mind.

Then we passed through a car wash. I enjoyed the sense of being in a watertight capsule as the van passed under the high-pressure water sprays and was slapped by the multi-colored ribbons of the gyrating cloth wraparounds. It reminded me of Sunday afternoons with Dad. He used to take Robin and me out on drives around the city, perhaps stopping at a park or a museum, and we always finished up by getting the car cleaned at the automatic carwash around the corner from our house. Every time he would buy us an ice cream. I liked one scoop each of vanilla and bubblegum, while Robin's favorites were caramel and choc-mint, and Dad preferred plain chocolate. We'd lick them down to the sugar cones while sitting inside the car as the conveyer belt pulled us through the bubbles, past the blue bristles and under the drying cloths, all the while discussing mean teachers and new friends, and why leaves turned red in autumn. Dad never gave a simple explanation when he could invent an outrageous story, and wouldn't stop his exaggerations until we were wriggling and giggling. Then we would drive home in the gleaming car, him singing his favorite show tunes, Robin nibbling his cone and reading, and me licking around my lips for any remaining traces of sweetness. Damn, I missed Dad. I missed those times.

Graham, I noticed now, did not seem to be enjoying the carwash. He had stopped fidgeting and was gripping his knees, staring fixedly at the floor. Claustrophobic? The boy was tightly wound, no doubt about it.

We emerged from the decontamination bay and took the road leading around the right of the main building, following colorful signs reading "To the Gaming Zone", and finally pulled to a halt outside what looked like a supersized warehouse.

We climbed out of the van, Graham jiggling, Bruce cricking his neck, and Leya and I stretching the kinks out of our muscles. A middle-aged man was waiting for us at the entrance, standing very straight and tall, with his feet apart and his hands clasped behind his back. Beside him stood a younger man and woman. All three wore black jump-suits, with the small red-and-yellow PlayState logo high on their right sleeves, as well as protective gloves and black respirator masks. The older man was completely bald, or perhaps he shaved his head. It shone as brightly as his polished boots in the sunshine. His eyes were a very dark brown, maybe even black, and they studied each of us in turn. Then he pulled his respirator to rest below his chin, and a wide smile, startling in its suddenness, cracked his mouth below a neatly-trimmed, dark mustache.

"Welcome, gamers," he said. "Welcome to PlayState and to your sniper simulation exercise — the prize for your exceptional abilities and achievements. This here is Juan and Fiona. I'm Wayne Adler, but you can call me Sarge. We'll be your guides, instructors and opponents today." His smile vanished as rapidly as it had appeared.

"Pleased to meet you, sir," said Bruce, stepping forward to bump elbows.

Leya followed suit, but I settled for a nod — I hadn't been within sneezing distance of an unmasked person, other than my brother and my mother, in years — and Graham stared at the ground, where his foot rubbed at some gravel.

"Come on inside," said Sarge. "Y'all can grab a cup of coffee and a bagel, and get geared up before we start killing each other." He barked a laugh and pulled his mask back over his nose and mouth.

Once we'd each passed through the decon unit at the entrance, Sarge took us to a changing room of sorts and told us to help ourselves to coffee and snacks from a refreshment table in the corner. I grabbed a bagel with cream cheese filling and popped another, unsliced and unfilled, into a side pocket of my suit along with a bottle of water.

While we ate, pulling our masks down to take bites and sips, Sarge tossed us each a package with a luminous green *STERILIZED* sticker on the outside. Inside was a pair of protective goggles, a helmet and a disposable jumpsuit to pull on over our clothes. My jumpsuit was blue, Leya's was green, Graham got yellow, and Bruce was given a red one. The bright colors would stand out in any game that involved finding and taking out targets. Sarge and the two other instructors kept their black suits on, which would give them a real advantage in the exercise, because Sarge had explained that we four would be playing in a team against the three of them.

"You look hot in blue, Jinx. It makes your eyes, like, really blue," said Bruce.

I had no idea how to respond, so I said nothing. I pulled on my goggles, readjusted my mask, and fastened the strap on my helmet.

The female instructor, Fiona, gave us protective vests to fasten on the outside of our suits. These, at least, were black.

"They're not proper body armor or anything," she said, "but they'll give you some protection — those peas sting! The rifles and the game arena are as sterile as we can reasonably get them, but you are advised to keep your goggles, masks and gloves on at all times during the exercise."

Finally, Sarge handed us our weapons.

"Here, Blondie," he said as he passed me mine, "or maybe I should call you Blue?" he said, pointing at my streaked hair and suit. And eyes, I suppose.

I held the rifle between my knees while I quickly braided my hair and doubled up the loop to tie it up against my neck, so as to make it less conspicuous and keep it out of my way. Then I picked up the rifle and weighed it in my hands, testing the heft and size. Although it was about the same size as the simulation rifle of The Game, it was definitely heavier, and the metal grips were cool under fingers used to the plastic gaming weapon. I lifted it to my shoulder and looked through the scope, though it was meant for distances exponentially greater than the length of a locker room.

All four of us were doing the same. I wasn't sure if any of the others had ever held a real rifle before, but for me this was the first time. I was a real-rifle virgin about to fire my first real shot. Only, of course, I wasn't.

"What you got there," said Sarge, "is what we call a pea-shooter. It's a decommissioned M24 sniper rifle modified to fire paintball ammunition."

Beside me, Bruce groaned in disappointment. What had he expected — that we would be turned loose to fire live rounds at each other?

"All the rifle scopes have been zeroed to fifty meters for you. Go collect your ammo from Juan. Three magazines of twenty rounds each, two for practice and one for the game, and in the same color as your suits. That way we know who took which shot."

"This is beyond radical. This is wicked!" said Leya.

I fell in line behind the others and collected my perfectly round, pea-sized ammunition balls, then watched carefully as Sarge showed us how to click the magazines of ammunition into the base of the rifle. Bruce's practiced movements told me he already knew how rifle parts fitted together, but I didn't. In The Game, the magazines and the rounds had been virtual. You reloaded by clicking on an icon on the screen. I imitated Sarge's actions, then tucked the spare magazines into the breast pocket of my suit.

"You've got all the ammo you're going to get, so don't go wasting it." Sarge fixed his eyes on Bruce as he said this. "As we used to say in Afghanistan: each shot a kill shot."

"You were in the war over there? As a sniper?" Bruce asked, keenly interested.

"I was."

"Respect," Bruce said.

What a suck-up.

Adjacent to the locker-room was a long shooting alley with black human-silhouette paper targets at the far end, about fifty meters away. For the first time in my life, I was about to aim a weapon at something that wasn't merely a figure on a screen, and I couldn't wait to try and see how I did. All four of us loaded our weapons and started shooting. I was startled by the kick of the rifle's recoil into my shoulder and the half-deafening sound of its report, and surprised that the trigger yielded to less pressure than The Game console weapon. The scope was hardly necessary at this distance, but amazing. Looking through it, it was as if the targets were a mere arm's length away, and it made shooting accurately as easy as the newbie setting on The Game.

My rifle was fantastic, well balanced and accurate, and after a quarter of an hour of practice, I was hitting the dead centers of the targets, as were Graham and Bruce. Leya's green splashes were a few inches outside the tightly clustered red, yellow and blue splats, but otherwise there wasn't much to choose between us.

"Right, looks like you've got your eye in. Follow me now, and listen while I explain the rules of the exercise," said Sarge.

Graham fell into step beside me, muttering about how basic the rifles were and how he'd hoped to be using more advanced equipment, and computerized scope-dopers to fine-tune our aim. I nodded, but my mind was on the game ahead. Would I be any good? Would any of us? If the practice rounds were anything to go by, then all the "shooting" of my last three years as a game sniper had trained my eye, but it was time to test myself in "real-life" shooting.

"Here we are — the urban arena," said Sarge, as we emerged from a short corridor.

I gasped. I mean, I knew we were actually on a constructed set like a movie back lot, located entirely inside a massive warehouse, but you could have fooled me. We were standing in a long, narrow alley which ran between the rear of two tall buildings. Above us was a blue "sky" brushed with clouds turned pink as if by a setting sun. The alley was dark with shadows in the dim, late-afternoon lighting. Old posters of rock concerts clung to the walls of the building on the left, and the steel ladder of a fire escape hung unevenly off the red-brick wall of the building on our right. My eye was caught by a scurrying movement between the overflowing trash cans and dumpsters which lined the alley. Were there repbots in this game? The alley ran straight down for a few blocks and then ended in a T-junction. Through my scope, I could see the distant shop-fronts and parked cars in the section of road visible from where we stood. The noise of distant traffic competed with shouting voices, dull thumping music and even, from somewhere close by, a chirping cricket.

"This is awesome!" I said. It was like I'd run away from home and been turned loose — with a rifle — in the back streets of a faraway city.

"It is, Blue," said Sarge. "It could be downtown anywhere USA."

He gripped my shoulder with one of his hands and gave it a firm squeeze. A very firm, almost painful, squeeze. I suspected he might be flashing me another fast smile, but the corners of his eyes above the respirator didn't crinkle.

"Right, listen up, y'all," said Sarge. "This is how it goes down. Juan, Fiona and I are your enemy. We are going to get a five minute head start on you four, but you may enter the field of action and begin your mission when you hear this sound." He pulled a small air horn from his pocket and pressed the button on top of the canister. The loud siren blast made three of us jump. "Your goal is to drop us before we drop you. A kill shot is a head shot, or one that hits within the golden triangle — nipple to nipple to throat and back again." With the hand not holding his own rifle, he sketched a triangular target over his chest and neck. "You get hit with a kill-shot, you're out of the game, even if you're only two minutes into it. This experience is meant to be as real as we can make it for you. If you get hit anywhere else, you can keep playing. At the end, I'll sound the siren again. We'll tally up the shots and the top scorer among you wins bragging rights. And fifteen thousand dollars."

We all looked excitedly at each other. I'd thought the prize was the opportunity to play in such a fantastic game, but 15K was a real sweet cherry on the top.

"Any questions?"

I was surprised when Graham, who hadn't yet even made eye contact with Sarge, let alone said anything to him, asked, "Do we get any scope calculators or laser range-finders?"

"No you do not. This is a game for snipers, boy, not a class for programmers or code-breaker geeks. But since you kids may not have had any shooting experience with real distances, I will give you one clue for yardage. From where we're standing to the end of the alley over there is a distance of 525 meters. Y'all will have to extrapolate to the rest of the arena based on that."

I immediately calculated the distances of objects and landmarks between where we stood and the end of the alley and memorized them.

"Any other questions?"

"Once we've taken out you three," Bruce indicated the team of instructors, "do we then become targets for each other?"

I exchanged a glance with Leya. Bruce was gung-ho to the point of unsettling.

"*Once we've taken out you three* — listen to him. Not lacking in confidence, are you, son? It may interest you to know that I've never yet been taken down by one of you gamer punks. And I was never hit in my tour of duty either. But you're welcome to take a shot. Just remember, the aim of the exercise is to take as many of our lives as you can, *while keeping your own.* You get hit by a kill shot, you're out of the game, no matter how fancy your shooting until then. And no, son, you are not to shoot each other. You hit one of your own team members, that's an own-goal and you're immediately disqualified. A sniper does not jeopardize the lives of his fellow soldiers. Squad before blood, comprehend?"

"Huh?" I had no idea what the phrase meant.

"In war, your squad, your fellow soldiers, comes before everyone and anyone, even including family. Get it?"

I nodded. But looking at Graham fidgeting and Bruce cracking his neck, and thinking of Mom and Robin, I figured it was a good thing this was only a game. Family would always come first for me.

Leya looked hopefully at Sarge and asked, "Can we begin now?"

Chapter 5

Rats

Sarge consulted his co-instructors. "I forgotten anything?"

"The rats," said Juan.

"Ah, yes, the rats."

Graham, who had been fiddling with his rifle, setting the safety catch on and off and on again, looked up at this.

"We have some rats in the arena, and you get bonus points for hitting them."

"Real rats?" Graham swallowed hard.

"Well, they ain't stuffed toys, boy."

"But are they plague rats or ordinary rats?"

Plague rats were disgusting mutants, genetically modified crosses between Gambian Pouched rats from West Africa, Argentinian Nutria, and a few other things the scientists were still trying to figure out. They were as big as cats, the biggest weighing up to twenty pounds and measuring over three feet in length, nose to tail. They had been carefully bred by the terrorists who launched the contagion, and then infected with rat fever and released into towns and cities across the nation. Naturally aggressive and themselves apparently immune to the virus, they spread the contagion to people and other susceptible mammals with their vicious bites. They made lethal and efficient carriers, and they bred faster than they could be trapped or poisoned. Every mutant rodent was potentially death on four legs. Everyone hated them. They freaked me out big time, and I'd never even seen one except on T.V. Good thing they hadn't mentioned rats in the letter to Mom, or she would never have let me come.

"They're plague rats, but they're lab-bred and ain't infected, so don't you worry about that. But they add an element of realism to the exercise, and they're a good measure of your skill — big enough to hit, small enough to be a real challenge, and likely to be moving. Right, that's it," said Sarge, hoisting his rifle onto his shoulder and turning to go. "Good luck, and may the best man win."

"Or woman," I said softly to his back.

He turned around and looked at me for a few seconds. Then he suddenly pulled down his mask, flashed me a manic grin and said, "I stand corrected. May the best man — *or woman* — win." The smile was gone before he returned his mask into position. He, alone of all of us, left off the protective eyewear and helmet. Cocky? Or just confident?

The three instructors took off down the alley at a jog.

"Are we going to play together as a team, or separately as individual snipers?" I asked the others.

"Together," said Leya and Graham.

Bruce shrugged. "Whatever."

"We can split up later, if we want to," suggested Leya.

"I'm good with that." I checked that the safety catch on my rifle was engaged, adjusted my goggles and said, "Let's go."

From somewhere down the alley, the siren screamed, echoing strangely off the painted sky roof.

We set off, dividing into pairs and clinging to the walls on opposite sides of the alley as we made our way deeper into the game arena. At first I was surprised that Bruce chose Leya to be his partner — until now, he'd been keen to stay as near to me as possible — but then I realized he'd made a smart decision. This game would not only be about accuracy, it would also be about strategy, and it was a piss-poor strategy to be paired with Graham. He must be a top-scoring online player in order to have qualified for this prize, but he was a liability as a partner out here. He twitched and fidgeted, focused more on the gun than on searching for targets, and seemed mostly oblivious to the need to stay behind cover. Before we'd crept ten feet up the right side of the first block in the alley, I had to shove him back into the shadows cast by the building.

"Keep back, right up against the wall," I told him, speaking as softly as I could.

Bruce was monitoring our exchange, and judging by the crinkle of his eyes above his mask, he was grinning at us. He'd deliberately let me go with Graham, probably hoping the fool boy would get us both spotted and taken out of contention, leaving him with only Leya as his competitor. Bruce might be annoying, but he wasn't stupid.

I had just eased forward a few paces to take cover behind a high metal dumpster reeking of rotting garbage, and motioned to Graham to get behind me, when Leya whispered from across the alley.

"There!"

I saw it at once, a small movement between the trash cans about halfway down the left side of the alley. I lifted my rifle to my shoulder, brought my eye up to the telescopic eyepiece, and studied the scene. The rat — if that's what it was — had disappeared behind the bins.

It looked like the others were all going for a shot at the rat, but I hesitated. This game would be more easily lost than won. Hitting a target might score you points, but it would also reveal your position. Getting hit bounced you out of the game immediately, so surely it was more important not to be seen than it was to hit a rat. Taking the risk that I might be losing out on the chance to score a few bonus points, I lowered my rifle and looked around. Bundled against the bottom of the peeling green paint of the dumpster's side was a length of discarded cloth. It may once have been a brown bath towel, but now it was a ragged, dark cloth, patched with dirty stains. Perfect.

Forcing myself to ignore the stink, I pulled it over my helmet and braided loop of hair, and around my shoulders. Later I might drape it over my rifle to camouflage that, too. Then I scraped my hand into the dirt at my feet, and smeared the muck in rough stripes and patches across my face, mask and the rim of my goggles, breaking up the distinctive face shape to anyone who might aim their scope in my direction.

I picked a spot at the corner of the dumpster that jutted into the alley, and sat down, angling my body to keep most of it hidden behind the protective metal. Next, I fished the spare bagel out of my pocket, browned it all over with dirt and then balanced it on my left knee. As I'd hoped, it made a perfect brace for my rifle to rest on.

This was it. I was actually going to try shoot something real and moving. Something alive. Finally. And I found I didn't like the idea of hurting an animal, especially just for the sake of a game. The paintball probably wouldn't kill the critter, but it would hurt it, surely? I didn't know the muzzle velocity of the paintballs from these rifles, but it would be enough to bruise. It was a weird moment. I'd spent years playing The Game as a marksman, but I'd somehow never connected the gaming to actual shooting. The enemy soldiers and repbots and explosive devices that I'd taken aim at on the computer screen had simply been targets — some easier and some harder to hit, a fun challenge for my skills. This was real.

A quick glance to either side confirmed that the other three each had their rifles trained on the target, and apparently they had no second thoughts about paintballing a live animal. Maybe I was being silly. Head in the game, Jinxy.

Across the way, Bruce and Leya tensed up, signaling that they'd spotted the rat again. My scope was at my eye just in time to hear a shot and to see the end of a tail disappear behind an old oilcan which lay in a small pile of rubble in the center of the alley. If my ammo was real I could have shot it through the can, but paintballs wouldn't penetrate metal. Heck, the target practice had shown they couldn't penetrate cardboard. I'd have to hit any target directly. I sat still, doing my tactical breathing, scanning the alley.

Graham, however, was incapable of sitting still or staying quiet. A sudden fizz of escaping gas startled me. I glared over my shoulder at him. He stared back at me guiltily, his hand frozen in the act of twisting the cap off a bottle.

"You brought sparkling water? *Sparkling*?" He was beyond help. "Just sit still and be quiet," I hissed at him.

I was probably being very rude, but I didn't know how to tell him tactfully. He might be a genius at the math and science of The Game, but no way was he a natural sniper. He lacked any semblance of patience and control. I had a sudden mental flash of him behind his PC, thinking up formulas and doing calculations to while away the downtime of stalking and observation. As soon as I could, I needed to peel away and play my own game. It was only a matter of time before Sarge, Fiona or Juan spied Graham and took him down, and I needed to be far away from him when that happened so that he didn't give away my position, too.

I took a deep breath, blew it out and went back into observation mode. With my rifle resting on the bagel on top of my knee and braced against my shoulder, I studied the alley systematically through my scope. Side to side, near to far. The goggles were a nuisance, but at least I was used to playing The Game wearing virtual reality eyewear. The gloves were plain horrible. I never wore gloves at home so I wasn't used to shooting with them on, and was frustrated that I couldn't feel the trigger properly beneath my index finger. The layer of latex separated me from my weapon, stopped my being one with it.

Then I saw it. A rat as big as a lapdog scuttled in short, tentative bursts away from the rubble. By my earlier calculations, the rubble pile was about halfway down the alley, which would put it at approximately 260 meters. Quickly, I adjusted my scope and took aim, leading the target fractionally to the right to compensate for its movement. Then I gently pulled the trigger.

It was a direct hit. Through the scope I could see the splatter of blue paint directly between the horrible creature's eyes.

"Pity — so close," Leya whispered across the alley to me.

It wasn't close, it was exactly on target. I'd hit the rat right where I'd been aiming and was indignant that she counted it a miss. If I'd been shooting with live ammunition, it would have been a kill shot.

I frowned at her but she wasn't looking at me. Both she and Bruce had taken a bead on the rat which now sat still, momentarily stunned by the blow. They both pulled off shots simultaneously.

"Yes!" Bruce said quietly, bumping gloved fists with Leya.

I peered through my scope. He'd shot the rat right through one of its eyes. It was an impressive shot, but I felt sorry for the creature lying on the ground. Paintballs probably wouldn't do more than bruise us, but they had enough force behind them that a direct hit into a rat's eyeball would do some serious damage. And it had. The rat writhed and twitched on the ground. Blood and some thick goo oozed from the red, paint-rimmed eye socket. Nausea threatened as I witnessed its suffering.

Beside me, Graham knelt with his head between his knees, making dry retching noises. Sure that his head must be protruding beyond the edge of the dumpster, I stretched out an arm and thrust him back, a fraction of a second before a movement of air past us and a thud behind us indicated that a bullet had just missed him.

He sat back, leaning against the wall, holding a hand over his mouth. He was as pale as paper, and a fine sheen of sweat covered his face. He was losing it.

"If you freak out, you'll get taken out. Just breathe, okay, Graham? Breathe. Slowly."

I inched back along the side of the dumpster, squeezed myself into the narrow gap between it and the alley wall, and crawled along. Graham followed me until we emerged from its cover. I crept down the alley, carefully hugging the wall, keeping my rifle up against my chest. At the end of the first block, I crouched down on my haunches and peered around the corner — scanning the road, the buildings, and windows for something that didn't fit in its surrounds. The thumping rap music was coming from down this cross-road.

A volley of shots from behind me made me spin my head around.

"Man down! That's a kill-shot."

Chapter 6

A Small Square Inch of Flesh

Juan emerged from behind a dark doorway down the street perpendicular to Bruce and Leya's corner of the alley. He had a green paint smear on the right side of his chest. Bruce had a black splatter on his left thigh.

"Good shot," Bruce said grudgingly to Leya, as the "dead" instructor walked past us down the alley, back in the direction of the entrance.

I used the moment of distraction to cross the gap of the road and pressed up against the alley wall again. Graham trailed behind me, tripping noisily over a cola can and sending it spinning down the cross-street. A round coming from straight ahead hit the spinning can and sent it bouncing down the alley. Sarge?

We edged up alongside the brick wall for another block, all the while scanning the buildings and alley for possible hides, and came to the small pile of rubble where the rat had been shot. It had stopped jerking now. It lay on its side, the red hollow of its oozing eye turned to the deepening pink of the false sky. Beyond it, just behind the oilcan, was something far worse. A dead rat, split open along its middle as though by a knife, lay decomposing on top of a couple of broken bricks and cement chunks, its stiff feet sticking into the air. Flies buzzed around the corpse, and the putrefying flesh seemed to be moving. I looked closer and saw that it was riddled with stirring maggots. The disgusting smell — horribly sweet with an acrid sharpness — caught at the back of my throat.

Majorly squicked out, I pulled back instinctively. Not Graham, though. He leaned forward, tearing at his mask. For one crazy moment I thought he wanted to study the rat up close, but then he was bent over and puking, adding to the stomach-churning sights and smells. I heard a crack at the same moment as a black splat appeared in the dead center of Graham's helmet-top.

Swinging my rifle up in the direction of the rifle report and bullet trajectory, I focused in on a movement in a window in the main cross-street, and took one shot. Then another.

"It's a kill. I'm out," came Fiona's shout. "Hold your fire while we clear the field."

She emerged, a few moments later, from one of the buildings in the main street at the end of the alley. I was pleased to see, as she came closer, that the blue splash of my paintball had hit squarely in the middle of her protective vest, directly above her heart.

"Nice shot," Fiona told me. "Come on, Graham, you're out, too." She marched up to where Graham still stood, bent over and retching, grabbed him under an arm and hauled him off down the alley. As they reached the exit, she called out, "Resume play."

"We've only got to get Sarge now, and maybe there'll be a few more rats. Let's split up and go in three different directions to maximize our chances," said Leya.

"Yeah, I'd like to get him," said Bruce.

I nodded and slipped off down the side street to the right. Leya took the left, leaving Bruce to continue down the alley toward the main cross street. I moved faster now that I was without Graham, slipping between the cover of parked cars and doorways, carefully studying darkened windows, doors, and small holes in walls behind which a sniper might lurk. My eye was caught by a fluttering curtain, and a low movement which might have been another rat, but I saw nothing that could be Sarge. Of course, that didn't mean he wasn't well-hidden somewhere with the crosshairs of his scope trained on me even at this moment. My back itched as if sensing an incoming hit, but I made it to the end of the block unscathed, only to scare myself stupid by bumping straight into Bruce as I turned the corner.

"Hey, if you want me to hold you, you only have to ask me, Blue," he said, opening his bulky arms wide as if to embrace me.

"Don't call me that." I righted my balance and stepped back from him.

"So, it's just the two of us at last."

"It's not just the two of us. Sarge is out there somewhere, probably taking aim at us right now. And so is Leya."

No sooner had I said her name than I heard her scream.

"Help! Help me!" The yell came from behind us, down the main street.

Bruce swore. "Are we supposed to help each other?"

"I guess. We're supposed to be a team of soldiers on the same side."

I stepped around him and made my way along the main avenue, in the direction from which Bruce had come. He was quieter than Graham and stuck close to my shoulder as we ducked behind parked cars, trash cans, tall trees and whatever other cover we could find until we saw them.

At the end of the avenue, about sixty or seventy meters away, was a traffic circle with a statue of a cavalryman astride a rearing horse in the center of it. Easing himself around the base of the statue was Sarge. With one arm, he held Leya tight up against his body as a human shield, with the other, he aimed his rifle in our direction. We didn't need our scopes to see that much.

"I have taken your comrade hostage. I know you're out there, so lay down your weapons and step out slowly, hands behind your heads," he shouted at us.

Now what? I glanced at Bruce. He shrugged. Neither of us responded to Sarge. I hadn't expected this to be part of the game.

"Surrender or she gets it!"

Crap. I had no choice. I would have to put my rifle down on the ground, kick it out into the street, and step out from behind my cover to stand beside it. If this was real, no way would I risk Leya's life, and we were playing this game as if it was real, weren't we? I began bending to lay my rifle down, already feeling the sharp disappointment of how the game had ended.

"No effing way!" Bruce whispered fiercely. "She got herself into that position, she can get herself out. I'm not losing because she was stupid enough to get herself taken hostage, no way."

"But —"

"You're too soft-hearted, Blue. You win the game by surviving, not surrendering."

"But if we don't surrender, he'll shoot her."

"With a paintball, Blue. Just a paintball," he said. "You do what you like, I'm out of here."

And with that, he melted away into the lengthening shadows of the avenue, leaving me alone, crouched down behind a rusty, old-model Ford.

Should I follow him? That was the smart course, probably what we were supposed to do. But it didn't feel right to leave Leya behind. It would be like leaving a friend in danger, or a fellow-soldier behind on the battle-field. A betrayal of sorts.

I should surrender. Maybe as Sarge released Leya, Bruce would be able to take a shot. It meant I would lose the game, of course, and Bruce would win, but at least we'd have gotten Sarge.

But there was no guarantee that Bruce would get Sarge. No

guarantee, even, that Sarge would release Leya if I surrendered. I could just as easily see him shooting me as soon as I laid down my weapon, then taking out Leya at short range, grinning maniacally all the while. Maybe he'd only captured her to lure us in. What had he said about the rules before we started playing? *Drop us before we drop you … the aim of the exercise is to take as many of our lives as you can, while keeping your own.* Oh yeah, he would drop us both, alright.

"I'm going to count to ten," Sarge called from behind Leya. "If you haven't surrendered by the time I get to ten, I'm going to add another kill to my count."

And if I did surrender, he'd add two kills to his count.

I lifted my rifle, rested it on a spare tire leaning up against the Ford, and studied him through the scope. I found myself running calculations through my head, even though there was no possible way to take him down without hitting Leya.

"One … two …"

He held her so that her body covered the whole of his, with his head tucked behind hers. The hand holding the rifle was the only part of him not protected, but a shot to his hand wouldn't be a kill-shot. Even if I could hit him there, he'd just take out Leya immediately.

"… three. You're beginning to make me ma-ad!" he called, in a sing-song voice.

The hand was exposed. And a small area of skin where the side of his neck protruded beyond the edge of hers. Damn these goggles — they did more to obscure my vision than protect my eyes. I yanked them up onto my helmet, locked my cheek against the stock, aligned my right eye with the eyepiece, and found that spot again.

"Four … five … six …"

It was a scant square inch of flesh, the tiniest target I would ever have aimed for. An impossible shot. And if I missed, I would either hit bare air and give away my position to Sarge, or I'd hit Leya and be instantly disqualified.

"Seven …"

But if I hit? If I hit that nickel-sized target directly above his jugular, it would be a kill-shot for sure. We'd have taken out all the instructors, while we three would have survived. And I would win the game.

"Eight," Sarge called, his voice rising high. "Poor little girl, she's running out of time."

So was I. I needed to make a decision. But it seemed my body had already made it for me. My breathing had slowed down, my shoulders moved down into their relaxed position, the pad of my forefinger was on the trigger, and a freckle in the exposed patch of my target's neck was at the dead center of my cross-hairs. My finger tightened on the trigger until I reached the point of resistance. I breathed in, held it, breathed out slowly.

"Nine …"

As gently as though I was touching a raw wound, I squeezed back on the trigger.

The recoiling rifle stock slammed into my shoulder. A vicious expletive from down the avenue told me I'd hit something. Quickly, I lifted the scope. An arm in a green jump-suit. Up. Leya's stunned eyes and open mouth. Down a bit. Her neck, a small splash of blue on the side. To the right. A neck above a black jump-suit — a neck splattered with blue paint. A hand moving to touch it. Up. Eyes above a mask, looking down at the hand. Then lifting to look down the avenue in my direction. Eyes livid with anger.

Uncertainly, I lowered my rifle and stood up behind the Ford.

"Uhm … Man down?" I called out.

Sarge cursed again, violently. Then the game-over siren sounded loudly through the arena.

Holding my rifle at my side, I walked toward the pair in front of the statue. The sound of running feet behind me on the road meant Bruce must be jogging to catch up with us, but I kept my face neutral and my eyes on Sarge, not sure of how he was planning to react to me. He didn't look too sure, either, as he nodded silently at me, then shook his head as if in disbelief, then nodded again. I shot a glance at Leya as I drew near. She was grinning from ear to ear and had both thumbs raised in the air to me, but she stood to the side and behind Sarge where he wouldn't be able to see the congratulatory gesture. Bruce caught up to me.

"What the hell did you do, Blue?" he said. His voice was a mixture of amazement and accusation.

"I took the shot," I said, closing the distance of the last few meters to Sarge and Leya.

"Well, damn me if that isn't a first," said Sarge, rubbing a hand over his gleaming head. "I don't know whether to shake your hand, Blue, or kick your ass into next week."

"That was an ace shot!" said Leya, coming to my defense.

"It was if it wasn't dumb luck," said Bruce.

"I could never have made that shot," said Leya, "I would have retreated."

"That's what you're *supposed* to do in this game. You're supposed to be smart enough not to be lured in, and tough enough to walk away. Keep yourself safe and hope for another chance. Like Bruce here did," said Sarge.

Beside me, I could just about feel Bruce preening under this endorsement of his actions. But Sarge didn't spare him a glance. He was too busy studying me. He pulled his mask down, looped it back under his chin and flashed that sudden grin that was more intimidating grimace than reassuring smile.

"But you, Blue, you are one cool customer. Detachment under pressure — that's an asset in the battlefield. No surrendering for you."

I'd very nearly surrendered; it had been my first instinct. And I hadn't taken the shot because I'd been cool or detached, I'd taken it as a last resort. It was something I'd never have dreamt of doing if we were in a real battlefield with live rounds. But I didn't correct his misapprehension. Already he looked like he was walking a fine line between admiration and severe pissed-offness. That shot must be stinging like a mother, right now.

The two other instructors jogged up then, with Graham trotting behind. He had a fraction more color in his face, but he looked deeply embarrassed. Sarge ignored him as if he wasn't there.

"Well done," Graham said to me.

"Thanks."

Juan and Fiona were staring at the side of Sarge's neck in amazement.

"Yeah, yeah. I got hit. By a dirty-faced little Blondie. Learn from this, soldiers! There's a weak spot, an exposed bit of flesh on every target. You just have to find it and hit it."

"Yes, sir," Bruce and I said.

"We got ourselves a winner, here." There was grudging respect in Sarge's voice, but something else, too. "So what are we going to do with you, Blue?"

"Give her 15K?" suggested Leya, her brown eyes full of mischief.

"Give her a congratulatory hug," said Bruce, grabbing me and squeezing me tight. I swear his hands brushed against my ass.

"Or something," Sarge muttered.

Part Two

Chapter 7

A Little Death

The picture on the T.V. in my bedroom flared and flashed as I scrolled through hundreds of channels. A soap opera with a rat-fevered hero, infomercials for ozone sterilizers and homeschooling supplies, reality shows featuring Doomsday preppers with *we-told-you-so* smugness written all over their faces, and endless reruns of unfunny sitcoms. I tossed the remote aside — four hundred and forty-two channels, and nothing interested me.

I could always spend some time on guitar practice. I'd been wrestling with a piece called *Andante* in my music classes — online tutorials, of course, no way would Mom allow a tutor in, or me out, for real lessons — but that day I wasn't in the mood for the slow, melancholy piece. Maybe I should go online and do some shopping, spend some of my sweet prize money.

I'd been feeling like this — bored and unsettled and unsure what to do with my time — ever since I'd won The Game. For so long, I'd been playing toward that one goal, and suddenly I'd achieved it. Now what? There didn't seem much point in starting from scratch and playing essentially the same game again merely to take out the new enemy leader. There ought to be another level or a different challenge for once you'd won, though I suspected that nothing would come close to being as exciting as shooting Sarge in the neck.

I was still so proud of that shot. Robin had threatened to tell Mom I had a headache and fever if I didn't stop bragging. Since that would have brought a busload of fussing, I quit bragging about it, but in bed at night, in the minutes before I fell asleep, I relived those moments in all their exhilarating detail.

Without gaming to distract me, I'd spent my time completing my online school units, submitted all assignments due for the end of the semester, and even completed seven of my eight online junior-year examinations. I wasn't much interested in school. When I tried to imagine what I'd do after my senior year, I came up blank. The idea of spending several more years at home studying online filled me with dread. I had never been interested in becoming a doctor or a mechanical engineer, but I might be tempted to register for a degree in one of them — at least then I'd get out from under Mom's thumb for the annual four-month on-site training at the college's quarantined facility.

I'd always longed to travel, to see the places I'd learned about in history and read about in English Lit. But with the borders sealed, I wouldn't be seeing the Eiffel Tower or the Great Wall of China any time soon. The government encouraged us to travel locally — someone had to support the tourist industry now that most foreigners weren't allowed in — but Mom made us stay home, "safe and sound". I'd had a pre-plague BFF whose mother had embroidered a pillow for her bearing the homily "There's no place like home". If my mom were to embroider a pillow for me, it would read, "There's no place *but* home".

I was looking forward to the social later that day because it would get me out the house for the first time since the simulated sniper mission. Being cooped up at home had always bugged me, but at least with The Game I'd been able to immerse myself in virtual spaces and vistas. Now the house was too small to bear. I wished I could see Leya again, or get out and meet other people — real people, not my e-friends from BackChat. And really talk to them, not just message them in texts and online chat rooms. I was bored stiff with my mom, and even Robin was getting on my nerves.

Some teens occasionally snuck out at night to hook up or party, but I was too nervous. The Plague was out there. Even if I wasn't actually attacked by some rabid nocturnal varmint or caught by the patrols enforcing curfew, my mother might find me out. And if that happened, I'd be "virtually grounded" for months. It was bad enough to be on what practically amounted to house-arrest, but if I lost connectivity, I'd go insane within a week.

When I went downstairs to the kitchen to grab a cup of coffee, Mom was sliding a baking pan into the oven. The kitchen T.V. was tuned in to the live transmission of the Oscars, which for the last two years had been held in April. Some stick insect of an actress was accepting her award for Best Actress in a digital composite feature film. She wore a spectacular gown of yellow and sat in what looked like her living room, delivering her acceptance speech over VideoCall, clutching the statuette which had been delivered to her door mere moments before. Canned applause followed.

"It looks so ridiculous," I said, stirring sugar into my coffee. "Why don't they just announce who won and show clips from the films or something? Why bother trying to have an awards ceremony?"

"Do you remember when they still held the ceremony in that magnificent old theatre in Hollywood?"

"Vaguely. I remember that they used to start playing the music when the acceptance speeches went on too long."

"They all swanned down the red carpet, and everyone who was anyone was in the audience. It was so glamorous, and the fashions were so beautiful," Mom sighed.

I'd never been much interested in fashion. As a kid, I'd found jeans and sneakers comfortable enough. I knew teen girls were supposed to be obsessed with clothes, but really, what was the point when nobody outside of family ever saw you in anything but a PPE suit?

Mom cast the odd glance at the screen as she packed away the weekly groceries — ordered online and delivered by sterile drones — then spritzed and wiped the kitchen counters with anti-microbial spray. I stepped aside as she made her way to where I leaned against the refrigerator; she was quite capable of spraying me, too.

"Well, now it totally looks pathetic." I peered into the oven. "What are you baking?"

"It's a picnic, so I thought I'd make brownies. Remember?"

I did. When Robin and I were kids, before my father died, before the world went mad, we used to go on family picnics in the city's parks. Before we ate, we'd always have a jousting contest. Robin would climb onto Mom's back and I'd piggy-back on Dad's, and then we'd run at each other like knights of old, trying to score hits with lances made of long loaves of French bread until we collapsed — Robin and me in giggles, and Mom and Dad in breathless exhaustion. Then we'd break out the hot dogs and coleslaw. And always, for dessert, we devoured Mom's homemade brownies.

But the socials didn't allow members to bring their own food, even for picnics. The risk of someone secretly being a terr cell-member and spiking the food or drink was too great. All food, checked and sterilized and sealed, would be provided by the Social Program and doled out by the SP hosts.

"You know you can't take it along, right?" I asked Mom.

"I know, I know. I'm being a bit silly, I guess." Not silly, no.

Mom was getting anxious as she always did when we went out, and baking soothed her nerves. "We can have it when we get home. I've got some good news for you. Well, you'll think it's good news, *I'm* not so sure. So I thought we could make a little celebration of it."

"What good news?"

Three sharp pips sounded from the T.V. Mom and I turned automatically to check the screen. There was always the chance it could be an announcement of an attack, or of a sighting of an infected person in our area with a caution to stay indoors. But this time it was merely a Public Service Announcement by Alex Hawke, President of the Southern Sector. I liked Hawke. He seemed like a strong, honorable guy, and I figured we were lucky to have him as the leader of our sector. When Mom hadn't been sure who to vote for in the last election, I'd persuaded her to vote for him.

"Why him?" she'd asked. "I know he's popular with you youngsters, but what precisely do you like about him?"

"I don't know exactly, I just think he's someone we can rely on, like we can trust him to do what's best."

Her look had been something close to pity when she replied, "I think he's something of a father figure to you, Jinxy."

Maybe she was right. But as father figures went, I thought — staring at his thick, wavy brown hair, beginning to grey at the temples, and strong, square face — you could do a lot worse.

"I think he's too smooth, a bit too slick." Mom never lingered on any conversation that might deal with Dad. "Then again, he is a politician."

A very successful politician. He'd swept into office with the largest victory margin in history.

Hawke was talking now. "In the Southern Sector alone, we have an estimated 1.3 million illegals living in the shadows, which leaves this nation vulnerable to a myriad of dangers. Do you suspect someone you know of being here illegally? He might be the person who delivers your groceries, or the woman you see on the street that somehow doesn't belong, or that anonymous commenter on your workplace's online forum who questions the need for immigration reform. For the safety of this nation, it is each citizen's responsibility, each citizen's national duty, to report suspicious activity or persons to the proper authorities. Be observant and stay vigilant."

It ended with the familiar jingle: "If you see something, say something. Call our tip-off hotline on 1-800-U-SEE-SAY."

My mother always watched these PSA's like they conveyed life-and-death information, which I guess they did, but she'd seen this one scads of times before and could probably recite it word for word. Even I already had the hotline number memorized. I tried not to let myself tune out the PSA's. As Mom often pointed out: complacency leads to danger. The terrorists counted on us letting our guards down, getting bored, and becoming unobservant and sloppy, and the virus thrived when we neglected our safety measures.

"What good news?" I asked impatiently.

"I'll tell you later — it's a surprise." She glanced at her watch and exclaimed, "Will you look at the time! The Fun Bus is due here in half an hour, and I haven't done my hair. Please, Jinxy, go and chase Robin for me. Check he hasn't fallen back asleep or gotten lost in a story or a program in that blessed game, will you? And make sure he puts on his PPE gear."

"What surprise?"

"Later! Here." She shoved a box of heavy-duty, double-thick latex gloves into my hands.

I trudged upstairs to Robin's room, while Mom hurried off to her own bedroom, presumably to do something intricate to her hair. So little of ourselves showed above the masks and jump-suits that people tended to go crazy with hair and eye decoration. I couldn't be bothered with braiding and twisting and spiking my hair into the outlandish styles so fashionable when people did get together. My blue streaks were distinctive enough, though for today I had also stuck long, indigo-colored false lashes over my own.

The image of the tattoo next to Leya's eye flashed in my mind. What was she doing today? Did she feel the same sense of anticlimax I did now that we'd played a real game? Then I remembered that Bruce had asked about today's social and groaned to myself. He'd said he lived a few blocks away, so it was quite likely he'd be in my group and on my bus, as they tended to organize these things in neighborhoods.

Robin was in his bedroom, folded into his favorite spot — the cushioned window seat beside the sealed window which overlooked the neighbor's yard. The Johnsons had a pool which they kept filled and sparkling blue, though I never saw anyone swimming in it. They also had a pretty daughter of about our age. Perhaps Robin sat there so often in the hopes of catching her in a bikini.

"Mom says I have to check you're ready for the" — I made jazzy star-fingers — "*social!*"

"I'm dressed, brushed, and as enthusiastic as a turkey at Thanksgiving," said Robin, not looking up from the spiral notebook in which he was writing.

His PPE suit and gloves were lying on the bed. I exchanged the lightweight gloves he had laid out for a pair of double-thicks from the box Mom had given me, and checked his mask for any tears.

"What are you doing?" I said.

"Writing a poem."

Robin was always writing poems — when he wasn't writing stories. Or reading. Inexplicably, he preferred poetry and reading about giant trees ambling around Middle Earth to gaming. I poked around his room, which was messier than my own, checked his digital reader for his latest downloads, studied his corkboard — a new haiku about the view of sky seen from a window, an old photo of Dad — and pulled a face at his old skateboard, which still hung on the wall directly above his bed. It had been Mom and Dad's gift to him on his eleventh birthday.

"Why do you still keep that thing?" I said, irked. The skateboard always reminded me of the time before. "What's the point? The skate-parks are closed, and no way would Mom allow you on the streets. You'll never get to use it again."

"I can hope, can't I? Things might change one day." Robin glanced out the window then wrote another line.

"Phff. It's like a leftover from the time before," I grumbled.

"A relic from ancient times … Maybe that's why I keep it."

Robin often said deep stuff like that.

As I plonked myself down next to him, my stomach growled a welcome to the smell of baking chocolate drifting up from the kitchen.

"Mom's making brownies." I peered over his shoulder, read the title of his poem. "An Unmarked Grave. What's it about?"

"A little death."

"Nice," I said. "Very cheerful."

Not particularly wanting to read further, I looked out the window. Beyond the fence, Mr. Johnson, our neighbor, was lowering a bulky bundle wrapped in what looked like white canvas into a large hole dug beside a huge rhododendron bush heavy with yellow flowers.

"What the heck's he doing?" Mr. Johnson was now dropping shovels full of dirt into the hole. He was working quickly; it would soon be filled up. "It looks like a grave, like he's burying hidden treasure," I joked.

"He is, in a way," said Robin. He put down his pencil and looked out the window, sighing deeply.

"What do you mean?"

"That was Maisy."

Maisy was the Johnson's dog, a friendly golden retriever with a gray muzzle, a loud bark and a perpetually wagging tail. She was one of the very few pets left in our neighborhood.

Because of the danger of contagion, most people who wanted pets had switched to animals that couldn't get outside, couldn't get infected and couldn't bite — tropical fish, seahorses, or reptiles like pet lizards which were resistant to the virus. Or, of course, robots. Robocats came complete with shed-free, easy-clean fur and purring function. RoboDogs barked and did tricks like sitting and back-flipping. Chatty Parrots repeated whatever you said. Mom was always a little freaked out by the neighbors' real live dog, and the fact that it was allowed out into their yard several times a day to run around and do its business really worried her.

"But, but, how did it die?" I asked, confused and beginning to get concerned. "And why are they burying it in the yard?"

"She was really old. And I guess they're burying her there because they want to keep her close in some way," said Robin, rubbing at the dent the pencil had left in his finger.

"Mom needs to see this."

"Jinxy, no, don't —"

"Mom!" I called out loudly. "Come quick!"

Chapter 8

Overkill

"Jinx!" Robin thumped his notebook down hard on the seat cushions. "What did you call her for? Now she's going make a fat fuss. Their poor old dog died, and they're burying her. It's not a federal offense!"

"Sorry to correct you, but I think it may well be," I said, my eyes still fixed on Mr. Johnson next door. He was patting down the earth on top of the grave. "It's definitely illegal. That dog could have died from the plague — it could have infected them. Heck, it could have infected us!"

"You are *so* your mother's daughter!" Robin's look was scathing.

"And what is that supposed to mean?"

Mom came running in, looking totally freaked out. She freaked out easily.

I pointed out the window, ignoring the stink-eye Robin was giving me, and explained what was happening.

"I can't believe some people! When they know full well what could happen." Mom immediately snatched up Robin's phone and called the hotline to report the death. "Which is what they should have done themselves," she said when she'd supplied the authorities with all the details and hung up. She said it a little defensively because Robin was glaring at both of us.

"You two are completely overreacting," he said. "And you're causing real problems for the Johnsons."

"That animal might well be infected. It needs to be disposed of properly, Robin James, and you know it. Otherwise it could be a risk to all of us," said Mom.

"How? She's dead! Is she going to turn into a vampire dog or a werewolf?"

"When its corpse decays, the virus could get into the groundwater."

"Mom, we don't get our water from a well in the back yard!"

"The contagion could still be spread —"

"A contagion it probably never even had," Robin interrupted.

"— if something digs it up."

"Like what?" Robin challenged.

"Like another dog — they do that, you know — or some foraging critter. A raccoon or a coyote" — her voice rose because Robin was pulling a contemptuous face and mouthing the phrase 'foraging critter' as if it was the most ridiculous thing he'd ever heard — "or even a *rat!* The point is, the laws are there for good reason, and this is against the law. And that," she said when Robin looked set to argue, "is the end of the discussion. The Fun Bus will be here soon, get dressed please."

"I am dressed," said Robin.

"I meant, put on your suit and gloves and respirator, both of you." Mom stalked out, looking annoyed.

Robin snorted and rolled his eyes at me in disgust.

"She's right, you know," I said.

"She's not. Nothing about this" — he swept a hand to indicate the sealed window, the neighbor's yard beyond, the protective gear lying waiting on his bed — "is *right.*"

All three of us were suited up and waiting in the living room when the Fun Bus's horn sounded its usual perky tune. We were all tense — Mom because she hated any of us leaving the safety of the house, Robin because he was still angry that Mom had reported the neighbors, and me because I didn't much feel like seeing Bruce again.

Mom, Robin and I each took our turns in the decon unit, then emerged, blinking in the sunshine, and headed down the front path toward the long Fun Bus parked in front of our house. Displayed on the side of the bus was the familiar official advertisement about the need to repatriate illegal immigrants to their countries of origin. In the photograph, a family, perhaps Mexican or Puerto Rican, welcomed a long-lost member into their open arms, above the slogan, "Support Immigration Reform, because families belong together."

But my gaze, along with Mom and Robin's, and every person's on the bus, was fixed on the three official vehicles parked in the street in front of the Johnsons' front yard.

Two techs in full hazmat suits carried a sealed level 4 biohazard bin to a white van, labeled *Purification Centre Disposal Unit*. I guessed Maisy's body was inside the bin, about to be taken off for testing and incineration. The second vehicle was a police car. Its blue lights flashed silently, while Mr. and Mrs. Johnson and their rosy-cheeked daughter were escorted by more full-suited techs to the third vehicle, a minivan marked *Q-Bay Transport*.

"Such overkill," muttered Robin, turning toward the bus.

"It's for their own safety," said Mom. "And ours."

I agreed with her — it was too dangerous to take chances with something like this. But I also felt bad for the Johnsons, who were not in for a fun time.

They would be kept isolated in quarantine until their test results were confirmed. The blood samples took twelve days to culture, which was a joke because, if you *had* contracted rat fever, you would be knocking on death's door by then, anyway. Until then, they were potential plague-spreading M&Ms — rat fever Mike and Marys. Mom had told us that the name came from someone called Typhoid Mary, an Irish cook who immigrated to the States in the early 1900's. She was a carrier of typhoid fever, and although she was never sick herself, she'd infected scores of people in the New York area before she was identified by public health authorities and taken away to spend the rest of her life in isolation on North Brother Island — the early-twentieth-century equivalent of Q-Bay.

Mrs. Johnson glared at us and shook her head as she was led to the waiting transport, but Mr. Johnson looked merely resigned, or perhaps defeated. Rosy-cheeks gave Robin a long look then trailed after her father. As the doors of the Q-Bay transport closed behind them, we climbed onto the Fun Bus and handed our social security cards to the hostess. She scanned their barcodes into the automated attendance register, misted each of us lightly with a spray from her decon aerosol can, and directed us to the hand-sanitizer dispenser. Someone waved from the back of the bus. Recognizing the short blond hair and heavily muscled frame of Bruce, I steered Robin and my mother to free seats near the front instead.

The picnic started off bad enough, with the same old bland, tasteless, sterilized food quickly slipped in under lifted masks, many of the same neighbors commenting how I'd grown, and the same exchange of rumors and stories about the war on the pandemic, all in the massive city park almost completely deserted except for our group. But then it got worse.

Mom walked off to go chat to neighbors she knew, probably to dish the dirt on the Johnsons or maybe to compare hairstyles. She was out of the running for the award for most extravagant look. One of the women had hair patterned with diagonal stripes all the colors of the rainbow, and she'd continued the look on her face, with furry rainbow lash extensions merging into vertical stripes of multicolored eye-paint stretching up over her eyelids and brows, and onto her forehead. She looked like an image from my science tutorial: *dispersal of the light spectrum through a triangular prism.*

Robin, still fuming, plonked himself under the shade of a tree and stuck his nose into a thick book, and I was left alone on our picnic blanket, lying in the warm sun with a protective arm over my eyes. This might have been pretty good, actually, but Bruce took it as an invitation to join me.

"Hey, Blue, how ya doing?" he said and plonked down next to me on the blanket.

I didn't feel comfortable lying down next to him, but when I stood up and said I was going for a walk to see the flowering dogwoods, he invited himself along. I had no idea how to tell him he wasn't welcome without being horribly rude, so I said nothing. He walked beside me, complimenting my hair and eyes and even my false lashes, and every time we came to a tree stump or boulder, he offered to help me over. The park was eerily empty. There were no ducks on the ponds, no dogs being taken for a walk, no children playing in the open areas. Dogwoods glimmered in the sun like ghost trees, their stark, dark wood stabbing through the masses of white blossoms.

The only interesting moment of the whole social came at the end, when Bruce and I were making our way back to the bus.

"That was a great shot you had in the game, when you hit Sarge. Lucky."

"I guess."

"I'm looking forward to taking you on again."

"How?" I said, looking at him directly for the first time. "Do we get to play another game?"

"Don't you know?"

"Know what?"

"Your mom didn't get a letter about you?"

"Not that I know of. Though she did say something about good news that she's planning to tell me tonight. A surprise of some kind. What do you know?"

"I won't say anything except that it's super-cool. You're going to be maxed out by the news. When my folks told me — dude! I was blown away."

"What? What is it?" I demanded, but Bruce would only tempt me with hints about what he knew, and taunt me with what I didn't, all the way back to the bus.

The minute I was in the seat next to my mother, I turned to her and said firmly, "Mom, you tell me that good news, right here, right now."

"What news?" said Robin, turning around from the row in front to face us. His mood had improved now that the social was coming to a close.

Mom smiled at both of us. "I was going to save it for later, when we have our brownies."

"Mother, now!"

"Tell us," Robin chimed in.

"No one else is supposed to know," she whispered. "I'm not even sure I can bring myself to let you go."

Robin and I pulled our heads in close to hear her. "The good news, Jinxy, is…" She reached into her pocket, pulled out a printed email and scanned it until she found the part she was looking for, then she read it out to us very softly, "Is that based on your performance in The Game and the simulation prize, you have been selected as a recruit for the Advanced Skills Training Program at the Advanced Specialized Training Academy, ASTA. On the first of May, if you so desire, you will begin your training to become a member of their first ever elite sniper squad."

"I'm going to be a sniper?" I whispered back, stunned. "What
—"

"Hold on, let me finish," said Mom, trying to find her place
on the letter. "Ah, here it is: 'to be deployed in the elimination of
dangerous rodents.'"

Robin cackled with laughter.

"You're not going to be a sniper, Jinxy, you're going to be a
ratter!"

Chapter 9

Pirate

I sat in the black Hummer, facing its new occupant, intensely aware of many things all at once. His long, lean frame and dark-mahogany hair — worn a little too long, so that the end bits curled against his neck. The silver ring threaded through one of the dark brows above eyes the color of slate, eyes which crinkled at the corners. The heat warming my cheeks. And an irrepressible urge to smile back building inside me.

He was wearing the lightest of protection — thin gloves and a basic surgical-style gauze mask which I knew from Mom's lectures on the subject would stop only particles and droplets coming at you from the front, and did little for airborne viruses. I could — almost — see the edges of his mouth smiling beyond the mask's loose-fitting sides. Risky stuff.

This morning, I had been determined not to be the only person wearing way more protection than anyone else, so I'd smuggled an E97 mask in my pocket to swap out before I got into the transport. I'd already said my goodbyes to Robin and my mother separately.

"Robin, please keep an eye on Mom. I know she'll worry about me, but don't let her get too anxious or, you know, go ... dark. Again. Come out of your cave occasionally and spend some time with her, okay? Promise me."

"Sure." He gave me a tight hug.

"And please do the waste incineration for her." The chore of lugging the contents of the bio-disposal bins to the basement and feeding them into the incinerator had always been mine. "You know how it freaks her out when she has to touch that stuff."

"Don't worry about us, Jinxy. Go and have fun with your rats." He was grinning.

"I totally intend to have fun," I said, ignoring his tease. "That's why I need to know you'll take care of Mom."

Downstairs, my mother made final adjustments to my respirator, zipped my PPE suit right up to my throat, and tucked a bottle of hand sanitizer and a pack of antiseptic wipes into my pocket. Her eyes were anxious even as she smiled down at me — the child who was Daddy's little girl but who for months had made Mom grilled cheese sandwiches or tuna salad for dinner, brought her water to take her meds, nagged Robin to get to school on time, and later, to log on for his cyber-tutorials. To her, I was still a little kid who liked Captain Crunch and watching old reruns of *The Simpsons*. And yet, apparently, I could shoot, and I was leaving home to learn how to shoot real live plague rats.

"To think my daughter is going to have such an important role in the war against the plague. I'm so proud of you!"

The words, "Your father would be so proud of you," hovered between us, but they remained unspoken. My mother never spoke about Dad, and if Robin or I mentioned him, her eyes would cloud over and fill with tears. When the two of us wanted to talk about Dad and the days before the plague, we did so in private.

"Don't be too soft on Robin, Mom. If you let him, he'll dream all day and read all night. Make sure he does his schoolwork and finishes the semester, and encourage him to do more programming units on The Game — he's really good and could turn it into a career, unlike poetry. And he needs hugs every day, even when he pretends he's too old for them."

"I know what I'm doing! I've been a mother for sixteen years, Jinx, I'm hardly likely to stop now."

You did before.

"Of course," I reassured her. "And don't worry about me. I'll be perfectly safe."

"I'll always worry. It's part of my job description as a mother. I suppose you'd better go now, they're waiting for you."

"Love you," I called to them.

"More!" they shouted back.

As soon as I was in the decon unit with my back turned to Mom and Robin, I swapped my half-face respirator for the lighter, form-fitted mask. When the decon unit door clicked open, I hurried off to the transport, not turning to wave. I didn't want my mother to see that I was hardly out the door and already I was breaking her rules.

It looked like the same twelve-seater Hummer, though its sides were a plain, glossy black with no PlayState logo. I was surprised to see that the official standing beside the open door, holding a clipboard and pen, was Fiona, one of the instructors from the simulation.

"Hi! How come you're here? Do you also work at the Academy?" I asked, confused.

"Stow your bag," she said, pointing to the trailer behind the vehicle.

As I hoisted my luggage into the trailer, I noticed that many of the other bags bore airline tags. This transport must already have collected new recruits from the airport. The recruits starting their training with me today probably came from all over the Southern Sector.

Fiona closed and locked the lid, then held out the clipboard and pen to me.

"As you were informed in the documentation sent to you, you need to sign a non-disclosure confidentiality agreement about today's proceedings. Also, before you get inside, please note that there's to be no talking on the transport to the Academy."

It struck me as a little extreme, but there must be a good reason for it, so I made no objection as I signed the form and then climbed inside.

Bruce had seated himself up front. I noticed that he had shaved some sort of geometric pattern into the strip of buzz-cut hair above his ears. He gestured to the seats opposite him, which were impossible to avoid since all the rest, except for the spot right next to him, were taken. It was awkward, being in one of the two seats that faced everyone else, including Bruce. Why did I keep finding myself in this hot spot?

Ten sets of eyes stared back at me — from faces that were black, white and brown, male and female, with a variety of different styles and colors of hair. One boy near the back had hair cut into a triangular scarlet afro. It was hard to tell because of the masks, but I guessed they were all a couple of years older than me. I'd made a good call on the face-mask because only one person, a slim Asian boy with a ponytail, was wearing a half-face respirator.

"Do you know if Leya is also coming?" I asked Bruce. I was keen to make a friend of her.

Fiona spun around from her seat up front and shushed me. "I told you — no talking."

I made a placatory gesture with my hands.

We didn't collect Leya. I hoped this was because she lived clear across town, and this transport was collecting recruits only from our side of town, and not because she hadn't made the cut. We made one more stop en route to the Academy — outside a small house in a low-income neighborhood closer to the center.

It looked like a scene out of a movie from before. There was an old-fashioned wooden swing-bench on the front porch, a low picket fence with peeling white paint out front, a basketball hoop mounted on the wall above the garage, and a blue-and-green toy pedal wagon lying on its side in the short driveway fringed with crimson azaleas. Did anyone actually swing on that seat or play in that yard?

Several people came out the front door at once — didn't they have a decon unit? — a tall teenage boy carrying a big, black duffel bag in one hand and a cat in the other, a shorter young man holding the leads of two dogs who were madly barking and leaping about, a much younger girl in an orange dress, and a middle-aged couple whom I assumed were their parents. The tall boy handed the cat to the little girl and then hugged each of the family in turn, even kissing the girl and the woman. I stared at them, shocked. None of them, except the boy now striding toward the Hummer, was wearing a mask or gloves.

He signed the form Fiona handed him, but when she warned him of the no-talking rule, he lifted his eyebrows in surprise.

"Really? Why's that?"

Fiona eyed him for a moment before sniffing then replying, "Because this transport includes recruits from across different … specialties. And you don't yet have security clearance to hear about them."

"Okaay," he said slowly.

Bruce craned his neck to see the new recruit, then his eyes registered the empty seat next to me and he swung himself territorially across into it, sitting right up against me and gesturing to the newcomer, when he climbed inside, to take the seat opposite us.

Which was fine with me, because now, as the vehicle pulled off, I got to study the smiling gray eyes, the wayward mahogany hair, and the dark tone of his skin. I couldn't decide if he was naturally olive-skinned or just deeply tanned, but together with the silver ring piercing his left brow, it made him look like a pirate. Black-and-white checkerboard sneakers stuck out below fraying denims — alone amongst all of us, he wasn't wearing a disposable PPE suit. He was wearing faded Levis and a long-sleeved gray T-shirt printed with the graphic of a stick figure who had a single, vertical line for an eye, and something written below. As I leaned forward to read the message, the Hummer bounced roughly over a pothole and I lurched forward almost into his lap. He caught me around the arms, steadying me. Bruce grabbed a handful of the back of my suit and snatched me back into my seat beside him.

"Would you like to sit next to me" — the pirate gestured to the space beside him — "or perhaps in my lap?" His voice was deep with a slight lilt to it, and one eye twitched as he spoke. Unless … Had he just winked at me?

Fiona turned from her seat up front and scowled at me. No fair — I hadn't been the one talking.

"No talking," she snapped.

"You're kidding, right?" the new guy said. "We were only playing around. I wasn't talking about anything sensitive. Well," he added with another wink at me, "not *security*-sensitive."

"I never kid," Fiona said.

Looking at her fierce frown, I believed her.

"And this isn't a game," she added.

The pirate raised his eyebrows at me. Then he leaned forward and stretched his shirt out from his chest so I could read the words printed there: "*It's all fun and games until someone loses an eye.*"

Then I did smile. Actually, I laughed. And so did he.

Chapter 10

Asta

The Advanced Skills Training Academy was located on the same private road on which the PlayState headquarters was located, but about half a mile farther down, right at the tail end. It was surrounded by the same dense woods and protected by the same massive security fence with guard huts on the perimeter, and floodlights and video surveillance cameras mounted in key positions. I figured the two had to be connected in some way.

The complex was laid out roughly in the shape of a daisy — if daisies could have rectangular petals and an oval center. The rectangle closest to the road (about a quarter mile down a narrow drive) was the main Academy building — five floors high, gray brick with long sealed windows that glittered opaquely in the morning sunlight. This was where we began our processing, first passing through decon units, then gathering in a large marble-floored foyer along with around fifty or so other young recruits, none of whom were talking. Weird.

Looking around in the hope of seeing Leya, I noticed that the pirate was standing a few paces behind me. Bruce still stuck to my side like a barnacle, nodding approvingly at a massive 3D hologram which was projected on the first landing of the wide central staircase leading to the second floor. A yellow-and-red logo of upward-pointing arrows, like the chevrons on a sergeant's insignia badge, rotated above the words Advanced Specialized Training Academy (ASTA) *Inform, Protect, Improve.*

When recruits from another transport were ushered in, I took advantage of Bruce's momentary distraction to move away from him, off to the side of the room. The sound of introductory music made me glance up to the landing, and I discovered that the pirate was now standing next to me. He turned to look down at me — he really was very tall — and I could have sworn those gray eyes were smiling again. When the hologram started speaking, he turned his full attention to the holo-zone. It was a live transmission from none other than Southern Sector President, Alex Hawke, who welcomed us warmly to the Academy and wished us the best of luck in our training.

I wanted to listen to the rest of Hawke's speech, but I battled to stay focused. I was too aware of the lean figure next to me. He was standing so close that our arms were pressed against each other, and I could feel the warmth of his body through my jumpsuit. I snuck a sideways glance at him. Although he seemed to be watching and listening intently, he somehow radiated an air of skepticism. Perhaps it was in the fold of his arms across his chest, or the small frown between his eyes, or in the evaluative tilt of his head. Once he shook his head very slightly and sighed softly.

It must have been a good speech, though, because when Hawke finished speaking the gathered recruits applauded and nodded enthusiastically. When the holo-zone reverted to the ASTA logo, gray eyes looked down at me, eyebrows raised as if to say, "Well, what do you think of that?"

I shrugged. I had been more focused on the guy next to me than the man on the screen, but judging from the odd phrases I had caught, the Pres had said more or less the same things he always said when he made a speech on T.V.: be vigilant, report suspicious people and activity, serve your nation in the war against terror and the pandemic, play your role as a loyal citizen.

Now a new transmission began playing. On the landing was a life-size hologram of a short, compact woman of around fifty years, wearing a navy skirt and jacket over a plain white shirt. The image shifted to a head-and-shoulders view, showing more detail: high cheekbones, dark eyes and an asymmetrically-cut bob of sleek black hair. When she moved her head, the underside of her hair flashed a deep iridescent violet, like the purple-skinned pokeweed berries Dad had pointed out to me on our family vacations in National Parks around the States. The woman was striking, but not beautiful. Her mouth was too small for her face, and the blood-red lipstick which was the only make-up she wore only emphasized the thinness of her lips.

"Welcome, new recruits, welcome. I am Roberta Roth, Chief Executive Officer of the Advanced Specialized Training Academy coming to you via live-stream from Washington. I'm sorry not to be able to welcome you in person. I want to commend each and every one of you for showing exceptional skills in your different fields of expertise. What I tell you next is confidential, and you are reminded that you have signed a legally binding contract not to disclose to anyone what you may learn here today."

She paused and let the warning sink in before continuing.

"Few beyond these walls know that the primary function of The Game, which all of you have been playing so skillfully for these last several years, is not that of mere entertainment."

The Game wasn't just a game?

"Yes, it is fun to play in your various gamer roles, and that is all it will ever be to most who play it. But for the last three years, The Game's real purpose, its most important function, has been to help us identify those gifted individuals who may be able to employ their valuable skills in serving the government and citizens of this great nation at a time when our very existence is threatened by heinous terrorists. In short, The Game is a recruitment tool."

A low murmur of surprise buzzed around the room at these words. I was pretty astonished myself. I mean, I'd guessed, from Fiona's presence at the game simulation and on the transport this morning, and from the fact that PlayState and The Academy were neighbors, that there might be some connection between them, but I hadn't figured that the Game's main purpose was to identify and recruit workers for the government. I snuck a glance at the pirate, but he was staring fixedly at Roth.

"You need to know this in order to make an informed decision about whether you wish to proceed with your induction and training here at the Academy. ASTA is a private agency mandated by our government to identify, recruit and train the brightest of this nation's teenagers. The goal is to train you to become skilled allies in the fight against the terrorists who have decimated our population with their evil disease, and reduced our freedoms and traditional way of life to shadows of their former selves."

Beside me, the pirate shifted his stance restlessly.

"Your skills have been developed through gaming. Your performance — online and in real-life simulations — has been monitored and your proficiency noted."

What the heck? All the time I'd been playing, some person or program had been monitoring my performance, comparing and evaluating me against other players? It sounded like even the simulated sniper mission had been a test of sorts. I thought back to that day, seeing everything differently in the light of this new information. Had Sarge, Fiona and Juan been observing us, to see if we could carry over our marksmanship and keep our cool in a "real-life" situation? If so, Graham had obviously disqualified himself by losing his nerve when under pressure. And had that disgusting dead rat been placed in the arena deliberately? I was sickened by the idea that someone had killed an animal and brought it to that precise and nauseating stage of decomposition merely to check how we would respond. Maybe the hostage situation had also been some kind of test. Would I have been ruled out of selection if I'd surrendered, as I had first wanted to?

"Some of you," continued Roth, "are our latest recruits to programs that already exist, but a few of you will be our first participants in a newly established unit. We believe that all of you have the talent and potential necessary to become skilled specialists in the service of your nation, and we would like to invite each of you to join our world of skilled and protective service. If you stay, you will be signing up for a period of training and employment of not less than eighteen months. During that time, you will be paid a small monthly stipend and will amass a wealth of training and experience which will stand you in good stead for getting an excellent job afterwards. If you are not wholly enthusiastic or willing to commit yourself fully to a program which will, I warn you, be challenging, then you are free to leave. Simply raise a hand now, if that is your choice, and you will be escorted safely home."

Everyone in the room looked around, but no one raised a hand. I hesitated.

I was being offered an out from the confined stir-crazy of home, as well as the chance to do something meaningful to help bring about the end of the war which had kept me trapped, kept all of us trapped, for the last four years. Part of me — the part whose job it was to worry about Mom and Robin — nudged me to raise my hand. But the rest of me, the selfish parts, I guess, wanted to stay here more than I had ever wanted anything. Maybe Robin would be late in submitting his school assignments, maybe Mom would work too late into the night designing websites for her clients, but they'd be safe at home. Besides, Mom would want me to serve my country, wouldn't she? And Robin knew how much I chafed against the restrictions made necessary by the plague. He escaped into his books; he wouldn't deny me a chance to escape using my skill.

I moved my hands, but only to clasp them together behind me. I was smiling widely behind my mask.

The pirate looked down at me, an odd expression in his eyes.

"You all wish to stay? How wonderful!" said Roth, her thin lips curving in a brief smile. Was *she* watching *us* via a live-stream, too? "Right, you will all now be taken to the medical and intake section, located down the corridor to your right, where you will be processed and assigned to your units. I look forward to getting to know you during your stay here. Please refrain from speaking to each other until processing is complete." With a final flash of violet, her hologram disappeared.

As we all trooped down the stairs to the intake and processing department, I followed behind the pirate, admiring the way his wide shoulders tapered down to his lean waist.

First stop was the registration table.

"Ladies first," said the pirate, stepping aside.

The uniformed official standing behind the table checked my registration slip off against an online list on his touchscreen computer, took my bags and labeled them. Then he issued me an empty cardboard box and a sealed package which he fetched from the packed tall shelves behind him.

"You're in the black unit," the official said.

"Thanks." I lingered behind to hear which unit the pirate would be in.

Blue. Crap.

Next, we were directed to the row of unisex decon shower booths. Another official, wearing the same sand-colored uniform, mask and gloves as the man behind the table, directed me to a booth as soon as the green light beside its door indicated that it was free.

"Shower, change into the garments in the package and put everything you are currently wearing into the box. When you are finished, exit via the door at the other side of the booth and proceed to the medical examination." She repeated the instructions to each recruit as they reached the front of the line.

I nodded and entered the booth, and the door swung closed behind me. In the tiny changing booth, I stripped and placed my folded clothes, underwear and shoes into the box. Both my box and package were labeled with black stickers bearing the same number: JJ20027. As soon as I stepped under the showerhead in the adjacent stall, the water turned on automatically. It was good and hot, but it was also yellow and smelt funny. Though it was probably only some strong sort of disinfectant, it felt like showering in pee.

The walls of the booth and shower were high enough not to be able to see over, but they reached down only to just below my knees. From where I stood under the spray, I could see under the booth walls into the lower section of the adjacent booth's changing area, where a pair of checkerboard sneakers lay on the ground. I was hyper-aware that I was naked and showering next to the pirate, with only the three-quarter shower wall between us. Now and then I saw a foot and ankle in the gap. Could he see my feet, with their long second toes and blue nail polish?

When the water stopped, I opened the package. Inside I found a disposable drying cloth, latex gloves and a new mask, as well as clothes — a bra and panties, a pair of black sneakers, socks and three black, all-in-one, zip-up jumpsuits. Everything was in my size.

I dressed, put on my gloves and mask, and tried to find a way to open the door at the other end of the shower cubicle, but apparently that was automated, too, because there was no latch or handle and it didn't open when I pushed. A few minutes later, it swung open with a soft ping. I exited and joined the next line, directly behind the pirate, who was now wearing a blue jumpsuit. When he noticed me, he stretched out a hand and brushed my dripping hair off my chest. I looked down to see that he had exposed the name embroidered in white thread and block capital letters over the breast pocket of the suit.

"Jinx?" he asked softly.

I nodded.

I read the name on his breast pocket. *QUINN O'RILEY.*

"So we're in different units?" I whispered.

"Looks like it," he said.

"What are you —" I began.

But Quinn held a finger up to his mask-covered lips and then, keeping his hand close against his chest, he pointed upwards and tilted his head a bit back. My eyes flicked above and beyond him. A small camera, like a dark, round fisheye, was mounted in the ceiling of the room. That was odd. Why would there be security cameras down here? Surely no one would want to break into the facility to use the showers?

I said nothing more but twisted my head to scan the line growing behind me. About ten positions back, I recognized the dark skin, short, spiky hair and temple tattoo of Leya. I was pleased to see she was also in a black jumpsuit, so at least I'd have a friend in my unit. We smiled and waved at each other. Soon Quinn was directed into a medical examination booth, and a minute or two later, I was sent into the booth next to him. Things worked like clockwork around here.

Inside the booth, a bored-looking medic with hot-pink hair and matching contact lenses took my blood pressure, stuck an infrared thermometer into my ear, and extracted a blood sample from a vein in my arm. Then she pulled down my mask and swabbed the inside of my cheek with something like a long, transparent mascara brush before twisting it closed in a glass vial. I felt exposed with my mask off — hers was still firmly in place — but not as exposed as when, a moment later, she told me to open my jumpsuit, peel it down to my waist and remove my bra for the examination. I did as she instructed, while she tossed the protective plastic nozzle-cover from the thermometer into a biohazard disposal bin.

I stood, rigidly uncomfortable and self-conscious. No one, as far as I could recall, had ever seen my body before except my mother. I hadn't gotten sick since we took to living inside years ago. A couple of years ago, I'd tripped and fallen down the stairs, landing hard on my wrist. Mom was worried I might have broken it, so she set up a consultation where the doctor examined my arm over video-call. He'd sent me for x-rays at the hospital, but no one had actually touched me, and I hadn't had to take off any clothes. I hoped the medic wouldn't mistake the blush of embarrassment I could feel spreading across my face and chest for the flushed rash of rat fever.

She checked my torso for the telltale spots and listened to my lungs through a stethoscope as I sat, naked from the waist up, all too aware of Quinn in the next booth. I could hear him speaking, asking something in his lilting voice.

"Two new masks and a box of gloves," replied another male voice, probably that of the medic examining him. "These will last you the ten days until your quarantine is lifted."

"Why only ten days? Don't the samples take twelve days to culture?" I heard Quinn ask.

"Are you complaining?"

"No. I was only wondering why the quarantine is shorter than normal."

"Because we have you under constant observation, that's why.

We'll soon pick up if there's a problem. Now please read and sign these forms."

My medic told me I could suit up again, gave me a package of gloves and masks, and then handed me three forms, preprinted with my details, instructing me to check that the information was all correct, before signing them.

The first form was a medical questionnaire and declaration of physical fitness, which came with a warning that it was a federal offense to lie or withhold information. The second was a waiver which indemnified ASTA against any legal claims in the event of me being injured or killed. Real overkill, as Robin would say. The third form was another confidentiality agreement.

I scanned the small print briefly before I signed. Though it was phrased in difficult-to-understand legalese, I figured I might just have promised, on pain of definite imprisonment and possible death or disembowelment, not to tell anybody, anything. Ever. More overkill. I was only going to shoot rats, and that surely couldn't be a state secret. Then again, I didn't know what the other divisions were up to. I had only The Game to go by. If we had been recruited according to the specialized roles we'd played, maybe some of these recruits would be helping with code-breaking or spying. That work would be much more sensitive than rat extermination.

"Do you understand what you have read and signed?" the medic asked when I handed back the papers.

"Not really," I admitted. "I'm not clear what I am and am not allowed to talk about, and with whom."

"You may not talk to anyone on the outside about anything — *anything*," she emphasized, "that you see, hear or do at this facility. You may speak freely to members of your unit once you leave this processing unit, but for the first six weeks of training, you may not converse about any aspect of your unit's specialized training or work to any recruit from another unit. If you can't cope with that level of confidentiality, then you won't be the sort of person we want working for us. Any breach of this rule will result in immediate expulsion from the program and, as you've seen," she tapped the contract, "serious legal consequences. You are free, of course, to liaise with recruits from other units as long as you talk about non-sensitive subjects."

"Such as?"

"Religion, money, politics," she said, with a brief laugh. "Plus there's always the weather."

"What happens after six weeks?"

"You graduate and are presumed to be trustworthy."

She countersigned the agreements, slipped them all into a manila folder with my name on it and stuck another of the black stickers on the outside.

"Left- or right-handed?" she asked.

"Right."

She grasped my left arm and wrapped a stainless steel band around the wrist.

"This is your ID bracelet. You are officially now an ASTA cadet." She sealed the band closed with a special clamp. "You are not to remove this under any circumstances."

"Right," I said, studying the band. It had the JJ20027 engraved into it, but not my name.

"Here's a map to your quarters and the whole facility. You're in room twelve, ground floor, west wing." She pointed to the highlighted rectangular petal to the left of the central oval marked *gymnasium*. "You may proceed to your quarters now."

"What about my clothes and stuff?"

"All your belongings will be delivered to your quarters once they've been through decontamination and inspection."

"Inspection?"

What were they looking for — rats? Syringes filled with contagion? I wondered what they would make of the bottles of vitamins and immune-boosters my mother had packed in my bag.

"We check for alcohol and illicit substances. You'd be amazed what people try to smuggle in."

Uh-oh. I wondered if my economy-sized pack of peanut-butter cups would count as an illicit substance? Maybe we weren't supposed to have brought in food.

"Right, Cadet James, that's you processed. Goodbye and good luck."

Outside the medical processing unit, Quinn was leaning up against a wall. He pushed off when I emerged and walked over, his hand extended to shake mine.

"Hullo, there, I'm Quinn O'Riley. Pleased to meet you."

I shook his hand shyly and awkwardly, unfamiliar now with the old ritual. It wasn't something most people did anymore. His hand was big and warm, even through the gloves, as it enclosed mine.

"I'm Jinx James. Um, pleased to meet you too."

We looked at each other over the tops of our masks for a few moments while other recruits brushed past.

"So, Quinn O'Riley? Is that an Irish name?" I asked.

"You sound surprised."

"You just don't look …"

"Not all Irish have milk skin, freckles and red hair, and look like they danced out of Brigadoon."

"I'm sorry. I didn't mean —"

"Don't worry yourself. I'm what they call Dark Irish, or Black Irish."

At my puzzled look, he explained, "We have darker hair and skin. Depending on who you believe, our ancestors were Viking invaders or Spanish sailors. Or fairies."

"Fairies?"

"The little people, you know. Apparently our ancestral mothers weren't too picky and were very … loving."

He had me laughing again.

"You look more like a pirate than a fairy."

"That's probably a good thing."

"And you sound a little Irish, the way you speak."

"I was born right here, but at my school we were taught by Irish nuns and both my parents are from the old country, County Cork, so I guess I've picked up a bit of the brogue, what with being stuck in the house with them for the last four years and all," he said. "So, can I escort you to your quarters?"

"Jinx! Hiya!" Leya ran up to me and gave me a friendly elbow bump. "We're in the same unit, isn't that awesome? C'mon, we're in the west wing. Blue is in the northeast," she said with a nod to Quinn.

"See you later?" I called back to him as Leya grabbed my elbow and tugged me away.

"It's a date," he said.

"Wooeee," said Leya, when we were out of earshot. "Brucey-baby has got himself some competition!"

Chapter 11

Surely, Goodness and Mercy

The first ten days of boot camp were a blurred hell of hard exercise, mind-numbingly long lectures, and hurried solitary meals carried on trays to our individual quarters, where we could remove our masks to eat. Ten days of sore muscles, blistered fingers, ringing ears, a bruised shoulder, brain fatigue, and bad food.

And Quinn.

Maybe my radar was stuck on pirate mode, but he seemed to be everywhere I looked — running ahead of me on the track in the gymnasium, playing pool or pinball in the rec room, and walking through the hallways between lectures.

At dinner the first night, I spotted him immediately — leaning up against the glass swing-doors to the cafeteria.

"Well, and if it isn't Jinx E. James," he said, as I drew alongside.

"Hi." I wished I could think of a cool way to greet him.

He held the door open for me to pass through.

"So, you'll be all settled in then?"

"I'm all unpacked."

I wouldn't call it settled. I felt nervous, out of place among so many new people, uncertain how to interact. I hadn't even been inside a cafeteria since the sixth grade.

"I figured we'd be getting sealed meals," I said, taking the tray Quinn passed to me and getting into the self-service line for food.

"They must be certain of their security. Besides, where's the fun in sealed meals? How could I tempt you with Irish delicacies that way?"

"There are Irish delicacies in the buffet?"

I scanned the display of food. I had no idea what many of the dishes were.

"Sure, yeah. Why, this now" — Quinn drew my attention to what looked like pieces of overcooked white fish — "is Cullen skink, an old family favorite. Here, let me help you to a morsel."

"Um, okay." I looked longingly at the roast pork tenderloin under red heat lamps across the way, but Quinn ushered me forward.

"Ah, now these are delicious." He was putting on a thick Irish accent for this guided tour through the home country cuisine.

"Really?" I peered dubiously into the dish of vegetables. "They look like miniature green cabbages."

"Phfa! Those are Colcannon crubeens. You'll be liking them."

He spooned a heap of them onto my plate. His own was conspicuously empty.

"You aren't having any?"

"I'll get my food after I've helped you. Ladies first, and all that. Ah! The cook must surely be an Irishman, for look, if it isn't Limerick Coddle."

Another ladleful onto my plate.

"I'm pretty sure that's okra."

I had a dim memory of my father once cooking the green, finger-shaped vegetables. It had ended with my mother pulling a revolted face and Robin and I hurling spoons full of the slimy mess at each other.

"You'll love it."

"Perhaps some salad?" I suggested.

"Not when there are tatties to be had!" He sounded scandalized and heaped a large dollop of lumpy mashed potatoes onto my already full plate. "There, now, you're set to go."

"Right."

Bruce, who was also getting his meal, stared down at my plate and said, "Blue, that looks beyond disgusting."

"They're Irish delicacies."

"Makes me glad I'm an American, born and bred," said Bruce. He said it to Quinn.

"As am I," said Quinn.

"Yeah, sure," said Bruce, brushing past us. "Don't forget, Blue, oh-six-hundred on the track."

"Isn't he a charmer? Well, Jinxy, I'll see you around," said Quinn, heading to the back of the line to get his own food. "Enjoy your meal."

"Okay, yeah, so long."

I made my way to one of the two checkout stations, noting that everyone else had more appetizing food on their trays than I had on mine. The checkout worker scanned my ID bracelet, placed my plate into a scanner, hit a few keys on a touch-screen, and then an analysis of its nutritional content was entered against my name in her system. She nodded, and I was free to head back to my quarters. I glanced back at the buffet as I passed and got a friendly wave from Quinn. I could swear there was a large portion of pork tenderloin on his plate.

The food was awful. The fish was overcooked and mushy, the okra was as slimy as I remembered, and the miniature cabbages were watery, bitter enough to make me shudder, and smelt of stinky feet. I resorted to eating most of my candy from home and feeling distinctly ick.

The next morning, Quinn was waiting for me again.

"Good morning to you, Jinx. And did you enjoy your uniquely Irish meal last night?"

"Uhm, it was definitely … unique."

"Excellent! Ready to try more, then?"

"Well …"

"Here, try some Boxty pudding" — lumpy oatmeal — "Irish oysters" — hard-boiled eggs — "and barm brack" — stale wholegrain bread. "Faith, we'll make a convert of you yet!"

By that night, I was on to him. He urged me to try some of what he called Blarney Stew, but to me it looked like chili swimming under a layer of oil.

"Then hurrah for an Irish Stew, that will stick to your belly like glue," he sang in his deep voice.

When he brought a heaping portion to my plate, I rapped his knuckles with the back of my spoon.

"Attacked — by a wench!"

"A *wench*?"

"The beautiful woman who is the object of a pirate's affections."

I looked down at the spoon, smiling behind my mask.

"You'll have put me out of business for the day," Quinn said, pulling a pained face and rubbing his knuckles. So he used his hands for his work? Maybe there was another sniper unit. Damn, but I wished I knew what his specialty skill was.

"Blarney stew, my eye!"

"Ay?" His exaggerated look of innocence only confirmed my suspicions.

"Quinn, I think you've been messing with me."

He burst into loud laughter. It was a deep, rolling, breathless belly-laugh, and it was contagious as hell.

"I was flabbergasted that you fell for it a'tall. You shouldn't believe everything you're told, you know."

"You, you —"

"I wondered how long it would take before you overcame your good manners and sent me to the devil!"

"Consider it done," I said.

"Ah," he said, dabbing at his eyes with the sleeve of his blue jumpsuit. "Well, it was fun while it lasted. Say you forgive me?"

"No. Those little cabbagey things? You're due some payback on those."

"Well, Jinxy, you tell me what you would like to eat, and I'll serve it to you."

I pointed to spicy tacos, green salad and lemon cake.

"And tomorrow, at breakfast, I'll want a chocolate muffin," I warned.

"I'll be sure and save you one." His gray eyes smiled down at me. "They do taste fantastic."

"While I was eating oatmeal and hard-boiled 'Irish oysters', you were eating chocolate muffins? Argh! I am going to get you good, Quinn O'Riley."

"I look forward to it," he said, and his eyes shone with something warmer than mere humor.

Suddenly unsure, I focused hard on the nutritional analysis at the checkout. When I snuck a sideways glance at him, he was still looking at me.

"Well, so long," I said, lifting my tray a little in explanation.

"Let me walk you to your wing."

"It's not on your way."

"Ah, you're wrong there, lass. It'll always be on my way."

For once, I was grateful for the respirator — it hid the blush warming my cheeks.

The next morning, Quinn walked me back to my wing again, each of us with a chocolate muffin on our breakfast tray. He had put two on my plate, but the checkout lady had frowned at me and told me my meal was too high in sugar and refined carbohydrates, and I'd sadly returned one of them to the baked goods rack.

Quinn cleared his throat and then said, "That fella the other night, the charmer, with the …" He sketched the shape of bulging neck and bicep muscles.

"Bruce?"

"The same. Is he —? Are you —?"

What was he asking?

"He's just another cadet in my division."

Quinn paused to open a fire door for me. At first I'd felt a little awkward when he did this for me, but it made such a nice change from being yelled at to go faster, run harder, hang longer by the males in my unit, that I soon grew to like it.

"He called you Blue."

"Yeah, because of my hair, I think."

He reached out a hand to twirl one of the colored strands.

"And, you know, my eyes."

"No, it can't be because of your eyes, else he would have called you Periwinkle, or perhaps Sapphire."

Was he flirting with me? Just the idea had my heart picking up speed. I *wanted* the pirate to flirt with me. Heck, I wanted to flirt with *him*, but I had no experience with boys, and no idea what to say.

"Do you like being called Blue?"

"Not really, but I got nicknamed in the —" I stopped myself. I'd been about to say in the Sniper Simulation Mission. You had to be so careful what you said here, no wonder most cadets hung out only with their divisional buddies. "I got the nickname early on, and it seems to have stuck."

"Do you mind if I call you Jinxy rather?"

"No. I mean, I like it. It's what my brother Robin calls me."

"Jinx and Robin. Those are very different kinds of names. Robin is pretty standard, but Jinx …"

"It doesn't mean what you think."

"Yeah?"

"It's from the Latin Iynx, and it means *magic charm* or *spell.*"

"Enchanting … yeah, that fits."

I was smiling again, unsure how to respond. "My father named me for his grandmother, and my mother named Robin for her grandfather. We're twins — Robin and I, I mean."

"Twins! You know, the Irish have some superstitions about twins."

"No doubt they involve something called Blarney Blinkety," I said, and because I was more interested in him than Ireland, I quickly got in a question of my own.

"Was that your family I saw on your porch?"

"Yup. I have an older brother, Connor; a little sister, Kerry; my mother and father of course, and two dogs — magnificent mongrels both — called Surely and Goodness. Oh, and a cat called Mercy."

"Surely, Goodness and Mercy — you're kidding?" He had me smiling again.

"I am not."

"And do they follow you about for all the days of your life?"

"They do try! Well the dogs do, but Mercy holds herself a little aloof — you know how cats are."

I shook my head. I'd had a hamster when I was in fourth grade. Mom shuddered now whenever she remembered that we'd actually kept a rodent as a pet inside the house. But it had stuffed its cheeks with food and run on its wheel for only a couple of years before going to the great seed bar in the sky. In the summer vacation before I started seventh grade, the plague had broken out, and any chance of ever getting another pet was over.

"We never had a cat," I said. "Or a dog."

"Never?"

"Nope. My mother never liked the mess, and after the plague began, no way would she allow pets. My mom worries," I added by way of explanation.

"Not even a goldfish? Or, say, an ant-farm?"

"She worries *a lot*."

Actually, I think the worrying saved Mom. The fear of the virus and the worry of contagion woke her from her flatlined state. Her obsession converted her numb depression into anxiety and transformed her grief over the loss of her husband into a fierce determination not to lose her children.

"I couldn't imagine not having pets. I love my animals!" Quinn's expression was a mixture of incredulity and pity. "Is it only the one brother you've got then?"

"Yeah, just Robin. And my mom, of course. My father died when I was twelve."

"I'm sorry to hear that," said Quinn.

It occurred to me that he was the first person here that I'd told about my dad.

"So you're sixteen now?"

"Yeah. And you?" I'd been dying to know how old he was.

"Just turned eighteen." He paused, then grinned and said, "D'you think that makes me too old?"

"Too old for what?"

"For you."

I blushed furiously. I wanted to say, "No, it makes you just right for me," but I forced myself to say only, "I'll be seventeen in November."

"Ah, perfect then."

We walked a bit in silence, then Quinn asked, "Do you miss him? Your father?"

"Yeah, I do. We were very close. My mother ... well, she's always connected better with Robin, I guess. I was closer to my father." Another swing door. "I really miss the good times we had when he was alive. It's kind of like life before the plague is all tied up with my memories of him. He loved to be out and about, doing things and meeting people."

I tried to call his face to my mind. Failed. Sometimes, when I wasn't trying, a memory would roll in — of Dad carrying a sleep-floppy me from the car to my bed after a long road trip; of Dad's laugh when I told him how my stuffed bear had eaten the last doughnut; of Dad running with Robin and me on the edge of the beach where the firm, wet sand met the foam-edged waves.

I sighed.

"He wouldn't have liked what the world has become."

"He sounds like a wise man." Quinn spoke so intensely that I glanced at him. "We've all lost a lot, haven't we? Our lives are so small, so limited now. And we're so tightly — Ah, listen to me spouting off on philosophy when you're still fresh with losing your father."

"It's not really fresh any more. But I miss knowing him at this age. Like I wonder what he would think of my work here? I wonder if he'd rather I stayed at home with Mom."

We were at the entrance to the west wing, now, where the black unit's living quarters were. Leya came out, followed by Bruce, and deposited their trays on the stainless steel trolley parked outside the door.

"Better hurry, Blue, we're due in Lecture Room Four in twenty minutes," said Leya as she headed back in the direction we'd just come from.

"Yeah, Sarge won't like it if you're late," added Bruce, with an unfriendly look at Quinn.

"I'd better go," I said to Quinn.

"I'll see you later," he said.

Then he leaned forward and pressed his respirator against

mine. If we hadn't been wearing the masks, it would have been a kiss.

I blinked in surprise and he was gone, walking to his wing. I touched my gloved hand to the mask.

"Jinxy!"

I looked up just in time to see and catch what Quinn had tossed to me. A chocolate muffin.

Soft and sweet as a hug.

Chapter 12

Hot and Bothered

Three weeks into boot camp, the streaks in my hair had faded to a paler sky blue. I didn't intend to color them again, even though they seemed to fascinate Quinn, who would occasionally twist one of the blue strands around his fingers and play with it. I loved it when he did that, but in one of our sessions on camouflage and concealment, Sarge had stressed the need to blend in.

"Anything that makes you stand out, anything that makes you memorable, increases the risk of your being made by the enemy and becoming a bullet magnet. Like your tattoo, Leya, or your hair, Blue."

"Rats can see blue streaks in my hair and know that makes me a sniper?" I said.

"You'll be amazed what those vermin can do," said Sarge with that flash of a smile.

I had learned enough about our unit commander not to mistake that grimace for an expression of joy. Sarge was the hardest, toughest, meanest SOB I'd ever met. Scratch that — I hadn't met enough people in my life for it to be a meaningful comparison. He was the strictest, most merciless, stony-hearted, take-no-prisoners SOB I could ever imagine. From day one, when he put us through our first "smoke session", that manic grin had flashed on and off every time he pulled down his mask to yell at me.

"Blue, you've got another thirty laps of the track. Pick up the pace, sweetheart — my grandmother can run faster'n you." Grin.

"Princess, they're called push-ups, not fall-downs. Tell you what" — grin — "add another twenty to the total. You need the practice."

"45, 46, 47 … Work those abdominals, Goldilocks!" Grin.

Failure is not an option, I will not quit, I told myself. I wasn't grinning.

Trying to suck enough air into my gasping lungs through the muffler of the mask was torture, especially when pushing through my own personal hell of pull-ups and monkey-bars. I had never known, until I started basic training, that I had absolutely no upper arm strength at all. None. Zero. Zilch. The guys in our group swung across the bars like orangutans and hoisted themselves up on the cross-bars with only the odd groan. Bruce's buff form was made for brutal exercise, and Mitch hardly broke a sweat. That didn't surprise me — he was a big, muscled nineteen-year-old from New Orleans who, but for the plague, might have wound up playing football for The Saints. But Tae-Hyun, the slim masked kid from the transport, and Cameron, a geeky-looking guy with glasses who came from Tennessee and who hardly ever said anything, also managed the upper-body workouts with relative ease. Even Leya, the only other female cadet in our division apart from me, had a wiry strength which kept her swinging and hoisting when my muscles were screaming or just plain giving out.

Failure is not an option. I will not quit. Failure is not an option. I will not quit. I repeated the lines over and over in my mind until they became my personal mantra.

Some nights, I was so sore I would have cried myself to sleep, but usually I was so exhausted, I fell asleep as soon as my head hit the pillow. One evening, as I hobbled stiffly back from dinner in the cafeteria to my quarters, holding hands with my pirate, Quinn shook his head at me.

"Sweet mercy, but this is pitiful. Would you like a massage and all, Jinxy?"

"A what?"

"A massage. A rubbing down of your sore muscles. They say it helps."

My heart tripped and stumbled. He wanted to touch me. With his hands.

"Where — here?" We were standing at the entrance to the west wing.

"No, Jinxy," he said, very slowly, his fingers playing with a pale-blue length of my hair. "In your room. Your bedroom."

I didn't know what to say.

"If you invite me in, I promise not to ravish you. Though now that we're on the subject, maybe I could just put it out there that you are most welcome to jump my bones anywhere, anytime."

I could feel my cheeks flame.

"Um, are we allowed in each other's rooms?"

"I don't see why not. This is a training academy, not a convent. No one's said we can't."

I'd often had Leya in my room, sitting on the end of my bed for girl chats while we painted each other's toenails, and once all six of us in the unit had gathered in my room to have a gripe-session about Sarge. But we were all from the same division. I couldn't, however, recall any rule on the lists we'd been given that prohibited a cadet from a different division visiting us in our rooms — provided we didn't speak about our work, of course. And somehow, I didn't think that was what Quinn had in mind.

"Okay, yeah, sure," I said.

My voice sounded high to me. A boy in my bedroom. A boy

about to touch my body. It was a first. I was terrified. I felt self-conscious as I sat on the edge of my bed with Quinn on the floor at my feet, rolling up the legs of my jumpsuit. I prayed that my legs were smooth, wished that my room was less messy.

"Now Jinxy, as the doctors say, this might hurt a little," said Quinn, warming a squirt of anti-inflammatory gel between his hands.

I smiled back nervously. Gently at first, and then more firmly, he rubbed the gel into my calves. Within minutes, I wasn't thinking at all. I was blissed out on sensation. The almost painful pleasure of his strong, warm hands kneading my stiff muscles left me limp as a noodle, and I flopped back on the bed. After my calves, he moved onto my arms.

"Oh, Quinn," I sighed, wanting something. Wanting more.

"Yes, Jinxy?"

His voice asked a question. But I couldn't answer with what I really wanted to say — *More! All over!* — so instead I murmured, "S'so good. Thank you."

One night after a particularly brutal day's upper-body workout, I was in too much agony to feel shy. I rolled up my T-shirt and he massaged my back and shoulders, working deeply into the sore muscles, moving his warm hands around and under my bra strap while I lay on my stomach, close to passing out. If anyone could have overheard my groans of pain and pleasure, they would have assumed that we were doing something else for sure. I woke up the next morning, alone, with the T-shirt pulled back down, the covers pulled up over my shoulders and my running shoes on the floor next to my bed. I wasn't sure if what I felt was relief or disappointment.

Every day, we spent hours honing our marksmanship with light and heavier-caliber rifles, semi-automatic weapons, and small sidearms. These were my favorite hours of the day, when we learned to shoot in all conditions — in low or bright light, from high and low angles. We practiced observing and detecting, estimating ranges and hitting targets (large and small, stationary and moving), at close quarters in the simulated urban arena at the PlayState warehouse, or over seemingly impossible distances in the wooded area behind the Academy, or on the target shooting range behind the screen of a concrete wall at the far back of the compound. When we weren't exercising or shooting, we were assembling, disassembling or cleaning our weapons; sitting through lectures on applied explosives or hide-construction; or playing Kim's Game — an exercise designed to train our observation skills by noticing what item had been added to, or removed from, a scene.

We pitted ourselves against each other constantly. The Game must have trained our snipers' eyes, because we were all pretty accurate, though Mitch was fastest in situations where we had to run to certain spots and then shoot, and Tae-Hyun was best at high-angled shots. Bruce was exceptional, his only flaw a tendency to pull his shots to the left when he got nervous or angry. Cameron was a good all-rounder, but he unnerved me. His impassive face showed no emotion, and he never said any more than was strictly necessary, so I could never tell what he was thinking. From the way his eyes followed Leya, though, I guessed he did have a heart. Leya was the weakest in marksmanship, but she was excellent at concealment, camouflage and stalking.

On a good day, I could outshoot them all — as long as the targets were made of tin or paper — but when the targets had paws and whiskers, I came unglued. Cameron and Bruce were not at all fazed when we began practicing on live targets. Rats.

"It doesn't bother you that these are perfectly healthy creatures we're about to kill?" I asked, as we trudged into the alley inside the PlayState warehouse. We only practiced with the rats there, where they could be contained and prevented from escaping into the wild.

"They're still freaking mutants," said Tae-Hyun.

"'Sides, I've shot plenty of perfectly healthy creatures before," said Bruce. "And prettier ones than rats."

"Really?"

"Hunting," said Cameron.

"Oh."

I'd never liked the idea of hunting animals for sport. It seemed kind of sick to stick dead, stuffed heads above the mantelpiece, and it had always struck me as unfair — pitting high-powered scopes and rifles against dumb bucks. Bare-handed moose-wrestling would have been fairer sport.

"We're not hunting the rats, though. I mean, we're not going to eat them. It just seems wrong, such a waste of life." At least with venison, the meat was used.

"Aw, you're the hottest greeny-beany bunny-hugger I ever met," said Bruce, giving me a squeeze and lifting me right off my feet.

He was always finding excuses to touch me and pass inappropriate comments, even though I made it plain I was in no way interested in him. I wasn't sure how to handle it. I'd asked Leya, and she'd advised me to ignore it.

"If you don't react, eventually he'll get bored and lose interest," she said.

"You think?" I had been ignoring it so far, but I hadn't noticed any slacking off in his attention.

"Sure. Even now, I think he only does it to rattle you. Not that you're not pretty, or anything," she added quickly.

"Why does he want to rattle me?" I asked.

She rolled her eyes and gave me a *duh!* look. "Because you're the best marksman in the unit. And he thinks that if he can get to you with his stupid comments and free hands he'll make you lose your nerve, and then your performance will suffer and he'll step into first place."

I thought about that for a moment. It could be true, I supposed.

"So you don't think I should complain to Sarge about it?"

"Hell no! Can you imagine how that would go?"

I could. I could just hear Sarge telling me to toughen up and stop being such a delicate snowflake, and that if I couldn't take the heat I should quit the kitchen.

"The thing is, Jinx, that females are still majorly in the minority here, especially in the sniper unit. We have to be twice as good, twice as strong, twice as tough, just to be taken half as seriously as the guys. If you complain about this, you'll only come across as weak. You need to handle this one on your own, not go crying to papa-Sarge. Though you know I'm always here for you if you need to download."

I knew she was. We tended to stick together in training and often hung out together afterwards, especially when Quinn wasn't free. I liked her a lot. She was clever and funny, and she encouraged me whenever I had doubts. If I'd had a sister, I'd have liked her to be like Leya.

"Okay, I'll keep ignoring Bruce," I'd said. "But he'd better not push me too far."

Right now I made a point of stepping away from him, taking up a position on the other side of Cameron. The others were still trying to help me overcome my reluctance to shoot a live being.

"Don't think of them as individual animals," suggested Mitch. "They're just tangos."

Tango was the phonetic alphabet word for T. *T* was for *target*. *Target* was for the thing you shot, but both my instructors and my co-cadets had a real aversion to using real words to describe live things about to become dead.

"Need practice," said Cameron.

"We could practice on little robotic rats, like in The Game," I said. "I mean, if they can build RoboDogs, they can build RoboRats, right?"

Bruce laughed like I'd said something hilarious. Cameron shook his head.

"It wouldn't be the same, though, would it?" said Mitch. "We need to train on what moves, sits, behaves, and looks exactly like what we're going to be taking out."

Leya nodded. "Jinx, I understand why this upsets you, I do. But sometimes the ends justify the means. Even if it does seem a bit cruel, the better we are, the more useful we'll be in the war against the plague. It's critical that we know our enemy."

Still I hesitated.

"Blue, we're not going to win this war unless we're prepared to take them out," said Bruce.

"I guess," I said.

They were right. I knew that in the rational part of my mind. But still, when I had to kill my first rat — a live, healthy, uninfected and even kinda-cute-from-a-distance rat, with perky ears and twitching whiskers that reminded me of my old pet hamster — my stomach knotted.

"Is this absolutely necessary?" I asked Sarge.

"Is a frog's ass watertight?"

I pulled on my ear protectors, raised my rifle, aimed, and hesitated.

"Do it, Blue! Don't be a goddamn pansy. You're a sniper, soldier!" Sarge shouted. "On my command: ready, aim, fire!"

I did. I took careful aim, then fired. And missed by about a mile.

"Our motto is 'one shot, one kill', Goldilocks, not 'one shot, one miserable piss-ant miss'!"

Sarge had me do fifty push-ups as punishment. "Pain is good, now feel the goodness!"

Up — *Failure is not an option.* Down — *I will not quit.*

I had to track the rat and set up the shot all over again.

"You can do it, Jinx," said Leya, smiling encouragingly.

I wiped my sweaty palms on the legs of my jumpsuit, then shook out my arms, which were trembling from the PT, made sure my rifle was stable, waited for the rat to stop moving — the little critter was munching on something to the side of a metal trashcan — and then sent a round down the chamber that blew off most of its head. It was the first time I'd ever killed a living being.

"Congrats, you've popped your rat-cherry," whispered Bruce into my ear.

The others cheered. I swallowed hard and wiped my ear against my shoulder.

Prickly with guilt, I spent the rest of the day killing time. I wished I could tell Quinn about it that night as we played a game of pool in the rec room.

It was the night we were given the all-clear on our test results and granted permission to remove masks and gloves. Everyone, it seemed, had gathered in the rec room to celebrate, reveling in the fun of being able to openly eat and drink the snacks and sodas we bought from the vending machines.

It was strange and wonderful to finally see everyone's faces. Everyone looked completely different and somehow naked without their masks. More vulnerable. We all shuffled about, staring at each other and grinning sheepishly, like newly stripped visitors in a nudist colony.

I discovered that Leya had a small rosebud of a mouth, that Bruce had a square chin and Cameron a faint scar through his top lip, and that Tae-Hyun's tongue was pierced with a red barbell. His habit of tapping his tongue against his front teeth explained the faint clicking sound I sometimes heard coming from him.

Quinn's face was lean, with a strong jaw and a faint, but totally fascinating, cleft in his chin. His mouth was wide, his teeth white and even, and his humor infectious. Every time I saw his smile or heard his deep, lilting voice clearly without the slight muffle of the mask, something tight and hard melted inside me, and a glowing bubble of happy took its place.

Quinn stared and stared at my face until, embarrassed, I eventually ducked my head so that my hair swung down to hide my warm cheeks.

"Something's really bothering you, Jinxy." He brushed my hair back from my face, twisting one of the fading blue strands around his finger before tucking it behind my ear.

"Yeah."

"Let's get out of here. It's too crowded and noisy to talk."

It was. There was a whole lot of shouting and cheering coming from the pool table, and the digital jukebox was at full volume. One of the blue unit recruits, a heavily tattooed girl called Dasha, was doing a roaring trade selling prepaid cash cards. Probably black-market.

The day before, Quinn had urged me to buy a couple of the cards in a few different denominations.

"Why?" I'd asked. "I have a credit card."

"You never know when you might want to buy something without it leaving a trail for someone to follow."

Nobody used cash anymore — it was too risky when rat fever was so easily spread — but people still wanted a way to buy stuff without it showing up on their charge cards. Teens especially wanted a way to buy booze, cigarettes, age-restricted apps, movies and reading material without tipping off their parents. They said you could even buy banned books and firearms with cash cards — if you knew where to look. I'd taken Quinn's advice, more to please him than with any real idea of ever using them myself.

It was a relief to get away from the loud music, the din of the pinball machines and the shouts of the crowd.

We headed to the huge indoor arena of the gymnasium and walked slowly around its silent floodlit track. Quinn kept sneaking glances at me as we walked. I was hyper-aware of the way his ungloved hand wrapped around mine — it was big and hard, and warmer than I could have imagined — and the way holding hands with him made me feel. Safe and confident. With my hand in his, I could have taken on the world.

"So, tell me about it."

"I can't. It's, you know, work."

"I got to say, I don't get this whole secrecy thing."

I looked up at him, surprised. I hadn't questioned the need for the rule.

"I can just about understand why they think we shouldn't talk about our work to the outside world. Though I think people would be pleased to hear that there's a program to train experts in fighting the war against the plague. But why can't we talk to each other?"

I thought about that, but couldn't actually come up with many good reasons.

"We might tell someone outside?"

"In case you hadn't noticed, we're locked in a super high-security facility — we can't run off and alert the media."

"We could tell them on a call or in an email."

"Jinxy," he said, laughing down at me. "You do know our calls and mails are monitored."

"*What*?" I hadn't known. I hadn't even suspected.

"Every communication coming in or going out from this place is scanned and checked for classified information."

"But, isn't that illegal, an invasion of privacy? They should have told us!"

"I think you'll find they did, somewhere in the fine print of those contracts we all signed."

I scanned back over my calls and mails to Robin and my mother and the few friends I'd had contact with since coming here, trying to think if I'd said anything very personal. I already knew I hadn't said anything classified — I'd been a good girl on that front. Embarrassment blazed hot when I realized that I'd gushed to Robin about Quinn. Whoever was monitoring our communications would know all about my crush on him.

"Hey, you're blushing! Have you been doing something you shouldn't?" he teased.

"Not really." Not nearly enough.

He stroked a finger down my cheekbone and trailed it down my throat to the opening of my jumpsuit. The pit of my stomach tightened.

"Can I tempt you to do so, then?" he said. He cupped my chin and tilted it up, so that I was gazing straight into his warm eyes, and rubbed his thumb over my lower lip. "Can I lead you well and truly astray?"

Yes, please, I wanted to say. I'd like that a lot. All I managed was a soft, "Uh …" But my parted lips seemed answer enough for him.

He lowered his head, by slow, halting inches, then touched his lips to mine. I hadn't kissed anyone since Mom and Dad back when I was a tiny kid, and I'd sure as heck never kissed anyone like this. It felt foreign and familiar, forbidden and necessary. Exotic. Dangerous.

His lips were firm and warm and opened up a current of energy which both electrified me and welded me to him. His mouth, when he opened it against mine, was like a channel into the heart of him. He tasted of coffee and, at the corner of his mouth, minty toothpaste. His hands moved down from my face, over my back, along my waist and down to my butt as he hugged me tight against him. I was icy, burning, desperate to breathe, determined not to pull my mouth off his. I wanted to melt into him, to stay there forever. My hands crept up to touch his jaw, his temples, the silver ring through the dark brow. His body shuddered against mine.

When finally we came up for air, I was different, changed. This was something else I'd never known, hadn't even suspected.

Quinn looked like he had been rocked too.

"Faith!" he said, his voice deeper, rougher than usual.

"Who's Faith?"

"It's Irish for *wow. Freaking wow!*"

I grinned. "Good thing we've been working on our aerobic fitness." My voice was high and breathy.

"Never reckoned I'd be grateful for the training," he said, lowering his head to mine again.

And while I allowed my fingers to explore his thick hair, his muscled arms and shoulders, we tested our aerobic capacity for a good while longer.

Chapter 13

Clocked

The next morning, before breakfast, Quinn knocked at my door.

"I wanted to give you this." He handed me a small jewelry box.

"Are you proposing?" I teased, and was delighted to see I'd succeeded in making *him* blush for once.

"Nah, no diamonds. But those" — he gestured to the box — "come in pairs, and I wanted you to have the other one."

Inside the little box was a silver earring, the mate of the one threaded through Quinn's brow. My eyes filled.

"It was getting a bit lonely, all by itself in the box." When I didn't respond, he continued uncertainly. "But you only have to wear it if, you know, you like."

"I like."

He grinned. I threaded the hoop through my right ear, and as I closed the clasp, it felt like I was setting the seal on us. We, too, were a pair.

I only wished my shooting was going as well as our relationship, because even with weeks of practice, I hadn't gotten much better at shooting live targets. Everyone in the unit had their own theory about why I could hit the bull's eye in a paper target at a thousand yards, but couldn't reliably take down a rat at a quarter that distance.

"You obviously don't *want* to hit them, and your subconscious sabotages your shots," said Leya.

"Maybe you want to leave here and go home," suggested Tae-Hyun.

"No way," I said.

"It's because you're fantasizing about me naked when you should be focused on the rat," said Bruce.

"Even less way!"

"Guilt," said Cameron.

"You're overthinking it, you're jinxing it," said Mitch.

"Funny one, Mitch," I said, not smiling.

"Stop thinking about what you're doing and why you're doing it, and if it's right or wrong. Just do it, man," he said.

Sarge's opinion? "You need to take a teaspoon of cement and harden the hell up, soldier!"

"I can hack it," I said. If I told myself that often enough, it might become true.

I was super fit from the daily runs and the workouts on cross-trainers and rowing machines, and way stronger from weight-lifting and resistance-training than I had been before I came here. But I couldn't figure out why we had to be so fit and so strong. A lot of the kids at ASTA had weight to lose — a result of living lives indoors in front of PC screens, I guessed — and all the divisions, black, blue, green, red and orange, had a daily physical exercise regime. But none of the other instructors pushed their cadets as hard as Sarge pushed us.

"You need to be prepared for anything. A high-caliber weapon system can top twelve kilograms — that's pushing thirty pounds including scope and ammunition, and not including the other equipment you might have to lug around, such as range-finders, spare magazines, specialized optics, GPS and comms equipment, hydration-packs, and your sidearm."

He never said this kind of thing in the gymnasium, of course, where cadets from other divisions might be running past on the track, or lifting weights on the equipment, or practicing fighting skills on the nearby mats. He was absolutely vigilant about keeping the work of our division secret until the day we all "graduated" from basic training. In our very first lecture, on our very first day, he had told us The Code — a set of rules that would govern our unit. Top of these was the code of silence. Under no circumstance were we to talk about our training with anyone outside of our unit, and we were not to ask cadets from other divisions about their training either. In fact, Sarge strongly discouraged us from what he called "fraternizing" with the others.

"If you socialize with each other only, you'll build a stronger team and won't be tempted to venture into classified information with *unauthorizeds*. Your fellow squad members are your new family: squad before blood."

I ignored this and spent every spare moment in Quinn's company. Because we had very little downtime, I made the most of mealtimes by sitting with him in the cafeteria.

Bruce scowled whenever he noticed me with Quinn, and often joined us, uninvited, at one of the steel tables where we ate our meals. He had set himself up as some sort of chaperone, guarding me to check I wasn't too free with either my words or my affections.

I wondered, sometimes, whether he reported back on us to Sarge, because Sarge's word was both law and gospel to Bruce. His every other sentence started with, "Sarge says," or "According to Sarge," or ended with, "… but I'll check with Sarge."

The first time he saw me eating dinner alone with Quinn, he came over and demanded to know what we were talking about. Perhaps he was worried that I was telling Quinn about the day's events. We'd spent that Sunday morning lying on our bellies on the ground, sopping wet and muddy from the hard rain, lined up in a row on the outdoor shooting range. We were working on our high-precision shooting — using heavier caliber bolt-action rifles stabilized on bipods and sandbags, shooting at cardboard targets a full kilometer away on the other side of a shallow, bushy gulley. Apart from the distance, and the rain which obscured our vision, a cross-wind complicated the shot.

Even worse, Roberta Roth had come out to watch us. Having her perched beside Sarge, the scalloped arcs of her umbrella like the dripping wings of great black crow, only added to the pressure. From time to time, they would lean in close to discuss something — probably us cadets, from the way their gazes latched onto each of us in turn.

"Right, cease fire!" said Sarge after we were all drenched and covered in mud. "Let's have some new tangos."

He gave the command over the radio to Juan, who was setting up the targets at the far end of the range.

"Earplugs out and listen up. How about a little competition to make this interesting, my piggies?"

He often called us pigs and had once explained, "That stands for Professional Instructed Gunmen — and gunwomen, princess, let us not forget the women! Once you graduate, you'll officially be HOGs."

"What's that stand for?" I'd asked.

"Hunters of gunmen."

"But we'll be shooting rats," I pointed out.

"I guess I'll have to call you HORs, then," said Sarge, and Bruce and Tae-Hyun had nearly bust a gut laughing.

Now he smoothed his moustache, staring at each of us in turn.

"Right, piglets, you each get three shots. Cadet with the tightest grouping on his target gets the afternoon off. Cadet with the widest cluster gets an extra two hours of PT, with an emphasis on upper-body strength training. I know how much you love that, Goldilocks."

I didn't know whether I was more motivated by the chance of spending a whole afternoon with Quinn, or by the fear of another two hours of torture, but I was determined to win. I might not be able to bench-press my own weight, but I could shoot straight. My waterlogged jumpsuit was weighing me down, though, and restricting my movements, so I unzipped the top, rolled it down and tied the arms around my waist. I was soaked to the skin, and my white undershirt may have been transparent, because Bruce goggled at my chest as though I was a contestant in a wet t-shirt contest. I guess he was still distracted when we received the command to fire, because his first shot went wide. He cursed, refocused and was better pleased with his next two shots.

I was pleased with all three of mine.

"You call this good shooting, boy?" Sarge said to Bruce, when we'd hiked across to inspect our targets, envious of Roth, who returned to the comfort of the compound. "My grandmother can shoot better'n this, with her eyes closed!"

Bruce's face darkened in an angry flush as Sarge continued, "I would say you shoot like a girl" — Sarge often made sexist comments like this — "only the girl has shot better'n you."

"No she hasn't, look! She only hit her target with two rounds. One of them clean missed the target."

"Look closer. All of you, come look."

We all clustered around my target. From close up, it was easy for them to see what I already knew. My second shot had passed through the hole made by the first, just nibbling off an extra crescent of paper on the edge of the perforation.

"Snake-eyes!" Sarge pointed at the double hole. "That's how it's done, son."

In disbelief, Bruce ripped the paper target off its backing

and peered up close at the target board, checking the holes that matched the target shots. Then, using a long blade on the multi-tool he always wore on his belt, he prized my rounds — both of them — from the hole and cursed again.

"Good shooting, Blue. You're dismissed, soldier. Enjoy the rest of your day. Bruce, Fiona will meet you at the track at 14h00 sharp. Embrace the pain, son. Because pain is … ? What is pain, piglets?"

"Pain is good, Sarge!" we all shouted back.

That night, when Bruce came over to where Quinn and I sat eating and chatting, he still looked mightily pissed. And exhausted.

"What are you talking about, Blue? Telling him how much better you are than me?"

"I'm not much better than you, Bruce," I said. "And I won't be the one to break the code."

Bruce looked only marginally mollified, but Quinn sat back and smiled, seemingly suddenly very relaxed, as if he'd heard something that pleased him.

"*Are* you better than him?" he asked, as soon as Bruce stomped off.

I hesitated, not wanting to appear big-headed. "Mostly," I said.

"Good. I don't like him. I hope you beat him every chance you get. Plus, I have a real soft spot for intelligent wonder-wenches!"

I was too glad that he considered me intelligent to wonder why he did. If anyone in our unit had the super-smarts, it was Leya. She had, she said, already registered for a college course in Political Science, and she loved nothing better than a good debate about immigration or civil liberties, or canvassing everyone's opinion on the best way to wage war against the plague. She, too, often joined us at mealtimes. And wherever Leya went, Cameron usually followed silently behind, though he didn't add more than a word or two to the discussions.

"You know," said Quinn one Friday afternoon as we finished

our lunch, "I can't say I like this."

He tapped the computer printout on the table in front of him. Every Friday, each cadet was issued with a report on their "physical parameters". It was an itemized list and nutritional analysis of everything we'd eaten in the previous seven days, a log of our time spent in the gymnasium, results of any exercise assessments we'd been put through (testing strength, endurance, aerobic capacity and flexibility), our pulse-oximetry, blood glucose and blood pressure scores, plus our weight and fat-to-muscle ratios, as taken before dinner every Thursday evening.

"I'm surprised they don't measure and analyze our output at the toilet."

"You don't think it's a good thing that they keep tabs on our health and fitness?" asked Leya.

"I simply don't think it's necessary that they note our every input and output," said Quinn. "Or that they know our every movement — which they do, thanks to those" — he cast a dark glance at the nearest fisheye surveillance camera — "and these." He flicked a finger against the steel ID bracelet encircling his left wrist.

"You think they monitor everywhere we go?" I found it hard to believe that.

"Well, obviously we get clocked going into and coming out of the gymnasium." Quinn pointed at the logged times on his report. "What's to say they aren't logging all our other movements?"

"Paranoid much?" said Leya.

"If you haven't done anything wrong, then you shouldn't have anything to hide," said Bruce, taking an uneaten half of a roll off my tray, wiping it in the gravy on my plate, and shoving it in his mouth.

If Robin had done that to me, he would have earned an elbow in the ribs, but I still wasn't sure enough of my way around people to feel confident doing it to Bruce. Besides, my elbow would probably bounce right off those bulky muscles.

"You're not paranoid if they are out to get you," said Sofia Medina, a pretty and petite girl from Quinn's unit, who occasionally joined him at our table. She had dark hair and soft brown eyes made exotic by intricate henna patterns ornamenting the skin on her cheekbones and temples. She looked like she was wearing the sheerest of filigreed masquerade masks.

Cameron made a soft noise which might have been a laugh.

"Who are 'they', and why would they be out to get you?" asked Leya. She was peeling an orange and breaking it into segments.

"You don't think that we've gone overboard with the restrictions and government control in the last few years?" said Quinn. "We've lost our privacy, censored our media, choked the free flow of people and ideas, had our civil liberties steadily eroded — it's banjaxed!"

"Sounds like you're a member of the Civil Libs," said Leya, offering Quinn an orange segment.

"Well, I wouldn't go that far," said Quinn, shaking his head and looking like he regretted saying so much. "But they do make some good points."

I wasn't sure what I believed. I'd never thought deeply about the politics of the plague, but now that Quinn had pointed it out, I realized how closely we were monitored inside the Academy, and how tightly we were controlled outside of it. Until this moment, I'd felt much less restricted here than at home. I'd met so many new people, learned so many new things and been so focused on the goal of getting out, that I had felt much freer. But I was probably even more closely watched here than under my mother's anxious eyes.

"I think the Civil Libs are full of crap," said Bruce. "And if you agree with them, then so are you."

"I think my brother would agree with you, Quinn," I said, wanting to give him some support.

"Would he?" said Leya.

I nodded. "My mother wouldn't though. She's completely obsessed with the virus and keeping us safe. She would say losing some privacy and freedom in exchange for gaining security is a good trade."

"Your mother is right. Safe is a darn sight better than sorry," said Bruce, licking the last shine of gravy off his fingers. "I agree with Sarge. He says those Civil Libs are a bunch of pansy-assed, rat-loving, terrorist-protecting traitors!"

"Bit of a sweeping statement, don't you think?" said Sofia.

Quinn was pinching his lips together, as if to stop himself giving Bruce a piece of his mind.

"Sarge says, one of these days those spineless maggots are going down. Ever since the plague began, this nation has been stronger and more united, we're better for it."

"What?" I couldn't believe what I was hearing.

"Not the deaths and stuff — like, obviously that's majorly bad. I mean that before, whatever the one side of the political field said, the other side disagreed with on principle. And vice versa. We couldn't get anything done. We were an easy target, man. A nation divided." Mitch nodded along to Bruce's rant. "But now we're all focused on the same thing. Nothing unites a nation like a common foe, that's what —"

"— Sarge says!" Leya and I finished for him.

"What do *you* think?" I asked Leya.

She shrugged and looked at Quinn then back down at her own report. "I think I need to spend some more time doing weight training if I ever hope to stop Cameron whooping my ass at arm-wrestling."

Cameron' face went pink, and the rest of us let the topic slide, though from the way Quinn ran a finger under his collar, he was still bugged by the conversation.

I could see his point. It was not only our weekly physical measures that struck me as excessive. Between theoretical lectures and practical exercises in observation, camouflage, observation skills and memory training, stalking, weapons care and sharpshooting, we got way more training than could be strictly necessary to take out the odd infected rat.

My theory was that Sarge thought he had something to prove. It turned out that our black unit was the newly established division that Roberta Roth had been speaking about in her welcome speech, and Sarge was no doubt determined that his new unit be the best, fastest, strongest and most highly trained of all the divisions. Either that, or the population had been protected from the full truth about the plague rats. From the way we were being trained — as if for a full-out war — I figured the problem was way worse than we knew.

Part Three

Chapter 14

The Choice

The Jinx in the mirror looked very different from the Jinx who had started boot camp here at the Academy six weeks ago.

I was leaner, my muscles more defined, and multicolored bruises marked my arms and legs and hips. There were calluses on my fingers and palms from constantly holding, loading and firing weapons, and I held myself differently — straighter and more alert, as if I was expecting something and was ready for it. My lips looked swollen. Of course, that was a consequence of Quinn and my continued exercises in aerobic capacity rather than a function of the daily drills in the vast gymnasium or shooting practice out in the woods surrounding the compound.

I pulled on a freshly laundered black jumpsuit, wondering if we'd be wearing the things for much longer now that we'd finished basic training. It would be such a relief to wear something — anything — different. Maybe we'd all be able to switch to civilian clothes soon; it would be so good to wear jeans and a T-shirt again.

Mom and Robin would be coming in for the graduation ceremony this evening, and I was looking forward to seeing them. I'd last seen them two and a half weeks ago, on the one and only family visit we'd been allowed. It had been kind of awkward — I had loads that I would have liked to share, but I wasn't allowed to tell them anything about my training. And they didn't have any real news since nothing much ever happened in the James household. So I'd told them about the cafeteria food and how fit I was getting, and Mom (who was wearing a half-face-piece respirator and had made Robin do the same, even while almost all the other visitors were merely wearing E97s) fretted about whether it was really safe for us to go about without protective gear and told me every detail of the decon process they'd gone through before being allowed in for the visit. Robin rolled his blue eyes — the mirror image of mine — while she spoke. I grinned. I'd missed him. Then I realized with a pang of guilt that I hadn't missed my mother very much at all. In the six weeks since I'd come here, I hadn't had more than a few fleeting moments of homesickness.

But that was good really, because I had no intention of returning home any time soon. I planned on being selected for sniping missions outside in the world, although Sarge had warned me that if I didn't up my game, I'd never get that far. Before the last family visit, he'd summoned me to his office — a small room, sparsely furnished with a desk, three chairs and two filing cabinets. A collection of miniature cacti in terracotta pots was arranged on the windowsill behind his chair. They reminded me of him: bald on top and prickly all over.

He sat behind his desk, bouncing his chin on his steepled hands while he stared at me for long moments. I tried hard not to squirm under the intense focus of those dark eyes.

"I'm wondering about you, Blondie."

It set my teeth on edge when he called me that. Or Goldilocks, or Princess. But I kept my face blank. I figured he'd only do it more if he knew how much it got under my skin. I fidgeted with the silver earring Quinn had given me, turning it through my ear.

"And do you want to know what I've been wondering?"

I suspected not. "Yes, sir."

"I've been wondering whether I made a mistake with you, whether I backed the wrong horse. What happened to that streak of cool blue that shot me in the neck the day we first met?"

"Sir?" I was confused. Was he talking about my hair?

"What am I supposed to do with you, Blue?" he asked.

"I don't understa —"

"You could be our top cadet, Jinx E. James. You could be our ice-maiden angel of death, our ace in the hole in this war. We could use someone with your unique combination of skills and attributes."

"Thank you, sir." I smiled, relieved that he wasn't about to chew me out.

"I said that you *could be*, not that you *are!*"

My smile disappeared as quickly as one of his own.

"Because you are worse than useless at shooting live targets. When it comes to doing precisely what we recruited you for, you are about as much use as a vegetarian at a barbecue. You have not improved in that skill-set at all, and we got no use for slackers here."

"I'm not a slacker! Sir."

"You need to piss or get off the pot, soldier. If you can't shoot rats, there's no point in continuing with this training."

"I can shoot rats."

"Coulda fooled me, Goldilocks!"

"Just not, you know, healthy ones. And with live rounds."

"If you think we're going to let infected rats run around the grounds and the compound just so's you can feel better about shooting them, or if you think we're going to turn you loose in the world without having practiced with live ammo on live targets, then you're sadly deluded, girl. And we're wasting our time here."

I stared down at my feet while he pinned me with his glare. A squished bug, a spider perhaps, smeared the tiled floor near my right foot. It looked like how I felt.

"*Are* we wasting our time with you, Blue?"

"No, sir."

My mouth was dry. Any minute now, he might dismiss me from the program. I'd be sent home. Back to Mom and our house and my tiny bedroom. Back to playing games while the real war waged on outside and people like Bruce got to fight it.

"Because if you can't shoot a rat, how in the hell are you going to be able to shoot the infected cats and dogs and other tangos that are running around out there?" Sarge tilted his bald head in the direction of the world beyond the window.

I grimaced at the very thought of it. Sarge leaned forward with one of his sudden movements.

"No one is making you do anything you don't want to, Princess. But you need to choose. Here and now." He tapped the desk with a down-pointed index finger. "What's it to be: shoot the freaking rodents — and let me be clear as crystal here, Blue, by "shoot" I mean shoot to kill — and be prepared to shoot other infected creatures and plague-spreaders, or go home with your momma this very afternoon?"

It was a no-brainer. No way was I going back to that house, to Mom hovering over me, nagging me, keeping me inside every moment she could. No way was I letting the rest of the unit advance while I went home with my tail between my legs. I had a shot at freedom, at really getting out, beyond the confines of the Academy which was now beginning to feel as stifling and constricted as home ever had. And I was going to grab it with both hands. Failure was not an option, and I would not quit over a bunch of mutant critters.

I looked Sarge in the eye and spoke firmly. "I'll do it, sir."

"Good man!" he said and shook my hand.

And I did do it. I took Mitch's advice and forced myself to stop thinking about what I was doing. I listened to Leya's encouraging pep talks and made myself believe her when she reassured me that what I was doing was right, that I had a gift and I should use it in the service of my country, that my skill and dedication were an example to her. I practiced until I could shoot those rats with as much accuracy as I shot the paper targets. I cringed and winced every time I did it, but only after sending the round down the barrel. And every time that peculiar mix of pride and guilt crept through me afterwards. At heart, I was not a killer, even of diseased rodents. But if it came to a choice between the mutants and me, then their days were numbered, because I was also not a quitter.

Now, as I closed the door of my quarters behind me and met up with Quinn outside the entrance to our wing, I hoped I'd be sent out on a ratting mission soon. How awesome it would be if sniper units like our own could really help stop the spread of the plague, if we could take the whole of our society a step closer to being free again.

"Where should we meet afterwards?" asked Quinn as we made our way to the foyer, where we'd be meeting our families before the graduation ceremony.

"Secret staircase?"

We often met in a small space under the staircase to the second floor that was located directly outside the entrance to Quinn's wing. I liked it because it was private — sheltered from the hallway where cadets and instructors were always walking past. Quinn liked it because it was out of the sight lines of the security cameras. Sometimes we'd take our cups of coffee and donuts there — the top of the fire alarm box made a useful surface to stow them while we had a quick hug or a kiss.

"It's a date."

"Look at that," I said, pointing down a deserted hallway that intersected with our own.

Leya stood outside one of the now empty classrooms, talking with CEO Roberta Roth. When she looked up and saw us, Leya said something more to Roth and then came jogging up to join us.

"Not in trouble, I hope?" said Quinn.

"Nah. She only wanted to know how I'm getting along with the job," said Leya, smiling. "I reckon Sarge told her that I was the lowest-scoring cadet in our squad."

I rushed to reassure her. "Only in, you know, that one skill." She was great in camouflage and stalking and tops at observation.

It would be great when, in just a few hours, we could talk freely.

"Yeah, but it's the one that really matters," she replied. "Still, at least I'm good enough to graduate. Oh, seems like everyone's here already."

The marble-floored foyer was full of people talking and laughing as families met with the graduating cadets. Some were wearing short sleeves and light dresses which spoke of a hot early summer's day outside, but most wore lightweight PPE suits. Quinn spotted his family at once and dragged me over to meet them.

"Mom, Dad, Kerry — this is Jinxy James. My Jinxy," said Quinn. He sounded — there was no other word for it — proud.

I smiled at them, searching what I could see of their faces above their masks for a resemblance to Quinn. He nudged me gently, and I saw that his mother and father had their hands extended. I hesitated — though they were wearing gloves, I wasn't. Then I reminded myself that they would have had to pass through a serious decontamination process before being admitted to ASTA HQ. Besides, Quinn had already hugged and touched all of them, so if they weren't "clean", then neither was he now, and I didn't intend to never touch him again. I reached over and shook their hands, hoping they hadn't noticed my momentary awkwardness.

Quinn beamed when I took his little sister's hand and shook it solemnly too.

"Are you Quinn's girlfriend?" Kerry asked with a lisp. She was missing a front tooth and had a sparkly temporary transfer of a sequined dragonfly stuck on her forehead.

"Now, Kerry, don't embarrass the poor lass," said her mother. Her lilting Irish accent was much more pronounced than Quinn's.

"Are you?" Kerry persisted.

No escape from the awkward today.

"I don't know," I said, casting a desperate glance at Quinn. "Am I?"

"Most definitely," he said, igniting a small golden glow in the region of my heart.

"You're very pretty," Kerry said, nodding at me in approval. "I like the blue in your hair. I want to make mine purple all over, but Mom says no." Then she asked her brother, "Are you going to marry her and make a baby?"

"Kerry!" said her mother and father simultaneously. Quinn tugged on his brow ring, looking half-embarrassed, half-pleased.

"I like babies, and I hardly ever get to see one," the little girl said, unabashed. "But my mother takes me to Freedom Park every day at four after we finish schooling, and sometimes a lady comes to the play park with her baby. She has yellow hair with green on the ends! We also go there on Saturdays and Sundays in the morning, but the lady with the baby doesn't come then. If you make a baby, you can take it there, too."

"Um," I said to Quinn, desperate to change the subject, "Didn't your brother come today?"

Quinn and his parents exchanged a glance, and then Quinn said, "No. No, he couldn't come here today."

"That reminds me, Connor sent a letter for you. Give it to him, Kerry," said Mr. O'Riley. He spoke softly.

I watched in amazement as Kerry took a tightly folded piece of paper out of the side of her shoe and slid it into Quinn's hand, taking the one he handed her and stowing it in the same place. In the press of the crowd, no one noticed the little girl crouching down to fiddle with her shoe. We were not supposed to exchange letters directly like this, I guess because, as Quinn had pointed out, they liked to check our communications for sensitive information. But I had no time to wonder about it now. If I missed seeing my mom, she'd never forgive me.

"It was nice meeting you all, but I'd better go find my brother and mother now," I said.

"Nice meeting you too," said Mrs. O'Riley.

"And congratulations on making it through to graduation," said Mr. O'Riley.

"Goodbye, Jinxy," said Kerry.

Quinn gave me a quick kiss, and then I was pushing my way through the crowd, making for a head of fair hair that might belong to Robin. I spotted Leya on the way — alone and half-hidden behind a tall potted plant. Didn't she have any family here to support her? Nearby, Bruce was introducing Sarge to his family. I could heard the phrase, "Sarge says …" as I passed by.

"There you are, Jinxy! I was so worried we wouldn't get to see you. You look thin. Are you okay? Eating enough? It looks like you've lost one of your earrings, honey. And shouldn't you be wearing protective gear — I don't like to see you all … *exposed* like that!"

It was my mother, of course, wearing full protective gear.

"Hi, Mom, I'm perfectly healthy." I bumped elbows with her. I knew better than to try hug her.

"Hiya, Jinxy." Robin gave me a tight hug.

"Hey, Robin. What's up?"

"Ah, you know, same old, same old."

"Yeah." I did know. I gave him a sympathetic grimace.

"Exciting day for you, though."

"Yeah!"

"You going to stay on and work for them?"

"If they let me, sure."

"Oh, Jinxy, do you really think you should? A year and a half! It'll be so dangerous, being out there. I wish you'd come home now," said Mom.

"You know I love you and I miss you, Mom" — the first part wasn't a lie — "but I've got a chance to do something really worthwhile here."

"I know, I know. But I worry."

"You? Worry? I never knew — you should have said something, Mom!" said Robin and we all laughed, even my mother.

"I know you think I'm overprotective. But with your father …" She hesitated, biting her lip.

"What have you been up to, Robin?" I rushed to fill the awkward silence.

"I've been doing a couple of programming courses, playing around on some sites."

"He's always on that computer, even late at night," said Mom.

"Have you been playing The Game?" How cool would it be if Robin was selected and could join me here. Immediately, another thought intruded. Would Mom cope if she had to live alone?

"There are other games in the world, you know, and some of them are very interesting. I'm learning a lot."

"That sounds cryptic," I said.

"We'll chat when you come home for a visit."

"My God — that mother just kissed her son!" said Mom, appalled.

A loud buzzer sounded — it was time for the graduation ceremony to begin.

Chapter 15

Hog's Tooth

My mother, Robin and I exchanged hurried goodbyes, with her begging me to write more frequently and him wishing me luck. Then we joined the throng making for Lecture Room 1, which was really more of an auditorium, complete with raked rows of seats and a small platform down front. The families were directed to chairs at the back of the room, while the cadets filed to the front, each division taking their seats in a different row.

Our graduation ceremony was way different from the ones I'd seen in movies on T.V. We all still wore our differently colored jump-suits, rather than academic gowns and mortarboard caps. No photographer took pictures of the graduates posing with their proud parents, and all cellphones and cameras had been confiscated at the front door. Afterwards, there would be no red-cup keg party around a swimming pool. Our only celebration would be one in the cafeteria, and I doubted there would be any alcohol or much fun allowed.

The black division was directed to the last row of cadet seats, behind the convicts — which was what we called the division who wore prison-orange suits — and since there were only six of us, half our row was left empty. I took a seat next to Leya, and Bruce promptly installed himself on my other side.

"I wish we could sit with our families," I said. Or boyfriends.

"No way. It's right that we're sitting like this — squad before blood," said Bruce.

He left his hand palm-side up on the armrest between us, as if hoping I'd take his hand. He never gave up! I crossed my arms.

Quinn was sitting in the middle of the ten blue cadets seated three rows in front of us. He was taller than all of them.

"I saw your brother. He's gorgeous!" whispered Leya. "How old is he?"

"We're twins, so sixteen."

"Leya is a cougar," Bruce chanted in a singsong voice.

Leya stretched an arm around the back of me to cuff him upside the head.

Roberta Roth stood up from the line of instructors sitting up front and addressed the auditorium, telling our parents how proud they should be of us, how she hoped we'd benefited from our vocational training, how valuable we would be in the war against the pandemic, how it was each citizen's duty to serve their country, blah blah blah. I wasn't really listening. I had my eyes on the back of Quinn's neck, where his dark hair curled a V into his nape. He was sitting next to Sofia, and as I watched, he muttered something into her ear that made her shoulders shake with suppressed laughter. I fought an urge to pluck a button off my suit and flick it at her pretty little patterned head. Where's a paintball rifle when you need one?

The sound of applause brought me out of my fantasy. Cadets from the green division were making their way down to the podium where Fiona now stood, calling out names. Each cadet shook Roth's hand, received a certificate, and then shook their instructors' hands and were handed a divisional pin. They lined up with their fellow graduates for one last round of applause before returning to their seats, and the next division's cadets were called up. When Quinn's name was announced, I clapped harder than anyone else. Leya giggled and whispered, "He *is* hot!" Bruce made a sound of disgust.

A few minutes later, I was up front with the rest of my squad. As Roberta Roth shook my hand, she leaned forward and spoke quietly beside my ear.

"We've got exciting things planned for you, Specialist James."

I only had a moment to say a brief thank you as I accepted my certificate. In italic gold lettering, it confirmed that Jinx E. James had passed with distinction the advanced training course in Marksmanship and Sniper Specialist Skills.

"Glad you finally got your ass into gear, Blue," said Sarge as he shook my hand hard and handed me my divisional pin.

Then he spun me around in front of him, and I held my hair up as he fastened something around my neck. I looked down at the long black leather thong with a wooden carving of a .5 caliber round threaded through it. Sarge had told us all about the old marine tradition of giving a graduating sniper a "hog's tooth" — the emblem of living life on the sharp edge. While Bruce and Cameron and Tae-Hyun were getting theirs, I fixed my pin onto the flap of the chest pocket on my jumpsuit. It was about the size of a dollar coin, made of silver in the shape of a scope's cross-hairs, with a rifle stretching diagonally across it.

"So cool!" I whispered to Leya, who was standing beside me.

"Arctic!" she whispered back.

I smiled out at Quinn and then gave a tiny wave to Robin and my mother sitting at the back. I had done it. I had succeeded. I hadn't let Sarge intimidate me or Bruce get to me with his endless comments. I had overcome daily exhaustion and feeble biceps. I'd learned to hide and stalk and shoot a dozen different weapons. I'd even come to terms, mostly, with shooting those damn rats, and now I was an expert, ready to go out into the world and make a real difference. I couldn't wait to begin. And I couldn't wait to hug Quinn and hear all about his work. I bet it was something brainy — code-breaking, maybe, or intel.

Once the last of us was back in our seats, Roth thanked the families, and then it was time for them to leave, and for us to be on the ear-end of more speechifying.

"Congratulations again — you are now officially specialists. As you probably already know," Roth concluded, "you all have the rest of the day off." She smiled her tight, thin-lipped smile at the cheers that followed, and then held up a hand for silence. "You are to meet at your Unit Commanders' offices at 09h00 tomorrow morning to receive your assignments. Some of you will be scheduled for additional training, while others will be deployed to other regions."

Uh-oh. Sarge had *not* told us about that. I was no longer smiling. What if either Quinn or I was sent somewhere else? I couldn't stand it if he were sent to one end of the country and I to another. Quinn swiveled in his seat and pulled a worried face at me — I could tell he'd had the same thought.

Roth was talking again. "… and some of you will immediately be deployed on assignments or active missions."

"Yes!" said Bruce, pumping his fist.

I might not be as enthusiastic as Bruce about killing critters, but I did hope I would be one of the ones sent out on a mission, though I hoped I'd be based in the same sector as Quinn. We'd been confined to this compound for the last six weeks, and I was totally sick of it. The main reason I'd been keen to sign up at the Academy was to get out, and I was looking forward to finally doing it.

"You are reminded that you are still not permitted to discuss your work at all with persons outside of this organization. Within the Academy, your projects will be subject to different levels of security clearance as advised by your COs. But for now, congratulations again, and enjoy the rest of the afternoon!"

Everyone cheered and scrambled for the doors. Bruce seized the chance to give me a congratulatory hug, and Leya asked whether I'd be joining them in the cafeteria.

"Sure, but later. I want to catch up with Quinn."

"Smoochy time!" she teased.

Bruce scowled and pushed his way past Tae-Hyun.

"Don't be long," Leya called as she followed. "There's a rumor going around that one of the convicts smuggled in a crate of beer."

"I call BS on that," I said. How would they get it past all the security?

Quinn was already waiting at our secret stairwell by the time I got there. He grinned and pulled me into a tight hug. The fire-alarm box pressed painfully into my back, but Quinn was the one who said, "Ow!"

He stepped back from me, rubbing his chest. I noticed the badge on his lapel at once. A magnifying glass perched vertically over the silver circle. As he lifted the thong to pull up the hard hog's tooth, the brush of his fingers against my chest raised a shiver of goose bumps on my skin.

"What in the name of St. Patrick is this thing around your neck?"

"It's a hog's tooth," I told him. "Not literally, I mean, this one's made of wood, so it's just a symbol that we've qualified, joined the squad and are ready for live shooting. Each of us'll get a real one — the casing on the round — when we make our first kill."

Quinn stood frozen with the carving in his hand. Only his face moved as the wide smile which had been there dissolved.

"Your first kill?" he repeated.

"Yes, from our first assignment."

Quinn's hand dropped the hog's tooth like it was hot then moved to brush aside my hair so that he could see my chest. This time he wasn't reading my embroidered name. His eyes were trained on my division pin, the rifle perched diagonally across the scope's crosshairs. His brows drew together and, for the first time ever, he looked pale.

"What are you?" he said.

"What do you mean?"

The hairs on the back of my neck prickled with the sense of danger drawing close.

"What division do you belong to, Jinx? What have you been training to become?" Quinn's voice was flat, hard, unrecognizable.

"I'm a sniper," I said, forcing an uncertain smile through my worry. Something was going horribly wrong.

"You're not."

"I am."

"You can't be!"

"Why not?" I was getting annoyed. "Because I'm a girl? I never figured you for a sexist."

"No, not because you're a girl," he said slowly, and without the hint of a smile. "Because you're a code-breaker."

"I'm not a code-breaker. Where did you get that idea?" I said, puzzled.

"You told me you were."

"No, I didn't."

"Yes you did. That day, in the canteen, with Bruce — you said you couldn't break the code."

"Oh, that?"

Relief washed through me. This was obviously a misunderstanding. He only looked angry because he thought I'd misled him.

"No, I said I *wouldn't* break the code," I explained quickly, eager to wipe that horrible expression off his face. "We snipers have a code of having each other's back, not telling tales on each other, and Sarge's number-one boot-camp code was that we were not to tell people in other units what it is we do. Not like we were allowed to anyway."

Quinn stared down at me. A muscle pulsed in his jaw.

"Bruce was scared I was telling you stuff you shouldn't know, so I told him I wouldn't break the code to, you know, reassure him," I finished lamely.

Quinn pulled the certificate out of my hand, unrolled and read it, and then handed it back to me.

"So you really are a ratter?" His face was tight with repugnance.

"A sniper, yes."

I jumped when Quinn cursed loudly and punched the wall beside me.

"What *is* your problem, Quinn O'Riley?" I demanded.

"Are you kidding me? Do you know what ratters do, what *you're* being trained to do?"

"Jeez, patronize much? Yes, as I am a member of the squad, I do in fact know exactly what I'm going to be deployed to do."

"And do you know that —" He paused and looked around to check we weren't being overheard, then continued in a whisper, "that you're going to be taking out live targets?"

"If I'd just wanted to play games, I could have stayed at home. I knew what I was signing up for when I started."

"And you really think that's acceptable?" he said, his voice a mixture of disbelief and disgust.

I knew Quinn loved his pets and probably hated the idea that they might be infected one day and have to be taken out, but he was taking things a bit far. It was one thing to be an animal-lover, but it was quite another to be so extreme that you thought it was a bad idea to kill infected rats.

"Okay, so I'm not 100% comfortable with it, but —"

"*Not 100% comfortable with it*? Listen to you!"

"But Quinn, we're not going to win this war unless we take them out."

"Who told you that — Sarge? So you want to be like him now? A killer?"

"I'm only killing a threat to our lives. What's the matter with that?" My own anger was growing now.

"What's the *matter* with that?"

He raked his fingers through his hair. He was staring at me as if he couldn't believe what he was seeing.

"The *matter* is that you'll be taking innocent lives."

"Oh, please don't be ridiculous, Quinn. You can hardly call them innocent when they pose a danger to us, when they've caused the deaths of millions of people. When the plague has caused us to become virtual prisoners in our own houses."

"That's not what has caused us to become virtual prisoners," he scoffed. "Faith! You've swallowed what they've told you hook, line and sinker. I thought you were someone … different. But I don't know you at all. Who *are* you?" He almost shouted the last three words.

"Who are *you* to judge me?" I shouted back, poking him in the chest with my rolled-up certificate. "What division are you in that's so lily-pure?"

"Intel," he muttered.

"I should have guessed. Nice and clean and indoors. And so safe."

"Are you implying that I'm a coward?" His eyes had paled to the color of frosted steel.

"No. I'm implying that you're a hypocrite. What do you think happens to the information intel figures out? You think your data and analysis won't feed directly into my dirty work? You think where we go and what we target won't be a direct result of your intelligence work?"

Quinn paused, scrubbed a hand across his mouth and shook his head ruefully.

"Ah, you've got me there, Blue."

"Don't call me Blue."

"How about I don't call you at all?"

"Fine!"

"Fine!"

He spun on his heel and stalked off. I was left alone, in the dusty silence under the stairs, clutching my crumpled certificate against my hog's tooth.

Chapter 16

Deployed

No Irish pirate slouched up against the cafeteria door waiting for me the next morning. I grabbed a tray and joined the food line, even though I wasn't hungry — I'd been sucking up a steady diet of tears served with a side of anger and self-pity sauce since the night before, and my stomach felt heavy from all the angst. I grabbed an apple and a cup of coffee and then noticed as I passed by the rack that always held the baked goods that there was exactly one chocolate muffin left. I stared at it bleakly. If Quinn had been with me, we'd have shared it, maybe even fed each other. Or he would have insisted I have it. I walked away from the racks to the checkout register.

"It's too low on calories, honey," said the operator who scanned my food. "According to the system, you're scheduled for active duty today, so you'll need to get more, preferably something with protein."

I took my tray and headed back against the stream of specialists headed for checkout, and nearly collided with Quinn. His plate was laden with eggs, bacon and toast. And the chocolate muffin. Obviously, *his* appetite was unaffected by our bust-up. He stared down at my apple and coffee, flicked his glance to my single earring, then met my eyes with his own flint-gray gaze.

"What? No appetite for killing today?"

I wanted to tell him where to get off. I wanted to cry. I wanted him to hug me. But I just stood there stupidly staring down at his checkerboard sneakers and remembering the day I'd first seen them. He moved off, and the throng of diners parted around me like I was a rock in a river. My face went cold, then hot. I dipped my head and snagged a protein power bar from a shelf before heading back to the checkout.

"Still not enough, dear. You need at least 150 calories more."

What the hell?

I spun on my heel and held my tray out to the nearest server.

"What would you —"

"150 calories of anything."

Back at checkout, the operator finally nodded approval — at the two hard-boiled eggs on my plate. Irish oysters. Now my eyes were burning as well as my face.

I had to pass Quinn again on my way to the table where my unit was gathered. He was sitting with the blues, though they all wore civilian clothing today, unlike our unit, who were all still in the black jumpsuits. Sofia looked up as I passed. I didn't think I imagined the deep satisfaction in her henna-circled eyes. Quinn ignored me.

I dumped my tray on the metal table, slumped onto the edge of the attached bench beside Leya, and contemplated my apple and eggs unenthusiastically.

"Hey, girl, you faded on a great party last night."

"Yeah."

"There *was* beer!" said Mitch.

"And" — Leya looked over at Quinn's table — "you're not sitting with your other half."

"No."

"Relationship status update?"

"It's complicated," I muttered. "No, scratch that. It's actually very simple — he dumped me."

Bruce, who was sitting at the far end of the bench on the other side of the table, perked up at this.

"Blue —"

"Not a word, Bruce," I said, holding up a hand as if to stop the traffic of his speech. If I was being rude, then too bad.

"But I —"

"Zip it!" I must have looked or sounded fierce, because he actually closed his lips. Though he tracked the rest of the conversation avidly.

"No way did he dump you! No *way*! That boy loves you," said Leya.

"Nope. Apparently he 'doesn't even know me.'" I sketched quotation marks around his words as I spoke them.

"What's that supposed to mean?"

"I'm not sure I understand it myself. He got it in his head that I was a code-breaker. He's intel."

"I know," said Leya.

"You did?"

"Well, I saw the badges on the blues — all, like, Sherlock Holmes. And did you know the convicts are spooks?"

"The oranges?" said Mitch.

"Yeah, they're spies, snoops and info-collectors. They work closely with intel."

"Greens?" asked Cameron.

"Programmers. I think they get to work on The Game eventually."

Apparently unable to hold back any longer, Bruce asked, "But what about the effing leprechaun?" He nodded his head in the direction of Quinn.

"Yeah," said Leya. "What's not being a code-breaker got to do with your relationship?"

"When he found out I was a sniper, he completely freaked out."

"Did he now? I wonder why?"

"He's some kind of major animal-loving pacifist and takes exception to the fact that I'll be shooting live rats, and maybe other animals. Don't know what he thinks we should do with them, since they're infected. Maybe put them in little hospital beds with blankies tucked around their furry little necks," I said bitterly.

Bruce laughed at that.

"He sounds crazy," said Leya, giving my hand a squeeze. Her sympathy soothed my wounded ego and fed my anger.

"He thinks *I'm* crazy — he called me a killer!"

"Huh," said Cameron who was sitting, as usual, directly opposite Leya.

"He did not!" said Leya.

"Said I was being trained to take innocent lives! I mean, honestly."

"That boy needs to shut up. And stop being mean to you." Leya turned around in her seat and gave Quinn's back a slit-eyed look.

"Do you want me to sort him out, Blue? Open up a can of whoopass and teach him some manners? Just say the word." Bruce cracked his knuckles.

"No."

"Moral of the story is don't have feelings for someone outside your unit," said Mitch.

"True story, bro," said Bruce.

"Moral of the story is don't have feelings for anyone, ever — especially in this line of work," muttered Leya. "Come on, eat your food, we need to go get our assignments."

Nothing would have gotten me to eat the eggs, but I forced myself to eat the apple and drink the now-cold coffee, and shoved the power bar into a pocket for later. Then we all trooped over to Sarge's office.

On the way, I ducked into the bathroom to remove Quinn's earring — I couldn't wear it now that we'd split. Problem was, I didn't know what to do with it. I should give it back to him, I supposed, but I dreaded another face-to-face confrontation. I could fling it in the trashcan or flush it down the toilet. But, dumb as it might be, I wanted to keep it, and keep it close to me. I tucked it into my chest pocket but then, worried that it might get lost, clasped it instead around the left strap of my bra, where it lay against my skin. Perfect — I could feel it, and no one else could see it. Then I hurried off to catch up with the others.

"Well, look at my sweet little piglets all grown up into lean, mean, fighting-machine hogs. Ready to get out and get shooting?" said Sarge as the six of us crammed around his desk. We all nodded.

Bruce, who as usual had managed to wedge himself into the spot next to me, said, "Sir, yes sir!"

"As of now, you are all on active assignment."

With all of us squashed together, Bruce didn't have enough room to do a fist-pump or a high-five, but I could feel his knees give a celebratory dip beside me.

"Today, we're going outside the wire. We've had reports of a nest of rats in Zone 21, and a possible infected cat. Blue and Bruce will be on point."

"Yes!" Bruce whispered.

I held myself completely still while Sarge's hard gaze pinned me, examining me for any sign of weakness at the prospect of killing rats. And a cat. After an age, he moved his glance to the others, and I could breathe again.

"Tae-Hyun, you'll be spotting for Blue. Mitch, you'll be spotter for Bruce. You're to proceed now to the armory, where Juan will issue you with your rifles, sidearms, ammo and optics. I've told him to zero the scopes to 100 meters for you. And when you get back, first stop is the armory again to return your weapons to lockup. And that is how it will always work, hog-people! Cameron and Leya — I want you to ride along and observe for today and also scope the field for civilians. Fiona will meet you in fifteen minutes in transport bay C. Now haul ass, you lot!"

"Um, Sarge? Should we wear gloves and masks?" I asked.

He stared at me for a long moment, tracing a finger over his mustache. "That's entirely up to you, princess. Think you can shoot a rat before it gets close enough to spit in your face?"

I had been thinking about more general contamination, touching the transport or objects in the outside world, but Sarge didn't look like he would have much patience for such concerns, so I simply nodded.

The armory was located at the rear of the compound, beyond the decon unit and doors which separated the main building from transport bay C. In the interests of keeping the nature of our work secret, I guess, we were the only unit who used either the armory or that exit. The only camera in the area pointed out towards the bay where our vehicles collected and deposited us.

Twenty minutes later, we headed out of the compound, and no one in the black van wore either gloves or masks. Bruce cradled his rifle in his arms like a baby. I stood mine upright between my knees where I sat, swaying, as we hurtled through the mostly empty streets. I stared out of the tinted windows. It was great to see something new and different.

Everyone peered out as we passed by a line of about twenty protestors, mostly women dressed in red PPE suits stationed outside an old abortion clinic. They had all been closed under the official Moratorium on Voluntary Population Reduction Act passed two years into the plague. The protestors were holding up cardboard signs, and I was able to read a few of the messages as we whizzed past: *Our bodies, our lives, our right to decide! Stop the war on our rights! Keep your laws off my body! Support Freedom, support Choice!*

"Effing civil lib traitors!" said Bruce.

What would Quinn have thought? Probably that when the government said it wanted to "save lives and ensure all human beings were protected by our laws," it meant fetuses, rather than the illegal immigrants who still tried to slip over the border into the US, despite the colossal wall that now ran the length of our border with Mexico.

Leya evicted Bruce from his seat beside me and took his place.

"Hey, girl, are you okay?" she asked softly.

I pulled a face and shrugged.

"Listen, don't worry about Quinn. He's overreacting, and he'll soon realize it. He won't want to lose you. You're some kind of special, you know that? Beautiful on the inside and the out. He'll come around."

"You think?" I wanted to believe her, but she hadn't seen Quinn's face.

"I do. And if he doesn't, it's his loss. And maybe," she said, winking at me, "Bruce's gain?"

That tugged a laugh from me. "No way!" I whispered.

"Now, we still have some time left in our session. Tell Dr. Freud what else is bothering you."

"Ah," I sighed, "the usual."

"Killing critters?"

I nodded.

"Worried you'll lose your nerve today and shoot like a blind Democrat?"

"Right again."

"And that Sarge will boot you out?"

"Three for three."

"Listen, sweetie, that is so not going to happen. I've seen you under pressure. And you're cooler and calmer than anyone I've ever known. You're a professional sniper, and when the time comes to take the shot, you'll take it like a true marksman. Besides, the critters you'll be shooting at today are infected. They're plague-spreaders — you *know* they need to be put down."

"That's true," I said. I was feeling a bit better.

"And if there's an infected cat, then I'm sorry about that, but better it dies a quick, painless death at the hand of an expert" — she poked a gentle finger into my upper arm — "than dying a slow, painful death full of suffering."

"You're right." She was. I really didn't need to have any moral qualms about today's mission.

"Sugar, I am always right."

I laughed with her at that, but when I said, "Thank you, Leya. You're a good friend, you know that?" I meant it.

Zone 21 was a pretty area northwest of the city. Middle-class and upmarket neighborhoods nestled in pockets between the urban forest and the old strip malls — now mostly boarded up with signs referring shoppers to new, online addresses. We had spent days practicing in the urban arena, camouflaging our faces with dark skin-paint and taking cover behind bins and dumpsters and burnt-out wrecks of cars, but this mission was in the middle of solid suburbia, and there was no need to hide or wear camouflage. We were all wearing the same black jumpsuits, with the addition of the badges and neckwear that had offended Quinn so mightily.

We would need to keep well back from the rats, so we didn't get bitten or scare them off with our noise and movement, and we would have to observe the field before we went hot. Sarge had trained us to scan for potential enemies — I guess that's what he knew from his war service years ago — but we would also be scanning for any civilians who might be endangered by our shooting.

The van pulled into a street which led down from the main road and into a crescent which looped through the subdivision. A deserted communal recreation area was located on the north side of the street. Weeds grew up against the walls of the clubhouse, several of its windows were broken and the front door hung ajar. Outside, the communal pool was empty except for a sludge of dead leaves and rainwater in the bottom, and the blue surface of the tennis court was cracked and bulging in places. Nature was reclaiming the places we had abandoned.

On the south side of the street stood a row of houses, each with a decon-unit at the front door. Most of the front and back yards had been cleared of vegetation and cemented over so as to leave fewer place for infected animals or M&Ms to hide. Only a couple of houses, perhaps abandoned, had let the rear of their properties get overgrown with weeds and bushes.

"As you can see," said Fiona, who was heading this mission, "the back yards slope down to a small stream which runs along the rear of the properties. We've had reports that there's an infestation in the wooded area beyond, and confirmed sightings of at least one pet suspected to be infected." She checked her notes on a handheld device. "A tabby cat called Marmalade."

"Soon he'll be toast," said Mitch, and Bruce and Tae-Hyun laughed.

We pulled into the drive of 11703 Peachtree Drive, a double-story house painted white with gray trim, and piled out of the van. I stood still for a moment in the fresh outside air, enjoying the warmth of the sun on my whole face and taking in the trees flowering nearby — magnolia and sourwood, going by our online introduction to local fauna and flora modules. Loose strands of hair moved in the light breeze, tickling my cheeks. I felt almost naked being outside without my mask and gloves, but no one else seemed fazed, so I acted like I wasn't bothered either. I stooped to pick up a fallen leaf from the drive. It was brown and crinkled, a veined and almost transparent pane when I held it up against the light, and when I crushed it between my fingers, it crumpled into dry dust which drifted sideways as it fell.

"Checking wind direction and speed? At least someone remembers the lectures," said Fiona.

I hadn't been. I was simply fascinated to be out, allowed to touch and listen and feel. I sniffed my hand. The earthy, musty smell was unfamiliar, and the dusty feel on my skin was a completely alien sensation.

"Blue, you set up in the drive by the garage. Bruce — up those side stairs," said Fiona, pulling out her phone, "while I instruct the occupants to move to the opposite side of the house. Leya and Cameron, check the field is clear."

We fell into our positions as we had been trained. I moved to the far corner of the house, loaded my rifle, then set it up on its bipod and checked the safety catch. I lay down on my belly close up against the protection of the side wall more from game-playing habit than necessity — there was no real need for cover here, since the rats would not be shooting back. Like me, Tae-Hyun lay down on his belly and adjusted his high-powered binoculars.

"Field of fire is clear of civilians," called Leya from somewhere behind us.

"Confirmed." That was Cameron, who had positioned himself behind the boys upstairs.

I scanned the bare, concreted back yard. The sun bounced off the hard surfaces in a blinding glare, so it took a minute or two to adjust my vision to the shady, overgrown patch of shrubbery and trees about 250 meters beyond.

"See anything?" Mitch called down from his perch on a balcony above us.

I peered through my eyepiece, looking carefully into the dappled shadows. Leaves moved in a slight breeze, and now and then one drifted to the ground. But other than that, I could discern no movement.

"Nothing," Tae-Hyun called back.

"So we wait?"

"So we wait. As long as it takes," confirmed Fiona, leaning up against the side of the house while she scanned her tablet.

It took the better part of an hour, lying in the increasingly hot sun with the rifle stock pressed up against my cheek and my eye trained on the eyepiece, listening to Tae-Hyun click his tongue-stud against his teeth until I snapped at him to cut it out. Sweat trickled down my forehead, and an ache grew between my shoulder blades. A fly buzzed annoyingly around my face, and I was waving it off when Tae-Hyun called the target.

"Tango at nine o'clock. Moving right." He spoke softly, for my ears only.

"Got it," I said. I was already adjusting the focus on my eyepiece.

Tae-Hyun called the range and the wind, and I entered the data into my scope. I eased the safety off and chambered a round as softly as I could.

"Do we tell the others?" I whispered.

"Sure," Tae-Hyun murmured. "After we've taken our first shot."

The rat, a large mutant for sure, was moving quickly from left to right, just beyond the first line of trees. I took a lead on it, aiming one mil-dot to the right of my crosshair intersection and then taking the shot. The rat walked into the bullet as the report of the rifle cracked the air.

"Hit!" called Tae-Hyun.

"Good job, Blue," said Leya. Their voices were muffled by the ringing in my ears.

I pulled the bolt of my rifle up and back, ejecting the spent cartridge, and then reloaded — Sarge had said that residents had reported a nest of rats, not just one. Fiona stooped down and picked up the spinning brass casing from the drive and handed it to me.

"Your hog's tooth, Blue. Juan will punch a hole in it at the armory for you."

I swallowed. I wasn't as enthusiastic about the symbol after what had happened with Quinn. But I tucked it into my breast pocket anyway.

"Just to the left of twelve!" Mitch called excitedly above us.

I returned to my shooting position and took the shot within a fraction of a second of Bruce. The reports cracked in overlap, and the poor damn rat exploded in a red blossom of flesh and blood and shattered bone.

"My kill!" said Bruce. "That was my shot."

"Whatever," I said.

Tae-Hyun caught the cartridge which fell down beside us and tossed it back up to the balcony. "Your hog's tooth, dude."

"Hell, yeah!"

We spent another hour cramped in our positions, with me growing uncomfortably aware of my full bladder. Bruce took out another rat, while I downed another three — wouldn't Sarge be proud? — before Tae-Hyun muttered a new set of coordinates, adding, "It's the rabid cat."

I could see it clearly, a blotched mix of yellow, orange and rust fur, staggering and falling on skinny legs in a patch of sun near a scrubby bush on the far bank of the stream. Unnecessarily, I checked that I had already chambered a round.

"Are you going to take the shot?" Tae-Hyun asked, with a sideways glance at me.

"Of course," I said. "Give me those coordinates again."

He restated the coordinates, and I repeated them back to him, louder than necessary, then fiddled a bit more on my scope. The loud report and cheers from above told me that Bruce had taken the shot. I looked away.

Bruce and Mitch came running down the stairs.

"Did you see the teats on her?" Mitch asked.

I had, and I knew what it meant. My stomach clenched.

Bruce placed his rifle behind where we lay and asked Cameron to keep an eye on it. He was already unholstering his sidearm as he and Mitch walked toward the patch of trees.

"You got my six, Blue?"

"Sure." I followed them, taking out my own handgun and tagging Tae-Hyun to watch my rifle.

I was okay to check that no rabid monsters pounced on Bruce and Mitch from behind — just as long as I didn't have to put down a litter of kittens. I moved after them, walking backwards, checking the way with glances over my shoulder, moving slowly and carefully, so as not to trip.

"There they are. Eyes not even open yet," said Mitch.

The soft mewling tugged at my heart. Maybe I still had time to run.

"Safety off. I am hot," said Bruce.

I kept my back to both of them, flinching with every one of the five shots. Then I led the way back to the house.

"Did you wimp out on taking that shot, Blue?" Fiona asked, her eyes hard on mine when I returned.

"No, sir," I said. We all called her that — she seemed to expect it. "I lost concentration for a moment, guess I was getting tired. Won't happen again, sir."

"It had better not."

After another half-hour of surveillance, I was desperate to go to the bathroom. When I could stand it no more, I rang the door of the house and asked to use their facilities. It was easy for the guys, they just peed against trees or, if they couldn't move, into bottles. But the jumpsuits meant being a girl wasn't easy — you had to take almost the whole thing off to go, and I had no intention of exposing myself to rabid critters, or the guys. The homeowner wasn't too enthusiastic about letting me in, but perhaps she could tell my eyeballs were floating, because she buzzed me through the decon unit and showed me to her bathroom. Sweet relief!

A folded newspaper lay on the counter beside the basin, and I scanned the front page as I washed my gloved hands to see what was happening in the outside world. Of course we had T.V. news and access to the internet at the Academy, but I'd been so busy, between the intensive training and spending time with the heartbreaker, that I'd lost touch.

Between the advertisements for germ-resistant copper faucets and doorknobs, respirators with filters containing both activated charcoal and a "selection of pleasant-smelling power-herbs guaranteed to repel rat fever", and an invitation to join the Church of the End Times in an online course about "apocalyptic revelations in scripture", were the sorts of articles that might have appeared any day these last few years. Headlines such as *Public Warned of Heightened Terror Threat*, *New Amendment to Immigration Reform Bill delayed by Civil Lib Filibustering*, and *Hulitechtron Worx secures Defense Contract*, were nothing new.

"My, but you're so young!" the homeowner said when I reappeared. "I must say, I think it's wonderful what y'all are doing. I hope you know that we are sincerely appreciative."

"Thank you, that's good to hear," I said. It was like a balm to my raw feelings that somebody approved of my killing skills and efforts.

Back outside, the unit was moving our post to the drive of another house two properties down. We kept the area under close observation for a further hour but spotted no more targets. Fiona called the Disposal Unit, and their white van and hazmat-suited techs arrived as we were packing up.

"That was a good job, people, well done," said Fiona from her seat up front once we were en route back to ASTA.

"We owned that kill-zone, man!" said Bruce. His eyes were shining with excitement. No doubt about it, the boy liked killing all right.

"It was great to get out and all," said Leya. "But it's not too exciting sitting around and watching."

"Next time," said Cameron.

"Yeah, you'll get a shot next time, Leya. It's not like this city's going to run out of plague-spreaders anytime soon," said Fiona.

I was surprised to see Leya pull out her phone and start texting — I hadn't considered taking my phone on a mission. Bruce polished his rifle with a soft cloth, and Mitch and Tae-Hyun stared out the window as we drove, while Cameron, as usual, watched Leya.

I fingered the casing from my first kill-shot on a live mission. It had been a good shot. Not impossibly difficult — the target hadn't been too far away, and conditions had been excellent — but still, a rat was a small target, and it had been moving. I was proud of myself. Today, because of what our unit had done, there were half a dozen fewer mutant rats in our city. And fewer cats, too, of course.

At the armory, Juan flattened the open ends of the casing together then punched a hole through the brass, and I threaded it onto the leather thong, where it lay alongside the wooden round. Sarge had said that in the wars he'd fought, snipers had recovered the next round from the barrel of the rifle belonging to the enemy soldier they'd shot — the round that had been intended for them — as their hog's tooth. Or sometimes they retrieved the actual round they themselves had shot from the body of the dead enemy soldier. I was glad that in our case, disease-control measures prohibited retrieving the round from an infected carcass. Wearing the casing felt like I was keeping a memento of the shot; wearing the slug would feel like I was celebrating the kill. It was a distinction that wouldn't have mattered to any of the others in the unit, perhaps, but it mattered to me.

Back at the compound that afternoon, everyone from our unit was still discussing the morning's mission as we jogged in a group around the track in the gymnasium. Bruce, who always ran directly behind me — so he could check out my ass, I suspected — made a frustrated noise.

"Can't he stay away? I thought you guys were over."

Quinn was striding across the AstroTurf center of the track toward us. As we came to a halt, Bruce moved to stand next to me and took my hand in his. Annoyed I tried to tug free, but he just held tighter. Quinn's hard glance flicked from our hands to the new addition to my neck thong.

"Congratulations."

I wish I could say that sneering made him unattractive. But it didn't. The words, "You're so cute when you're angry" bubbled up in my mind, but I managed to stop them spilling over my lips. Unfortunately, I couldn't completely suppress the hysterical giggle which accompanied the thought.

Quinn's eyes narrowed even further. What must he think I was laughing at — killing rats? Or at how he felt about my work? He moved his attention off me and spoke softly to Leya.

"I don't think it's wise to criticize your Unit Commander in communications which might be intercepted. And if you text anyone information about where and what your missions are, you'll be bounced out of here for sure."

"What? You saw that?" Leya said.

"Someone always sees everything, you should know that."

"Did anyone else see it? Will I —"

"I deleted the content and the trace, but I won't always be the one to intercept it. Just watch what you say, and especially what you text or mail."

"Thank you, Quinn. You saved my ass." Leya's gratitude was obvious on her face.

I wanted to thank him too. He'd helped my friend, though I couldn't think why.

"Quinn," I said softly, touching his arm and drawing his gaze back onto myself. "Thanks so much. I really —"

"I didn't do it for you!" he said, shaking off my arm.

"Then why?"

"This may be news to you and your little kill-squad, but some people do the right thing because it's the right thing to do."

And those were pretty much the last words Quinn spoke to me for the next month.

Chapter 17

Casualties

Sarge's office was empty when I reported for my one-on-one review session with him. I sat down on a straight-backed chair to wait. The cactus on the windowsill now had two neon-yellow blooms nestled between its thorns, and through the window behind it I could see the heat-haze of the summer's day shimmering over the front lot. I'd been ratting for a month.

Restless, I stood up and walked over to study the massive spreadsheet which covered much of one wall of the office. The names of our six unit members were listed in the far left column, and then each member's missions, confirmed kills (broken down into categories for rats, cats, dogs and "other") and kill ratios were recorded. The red star next to my name indicated that I was heading the pack in confirmed kills — though I had fewer cat and dog kills than the others — with Bruce, Mitch, Tae-Hyun and Cameron clustered tightly behind me, and Leya trailing behind. The blue star next to Bruce's name indicated that he currently held the record for the longest-distance shot.

My eyes tracked the entries to the right-hand side of the spreadsheet and came to rest on something I hadn't noticed on my previous visits to Sarge's office. On top of the filing cabinet in the back corner were a couple of small framed photographs. I moved over to study them. The first was of two soldiers in army fatigues and helmets, their arms slung around each other, smiling into the camera. The grime-smudged face on the left belonged to Sarge. It was much younger, but I'd recognize that frenzied grin anywhere. In the second photo, a platoon of young men stood or knelt on one knee in front of a dusty Humvee. In the background, a flat, beige, desert-like terrain stretched out under a high blue sky. Iraq? Afghanistan? On top of the glass, someone had drawn red crosses over several of the figures in marker pen. I shivered. The plague might be deadly, but our war against it was safer for "soldiers" like me. A bronze medal lay beside the photos. I traced its red, white, green and black ribbon, studded with a silver and two bronze service stars, then returned to studying the shot of the platoon, trying to identify which figure might have been Sarge.

"They were closer to me than my real family."

I jumped at the sound of Sarge's voice. He was standing in the doorway, watching me.

"I hope you don't mind me looking?" I felt like I'd been caught snooping.

"If I didn't want anyone to see it, then that would be a dumb place to store it," said Sarge.

He took his seat behind the desk and indicated that I should sit opposite him, then opened a folder and sifted through the papers inside. I fiddled with the hog's tooth around my neck and tried not to stare at the way the sunlight coming through the window gleamed on his head.

"Over a hundred confirmed kills. My, my, Blue, you sure have been a busy girl."

I had. It was no surprise that I'd been on the most missions and taken out the most targets, since I had volunteered for every assignment possible in the last month. When I was busy out in the field, all my attention was focused on tracking and taking out my targets. When off-duty, I spent my downtime on the target range or in the gym, completing my final school examination for the year, and generally doing anything that would keep me busy. Because when I wasn't busy, when I had time on my hands and my mind was free to wander, it inevitably wandered back to Quinn. Then the memories — funny and tender and exciting — would fill my heart with anger and my eyes with tears. Bedtime was feeble-time. But I'd found that if I kept busy exercising as hard as I had in boot camp, then exhaustion cut even this time short. So busy was good. Busy was much better than feeble.

I cast a glance at the spreadsheet, at the black-dot missions which had kept me out of the cafeteria and hallways, minimizing the number of times I could bump into Quinn. I missed him fiercely. I was lonelier than I could ever remember feeling. Looking back, it amazed me how quickly Quinn had gone from being a complete stranger to becoming my best friend. On graduation day, I had not only lost my boyfriend, but I'd also lost the best buddy who could have comforted me through the breakup. Every night I threaded his earring back through my ear, so that I could sleep close to something of his, and every morning I took it out again and clasped it around my bra strap. Pathetic.

I'd once read a book where the hero, a World War I soldier, had been hit in the thigh by a piece of shrapnel. Lodged too deeply near the bone, the shard had never been removed, and afterwards his leg would ache whenever it was due to rain. I felt like that poor soldier now, only the shard Quinn had left me with was stuck in the region of my chest, and it gave me a sharp squeeze of pain every time I saw him, or even thought of him. Like now.

"We're very pleased with your progress, soldier," Sarge continued. "You've been performing excellently on your missions, and I think we can safely say that you are now our top specialist."

"Thank you, Sarge."

Again, the old mixed feelings twisted inside me. Was it wrong to be proud about being efficient at killing things? Or was it plain stupid to feel guilty at taking out diseased mutants?

"We're so pleased, in fact, that we want to promote you."

That was a surprise. I hadn't known that there was anything to be promoted to. Did they want me to help run the operations, or plan them from the command center rather than doing the shooting myself? I hoped not. For one thing, I figured that would be a waste of my abilities. For another, it would mean that I'd spend much more time based at the compound — the same compound where Quinn was based.

"I'm going to give it to you straight, Goldilocks. You may be the best little ratter in the whole of the Southern Sector, but the war isn't against rats. You were prepared, recruited and trained to fight the plague, to target *plague-spreaders*."

Where was he going with this? He rested his folded arms on his desk and studied me as if assessing me. Come to think of it, he *always* looked at me as if he was assessing me.

"Sir?"

"Rats and pets are not the only plague-spreaders out there. They are not even the most important or the most deadly mooks."

I couldn't figure out what he meant. What else was there that could transmit the virus? And then it clicked.

"You're talking about … people?" I said, horrified. "You want me to take out people?"

"Not take out, soldier, take *down*. Tranquilize and bring in for treatment. M&Ms and rabids are out there spreading the plague when they should be in hospitals being taken care of and being quarantined. And you can help make that happen."

I stared at him. M&Ms and rabids. People. Quinn had asked me if I'd known what I was being trained to do, if I was okay with taking down live targets. Had he known, before I had, what they planned for me?

"And not just them, Blue."

"I don't follow." My voice sounded faint.

"We have to get to the real heart of the pandemic. We have to treat the cause, not merely contain the symptoms. The real plague-spreaders in this war are the terrs. They are the ones we need to bring in."

"I couldn't shoot a human, Sarge. I just don't think I ever could." I recoiled from the very idea.

"A tango is a tango, Blue." He thumped the folder down onto the desk and stood up abruptly. "Wait for me outside. I have a call to make, and then you and I are going to take a little drive into the city. I want to show you something."

I had never before been to Community General Hospital, so I couldn't be sure, but I was guessing that the Biocontainment Wing was newly built. It had its own separate entrance, its own intensive decon procedures and super-high security measures. Judging from the uniformed staff who manned the entrance and patrolled the corridors, the army was at least as much in charge of this facility as the medics.

The hospital room in front of me had its own decon unit with the red, triple-petaled biohazard blossom emblazoned on both of its two sets of auto-locking glass doors. A printed warning stated that only medical personnel in full hazmat suits were allowed inside, and a sign on the wall beside the door read *BSL 4, Negative-pressure biocontainment room.*

The room was situated on a corner, and the two walls bordering the hallway were dominated by large, sealed, heavy glass windows. Sarge and I stood outside one of these. Across the corner of the room, outside the other window, stood a small group of people

I assumed were the patient's family. Two women of about forty stared silently into the room. One of them pushed limp hair out of her face and then returned her hands to the shoulders of a small boy and girl standing in front of her. Was the man on the bed inside the room their father?

He lay perfectly still under the clean sheets and pale-blue blanket of the neatly made bed. He must have been heavily sedated, because he displayed none of the twitching, thrashing, muttering agitation typical of rat fever patients. Tubes from drips and machines ran into his nose and mouth and tattooed arms, and drained his body from somewhere under the bedclothes into bags hanging on the rails at the side of the bed. At first glance, all that suggested this patient was not merely recovering from an appendectomy or a bad bout of pneumonia was the color of the fluid in those bags, brown and purple and red-streaked, like liquefied bruises. Well, that and the rash of petechial spots spattering the skin on what I could see of his face and arms. When I looked closer, I saw the rash spots were oozing blood, red froth bubbled at his nostrils and a tear of blood trickled from his left eye down his temple into his hair.

"He hasn't got long to go now," said Sarge, his voice unusually gentle. "Ah, here she is now."

I looked across the glass panels and was surprised to see Roberta Roth had joined the little family. She gave each of the women a brief, consoling embrace and then crouched down to talk to the children. I was impressed — I hadn't pegged her as the sympathetic type — but confused as to why she was here. Maybe she was related to the dying man. She patted the little girl on the top of her head and walked around the corner to come stand with Sarge and me, tugging the jacket of her business suit straight.

"Wayne. Jinx." She greeted me with a nod which set the underside of her hair shimmering like ripe pokeweed berries under the bright fluorescent lights.

"Ms. Roth."

"Please, call me Roberta."

That was so not ever going to happen.

"So sad, isn't it?" she said, sighing at the man in the bed. "So sad the toll this disease takes on all of us."

"Yes, ma'am."

"And yet, how fortunate that this poor man's family are able to visit him and see him lying so peacefully, so well cared for. That must be a comfort, don't you agree? That they have this opportunity to bid him farewell, to make their peace and say their goodbyes. It is an opportunity they would not have if this poor man was running wild on the street, ill, uncontained, infectious.

"The infected persons whom we are able to identify and tranquilize are brought here," continued Roth, "where the doctors can treat them, manage their pain and restore some measure of dignity to their final days. They do what they can to keep the patients comfortable and to give their families a chance to achieve some small sense of closure. Isn't this a better final image for their families to carry in their memories than one of the demented and suffering person out there?"

I had to admit that it was. I was irresistibly reminded of the infected man we'd encountered on our trip into the sniper simulation — the crazed eyes; the split, bloody face; the blotched and naked body. The contrast between the two men could not have been more vivid.

"And while the medical teams treat them, they also learn from their patients. We advance our knowledge of this pestilence, which so far has been adapting and mutating faster than our virologists can develop a treatment or vaccine. And of course, there's also always the possibility of a miracle; someone might survive in a better state and give us a medical lead to pursue. And who knows?

Any day now we might find a cure, and those in the hospital at that time could be helped."

The man's family moved back from the window and walked slowly away down the hallway. There was no change and nothing really to be seen — which was a lot better than the alternative.

"ASTA plays such an important role in supporting our government. But we need our top specialists to help us fulfil this duty." She took one of my hands in both of hers and squeezed, as if she could press a sense of urgency and obligation into me. "So, will you help these people? Will you help us bring them in, Jinx?"

Chapter 18

Revelations

It was obvious that Roth and Sarge had brought me to the hospital and shown me the rat fever patient to convince me that taking down and bringing in infected people was a good option. And seeing it for myself, I had to admit that it was more humane — both for the patient and their family — than leaving them to suffer untreated. I couldn't argue, either, with their point that M&Ms should not be out in the world spreading the disease. Hell, if I was ever infected, I wouldn't want to be allowed to infect others.

"How do you get them in?" I asked.

I'd seen on T.V. news how difficult it could be to take plague victims in for treatment. There had been outraged protests from the Civil Libs at the measures police and disease control officers sometimes used. I'd seen T.V. footage of one case where police had tazed a rabid over and over again, but the man had kept coming at them.

"Until now, we've had to rely on the traditional method of injecting a tranquilizing drug, but to get close enough to inject the sedative means you have to get close enough to be injured or infected. M&Ms are unpredictable and aggressive — a sudden charge, a scratch or bite and we'd lose a valuable asset. Our

Research and Development department has come up with an elegant solution that allows us to connect with the target from a safe distance."

"What is it — a dart gun? Like I've seen on T.V. wildlife shows?" I said, thinking of wildlife veterinarians and toppling elephants.

"It's a little more sophisticated than that," said Roth. "A dissipating bullet fired from a modified sniper's rifle. The hollow round *im*plodes as it penetrates the body, releasing a major tranquilizer which downs the target instantly, and because it has low penetrating power, the slug is easily removed from the body, leaving minimal damage."

"Why do you need snipers — surely the police could do it?" I asked Sarge. "Come to that, don't the police already have snipers?"

"We need perfect marksmanship if we're operating amongst civilians in the cities and suburbs out there. But we also really want a low-key, small, maneuverable team that we can insert and extract with the least possible red tape, and a minimum of fuss and attention from the public. It's fine for the public to see patients being taken off by ambulance — that they'll understand. But I'm not sure everyone will like the idea of us darting people and having them hauled off by the cops against their will."

"If," interjected Roth, "if they can even be said to have a will. Legally speaking, they are not in their right mind, and so their personal liberties are constrained by society's right to safety."

"Point is, Blue, this is part of what your unit has been established to do, with a maximum of efficiency and a minimum of negative attention. Will you do it?"

I looked again at the man lying so still in the bed, thought again of the rabid in the street.

"Look, I can just about imagine myself helping to tranquilize these people so that they can be brought in and treated, and that their families can …" I gestured helplessly down the hallway where the family had gone. "But back at the compound, you mentioned terrorists."

"We need to bring them in, Blue. To arrest them, to question them about their operations and methods and plans, so we can take this war to them instead of sitting back like a bunch of dumb sheep waiting to be slaughtered."

"And we need to subject them to the full force of the law. These monsters need to be tried and punished for their heinous crimes," Roth added. She was hot on the law, all right.

"I can't argue with that, but I also can't see myself doing it. That's a job for a real soldier. What if something goes wrong? They're armed, aren't they? And there would be real shooting involved, with live rounds."

"We don't want firefights out there among our citizens, Blue. And we don't want to use live ammo — we need the tangos alive and talking. As soon as they come around from the tranq, we can start to interview and debrief them, learn their methods. We start using real soldiers for these missions, we'll have us some dead bodies, and we'll learn nothing."

Still I hesitated.

"I'm just not sure I have the heart for this. I'm not … It's not …"

I struggled to express my deep reluctance. I now realized that I had painted myself into a corner when I'd assured Sarge months back that I was capable of shooting live targets. When I'd made my choice to stay at the Academy, it had been for the wrong reasons. It hadn't been because I liked killing — far from it. And it hadn't been because I believed myself the right person for this work. No, if I was honest with myself, I had been motivated mainly by fear — fear of going back home and getting stuck in my mother's smothering net of worry, with all its unending sameness. I hadn't so much chosen to stay and snipe as I had chosen *not* to go home.

"It's not my fight," I finally said.

Roth and Sarge exchanged a glance, then Roth said, "There's something else you need to see. Follow me."

Roberta Roth set off briskly down the hospital hallway, with Sarge and I following, and led us to an office occupied by two white-coated doctors.

"Will you excuse us?" she said, and they left the room without a word.

Sarge closed the door behind them and took up position in front of it, as if guarding the entrance, and told me to sit in the chair at the desk. Roth sat down in the chair beside me, took a laptop out of her briefcase and fired it up. She hit a few keys then spun it around so that the grainy black-and-white image on the screen was facing me. Two more keystrokes, and the window was maximized to full-screen size, and the video began playing. I glanced quickly at Roth. Her mouth was pinched tight, her eyes looked back at me with something like pity.

It took me a few moments to realize what I was watching was footage from a security camera — from a couple of them by the looks of it, as the angle on the scene kept switching — monitoring the floor and counters of what looked like a busy bank. Behind the service counter, tellers were counting cash and keying entries into computers. The camera view changed to the security door that led from the banking floor to the area behind reserved for employees. A smiling young woman with a strawberry-shaped birthmark on her forehead looked up into the camera as she buzzed for entrance. The door clicked open and she passed through to the employees-only side.

I leaned forward to read the numbers in the bottom corner of the footage. Some of them rolled over continuously. I guessed those were the seconds of the time-stamp. Eight digits interspersed with slashes stayed constant — a date stamp. The footage was from a date in June four years ago. My heart gave a sudden, unpleasant kick against my chest wall and beat more quickly.

Something. Something bad. Something about this, about to happen.

Behind the counter, the young woman with the birthmark was now standing between two of the tellers. She was holding a stack of papers and a poster-sized bank advertisement, and laughing at something one of her colleagues had just said.

As the footage changed to the camera covering the main entrance, a group of five figures burst through the doors, training weapons on customers and tellers. The camera view shifted to the row of tellers behind the counter. All their heads snapped up. Their eyes were wide with shock. Stark terror constricted the face of the one closest to the camera, as a thick sheet of reinforced security glass slammed down between the tellers and their customers.

The view shifted again. One of the figures, a man who must be the leader of the intruders, fired shots into the air above his head. His mouth moved in a soundless stream of shouted commands. The video had no soundtrack, but in the noise and pressure building inside my head, I could imagine the reports of the weapon, the screams of the customers, the threats and orders as the civilians were corralled into a group in the center of the floor.

Without warning, the footage changed. Now it was full-color, sharp-focus, close-up and with sound.

"Now this is footage the terrorists took themselves, of their actions that day and in the days that followed. We've edited it so that we can show you what's relevant to you," said Roth quietly.

"We have brought this war into your temples of greed and into the lives of your men, women and children, as you have so often brought your unjustified military imperialism into our lands," the man on the screen shouted. He wore a scarf around his head, and above his bearded chin, his eyes glinted.

My heart was racing. I couldn't look. Something was about to happen — my thumping heart told me so. But I couldn't look away.

"An eye for an eye! A tooth for a tooth! A life for a life! Bring the first."

There was the briefest flash of a terrified child being handed to the man, and then the picture jumped with an edit and I was looking at a struggling man with wide, panicked eyes and arms bound behind his back.

No. No, please.

The scarved man held him around his neck, pressed a filled syringe up against his throat. Pushed in the plunger.

No-no-no-no-no!

"We will not stop our war until you do!"

Cold sweat broke out on my upper lip. My hammering heart was the whole of my chest. I couldn't breathe. I could only stare.

"Tell your leaders what you think of them now," they shouted at him. "Talk to your people!"

Then the man did talk. He said, "Jinxy, Robin, Marion. I love you."

Chapter 19

Fury

A moment to take it in, and then my whole body began to shake. I leaned over and retched into the bin Sarge held out to me. Roth passed me a clutch of tissues, and I wiped my mouth and blotted my sweaty face. They both stayed silent, watching me, waiting for my response. I had to clear my throat a few times before I could speak.

"That's my father," I said, though of course they already knew. Roth pinched her lips together and nodded.

"That's how he really died?"

"Yes, that is what happened."

"From the plague?" I still couldn't quite take it in. I felt like I had been catapulted into someone else's life.

"I'm very sorry, Jinx. I know this is distressing, but we felt it was time you saw for yourself." Roth gestured back to the screen and my gaze followed her hand. "As you see …"

And I did see.

I saw my father, filmed in bursts over the course of the next ten days, watched as he disintegrated in front of my eyes. I saw how the light of reason faded into a feverish mania, how the sheen that covered his face was overtaken by the rash of weeping blood spots and dark hematomas. I listened as his words of love and reassurance for me and my mother and brother fell into begging and pleading — "help" he kept saying, over and over again, "help me" — then tangles of meaningless utterances, random snorts and grunts and, finally, wordless screams. I watched as his familiar movements — fingers run through his hair, a wide yawn and even, once, a gentle smile — were replaced by endless cross-legged rocking, relentless beating on the front doors of the bank, vomiting of black blood, convulsive seizures, and attacks on himself — pulling out gore-clotted hanks of hair, and scratching at his forearms until they streamed with virus-riddled blood.

Roth froze the picture on a close-up of him turning to look directly into the eye of the camera, his head twisted impossibly far around his neck, his snarling lips smeared with red slime and black flecks, his red eyes empty of any trace of the father I had known. And loved. I looked away, aware suddenly that my face was wet with tears. A shudder ran through me. I was on the verge of losing it completely.

"Suck it up, soldier," said Sarge. "Snap to."

I swallowed hard, dug my nails into the palms of my hands and focused on that pain instead of the one that threatened to swamp me.

"Your father was one of seven innocent victims who were infected that day, all of whom were murdered in the same way. One was just a child. And they filmed it, the terrorists. They filmed it in high definition and full color so that they could release it on the net and to the newsfeeds so as to terrorize our population," said Roth.

"But I didn't know. I never even … How is it possible I've never seen this?"

"At the time, the government got together with the news organizations and agreed that no one's interests, apart from the terrorists, would be served by showing such graphic footage. We'd already learned in this country how deep a scar can be grooved onto the collective memory and psyche of the public by showing footage of terrorist attacks over and over again. Of course, there were some leaks in violation of the embargo, but we soon had a court order and were able to get the footage removed and the offending sites taken down. After a few successful prosecutions, people stopped disseminating it."

"And you left them in there to die? You didn't try sending in a SWAT team to rescue them?"

"We knew very little back then about this disease and how it spreads. We couldn't risk sending in a team of assets who might themselves get infected. And we couldn't blast an opening into that sealed building if that meant letting the contagion out. Besides, once the victims were infected, we knew they would die anyway. There was no cure. There still isn't."

"My mother, she told us he died of a heart attack."

I remembered it clearly. When she fetched us from school that day, her eyes were red and puffy, but she wouldn't say what was wrong until we got home. Then she made us both sit down and told us that Dad had had a heart attack and was very sick in the hospital, that he might not make it. She said we couldn't visit him because kids weren't allowed in the ICU. Then a few days later, she told us he'd passed away. We never got to say goodbye.

"She lied to us all these years?"

"Hell, Blue, would you tell someone you loved that this is how their father died?" Sarge dipped his head towards the screen.

I kept my eyes averted from that final sickening image.

"Yes," I said, aware now of an anger building inside me, coursing into my trembling hands, gathering behind my eyes. "People deserve the truth. She should have told us the truth!"

"I'm sure she was merely trying to protect you and your brother from the pain of knowing how he really suffered and died. A lot of people choose not to tell the truth about how their relatives passed away because it's such an appalling image to have stuck in your head. That's part of the reason for the work done in this unit" — Roth tilted her head back in the direction of the quarantine room — "and the establishment of your specialized unit. But you're old enough to know the truth now, Jinx. And old enough to make a decision about what you need to do, now that you know."

"Now that I know."

"Dammit, Blue, this *is* your fight. It doesn't get more personal than this," said Sarge. "But only you know if you've got the intestinal fortitude for the battle."

I looked down at my hands, as if expecting them to give me the answer. And they did — they had stopped shaking. I was still shocked, horrified, sickened. But mostly … mostly I was *angry*. Livid with my mother for never telling me the truth. Filled with fury at the men who had killed my father, that child, the bank teller. Enraged that human beings could do this to each other in the name of a cause, any cause. On fire with an icy flame of wrath at the cruelty of the disease, and the extremists who started it and still spread the suffering.

The plague was a darkly looming presence in the room — huge, powerful, evil. And real. Real to me in a way that it never had been before.

In spite of my fury, I finally understood my mother — how she'd crumbled and gone silent on Dad after his death. Finally I got her paranoia about the disease, her overprotectiveness of Robin and me. I even understood why she'd lied to us. It *was* unspeakable. But in refusing to speak about his death, she'd lost his life *and* her own, in a way. She'd stayed frozen in a lake of pain and silence and horror, Robin had got stuck in his window seat, lost in his stories, and I'd disappeared into a game. A game that wasn't even a game.

There were so many losses, so much pain rippling out and out from the center point of the plague. So many families out there were also trapped in grief and fear, living their constrained lives behind walls and latex and respirators. So many children might never get to play outside with the other kids in the neighborhood, or camp out in nature, or have pets. I thought of Robin's skateboard, mounted like the head of a dead animal on his bedroom wall, of the empty swing on Quinn's porch, and the deserted city parks, of the boy and the girl peering through the pane of glass at their dying father.

It had to end. And I had to help end it.

Part Four

Chapter 20

Committed to Target

The first person I shot was a young woman.

She was dark-skinned, maybe twenty or twenty-five — it was hard to judge ages once the rat fever took hold — and she was wearing the mismatched remnants of a former life: the top half of a cheerleader's outfit, the knee-length pinstripe pencil skirt of an office suit, and a red velvet stiletto on one foot. Her other foot was bare and filthy. Through the powerful magnification of my eyepiece, I could see a torn nail bent back and bleeding on one stubbed toe. While all of her clothes, like her skin and her matted hair, were filthy, that one beautiful shoe looked as good as new as she stumbled and mumbled her way through the litter and puddles of the back alley.

I finished assembling my rifle and weighed it in my hands. It felt cold and heavier than the usual weapons we worked with. Was that due to the suppressor fitted to its end, or the modifications that had been made to it to fire the dissipating bullets? Or was it due to my dread at having to put a tranquilizer round that looked pretty much the same as a small but live round into an actual human being?

I'd been trained, along with Bruce who'd also been approved for these missions, on two particular weapons. The first, the one we'd use to take down the terrs, was a tranquilizer dart gun suitable only for short-range distances. The second was this tranquilizer bullet rifle to be used on M&Ms because it was accurate over much greater distances. They didn't want us getting anywhere near the infected plague-carriers, especially as the "camouflage" we needed to wear for these jobs included nothing more than an E97 mask and latex gloves. No helmets, no protective ear- or eyewear, no flak-jackets and no full-face respirators.

"You need to blend in," Sarge had said. "That's the whole point of camouflage. You need to adapt your look so that you disappear into your environment."

And while there weren't many teens walking the inner-city streets in jeans and t-shirts, it wasn't so extraordinarily rare that anyone gave me more serious scrutiny than a casual second glance. Though what they thought might be in the big gym bag I was carrying was anyone's guess. My hog's-tooth necklace was tucked under my T-shirt, where no one would see it, and Quinn's silver earring was in its usual place against my skin.

I was dropped off outside a four-story industrial building whose roof overlooked an alley where an M&M had been sighted. Until now, our ratting missions had all been in the suburbs and in the undeveloped, wooded land outside the city, but this built-up environment reminded me of the simulation arena at PlayState. It occurred to me now that they'd probably built it with the express intention of training us for sniping in urban areas.

The comms earpiece connecting me to Sarge, who was directing proceedings from the van down on the street, crackled.

"Ready to go there, Blue?"

"Just taking my final firing position, sir."

It was an awkward position, poised behind a small loophole in the retaining wall at the edge of the roof, with my rifle angled steeply down at the target below. She was clutching her head and walking in small circles now, hobbling lopsidedly on that crippling crimson heel and her injured foot. I wished that Tae-Hyun was here, spotting for me — he was the best at these high-angle shots — but we'd been told that these take-downs would be solo missions.

As Sarge had said: "Maximum maneuverability, minimum attention, total success."

What would Quinn think of today's mission? He had obviously known from his work in Intelligence what the ultimate purpose of our unit was. He hadn't freaked out solely because we were shooting animals, he had known we were being trained to "shoot" humans. I needed to get him on his own, explain why we were doing this, how it was better to bring in infected people for treatment and containment. I needed to explain why I believed I had to do this work. I needed to tell him about my father. But every time I passed him at the compound, he was surrounded by a group of people — Sofia looked like she was moving in for the kill — and he either gave me an unreadable look or ignored me altogether.

"Soldier, are you in FFP and committed to target?"

I pulled my mind back from Quinn and my view back from the one red shoe, training my crosshairs on the woman's torso instead. We'd been reassured that the dissipating rounds were constructed for minimal penetrating power, and that it was safe to shoot at the usual target areas since the rounds would never punch through to the heart or lungs. I was relieved about that. During boot camp, Sarge had set up a terminal ballistics training session where we'd fired high-caliber, high-velocity rounds into blocks of ballistic gelatin — a tough, jelly-like substance that most closely mimicked the consistency of human and animal flesh. Afterward we'd been able to cut open the urine-colored blocks, to trace our bullet's trajectory and see exactly the amount of damage the rounds caused as they tore through the substance, exploding into fragments of shell that radiated out from the wound path.

At the center of one of the blocks was a large pig's heart sourced from a butcher or abattoir. Bruce had volunteered to shoot that block — no surprise there — and Sarge had filmed the shot. We viewed the footage in extreme slow-motion, watching the bullet punch into and rip through the block, sending shock waves pulsing and rippling through the gelatin as it discharged its impetus. The heart had exploded into bloody mush.

Watching the footage, the boys had whistled and cheered. I hadn't.

"Instantaneous incapacitation of any mook," said Sarge. "These .5 caliber rounds have total stopping power."

"Imagine what it would do to a person's head — deep tissue destruction!" said Mitch.

"Complete cranial evacuation, dude!" said Bruce.

"Decapitation," said Cameron.

Destruction, evacuation, immediate suspension, target suppression, immobilization. These were the terms we used instead of saying kill, maim, destroy. Whatever we termed it, there would be no recovering from a wound made by *those* rounds.

It was unlikely that there would be a return to health for this poor M&M, either, but at least she would soon be comfortable in the hospital. Clean and out of pain. I reminded myself of that, reminded myself that I was only darting, not shooting, reminded myself why I was doing this. But my mind kept bringing me back to the inescapable fact that I had a rifle aimed at another human being.

My heart was racing, my mouth as dry as dust. I was in danger of getting full-blown "buck fever" if I didn't calm down or get this done as soon as possible. I ran through the strategies we'd been taught to regain calm and focus. I checked my high-angle calculations, adjusted the elevation turret on my scope and steadied the rifle against my cheek. As I forced my breathing into a slow, steady rhythm, I cleared my mind of anything but the here and now. I stopped looking at the woman's dirty, bruised face, stopped looking at her as though she was a "her", and locked my focus instead on the golden triangle of her chest, adjusting my aim to the middle of the letter S on her cheerleader's top.

Failure — not an option.

"Affirmative. Shooter ready," I said, easing off the safety and putting the tip of my index finger on the cool curve of the trigger.

"Field is clear and we are hot. Send it."

I breathed out, paused, and squeezed the trigger, just as the target angled her body sideways.

I missed. A splash of dust and debris kicked up beyond the woman where the round had hit the ground. Damn! Static hissed in my earpiece, but Sarge said nothing. Maybe he thought I'd lost my nerve, that I couldn't handle these assignments. Maybe he was right.

I recalculated the angle, doped my scope, slowed my breathing as I tracked the torso turning circles below. Then I fired. The woman dropped like she'd had her lights punched out — which I guessed, in a way, she had. One hand fell across her chest, below where the small rose of blood bloomed. She wore a wedding ring, I saw now. I sighed and disassembled my rifle and collected my used cartridge cases as I'd been trained to do. Before I was back down on street level, the specially equipped ambulance — they called them "rabid hutches" — had arrived and taken her off to the hospital. All that remained of the mission was a teenager with a gym bag climbing into an unmarked black van. And a red velvet stiletto lying in a rain puddle against an alley wall.

I was still rattled that evening, and the congratulations and envy directed my way by the rest of the team didn't help. Leya, who could see that I was upset, finally pulled me aside to give me a talking to — a verbal hug and slap combo.

"This is hard for you, I can see that. I can understand it. Shooting people? That's heavy stuff. But you can't let it become personal. It's *not* personal — it's your job. We all have to do things we don't like in our work, but we have an obligation to do the best job we can. If feelings get in the way, you have to shut them down."

I tried to calm myself by picturing the woman lying calmly in the Community General Hospital plague ward. I even asked Sarge if I could go visit her there — a request which provoked a sharp bark of laughter in addition to an extra-maniacal grin.

"No, Goldilocks, you may not. Of all the sharp-eyed, steady-handed bleeding hearts, I had to land you! Next thing you'll be asking if you can go scatter the ashes of your poor little rat-kills in the woods, lay a rose at the kill-site, maybe sing Kumbaya. It's a *job*, soldier! Do you think you could possibly be a bit more professional about it?"

That stung. I resolved to dial down the volume on my tender-hearted and sympathetic impulses, but while I could make myself be coolheaded during the subsequent M&M missions in the city, afterwards I could only fake hard-hearted. Beneath the tough outer coating of don't-give-a-shit was a squishy mess of confusion and doubt.

Chapter 21

Blondes in Pink Satin

I had completed four human-target missions by the time I was sent on my first terr takedown. I thought it would be easier. It was harder.

Partly, this was because I had to take the shot from close-up. Partly, it was because despite all Sarge's talk about me being a professional soldier, they had dressed me like a little girl. They'd stuck me in a pink dress, and Fiona had brushed my hair up into a high ponytail. I even finally had patterned latex gloves — white with pink polka dots to match the girly ensemble.

"What the hell is this?" I asked, aghast, when I saw myself in the mirror. I looked about thirteen years old.

"Camouflage," said Fiona, unfastening the hog's-tooth thong from my neck and laying it aside on my bedside cabinet. "No one will guess anyone who looks like that might be about to shoot them."

I suspected that the truth of why I had been such a valuable recruit lay at least as much in my ability to pass as an unthreatening little girl as it did in my marksmanship skills. They'd probably chosen me to be the first sniper in human-target missions because I was the youngest and most innocent-looking. How would they be dressing me when I could no longer pass for a juvenile? I imagined Fiona styling me with a look somewhere between honeypot and hooker, and shuddered.

Sarge and Roberta Roth dropped in to check me over before I set out, and Sarge let out a cackle of glee. "Those mooks won't know what hit 'em!"

"You'll do," Roth said, giving me a sharp nod of approval before turning to Sarge. "Wayne, a word?"

Down in the hallway outside the transport bay, the whole unit was waiting. Mitch whistled when he saw me, Tae-Hyun and Cameron applauded, and judging by his appreciative grin, Bruce seemed to have a thing for blondes dressed in pink dresses.

"Shu-weet!" he said, stepping towards me. "Wanna —"

"Stop right there," I said, poking a forefinger into his chest to hold him at arm's length and giving him a death-stare. A movement in my peripheral vision caught my eye, and I turned my head to see Quinn was standing to my right, looking me up and down, from the tips of my pink-laced Hello Kitty sneakers to the top of my ridiculous ponytail.

"You're a real heartbreaker in pink," he said, shaking his head. "Literally."

"Piss off," said Leya loyally.

"Don't let the douchebag dent your confidence, Blue," said Bruce, as Quinn walked away. "I think you look —"

"Bruce, if you say another word, just one more word, to me right now, I swear on my *rifle* that I will break every single finger on your shooting hand." I spat the words out with such intensity that Bruce's mouth fell open.

He blinked. "Jeez, Jinx! Overreact much?"

"Actually, I don't think I've reacted *enough*. Let me correct that right here and right now. I'm sick of your stupid, sexist comments and insinuations. That shit stops now! Get it?"

"Loud and clear," he said in a mocking tone, looking around at the other guys as if hoping they'd back him up. When none of them came to his support, he muttered, "Can't even take a joke," and slouched off.

I let out an exasperated sigh. "Remind me why I'm doing this," I begged Leya.

"For the war against the plague. For the future of your country. For us," she said.

Again, I had that sense of the plague as a looming, evil foe. I straightened my back as I marched past amused and interested stares, through the decon unit and doors to transport bay C and into the armory for my weapons and ammo issue. Juan handed me one of the new dart guns. It looked like a semi-automatic pistol with a longer-than-usual barrel out front and an internal dart magazine, loaded with three darts, protruding out the back. There were sights on the barrel, but no optics — this was more short-range sidearm than long-range sniper rifle.

"Remember, the ideal range is less than five meters," said Juan. "After that, you start losing accuracy."

I stuffed the weapon in the shoulder-strapped denim bag Fiona had handed me and reported for duty. The take-down was due to happen on a street.

"It'll be easier to take him when he's on his own and outdoors. Luckily, this tango is cocky. He doesn't feel the need to exercise indoors on a treadmill. He runs like a rat on the roads, as if the plague doesn't apply to him. Thinks he *owns* the city," Sarge had briefed me. "Doesn't even bother to vary his route much, according to intel."

Had Quinn supplied that nugget of information? Or Sofia?

"Did intel say whether he was likely to be armed?" I asked.

Sarge paused a moment too long before replying. "In the man-hunting game, it's always a case of take before you're taken. You get me, soldier?"

"Message received, sir."

Now I was grateful for my absurd outfit. Anything that would buy me a few extra seconds' advantage was welcome. I only hoped that the target would be taken in by my girlish appearance, that he didn't have his own intel or a mole in our organization who had relayed our plans to him as efficiently as his had been passed on to us.

"And why can't we use the rifle with the dissolving tranq bullets for the terrs, Sarge? Then we wouldn't need to get so close." As a sniper, distance was my friend.

"We don't want to perforate them unless we need to, Blue. Time they spend recuperating is time we could already be questioning, getting information in time to stop their next attack. Doesn't matter so much for the rabids — they're going to be in the hospital anyway."

The insert vehicle was a battered old tan sedan that fitted inconspicuously among the two other rusting vehicles abandoned outside a derelict McDonalds in an abandoned strip mall located in a rough part of the city. I pulled up my small white mask, one of the lightweight surgical jobs that Quinn had been wearing the first time I met him, climbed out of the car and headed for an old playground nearby, directly on the target's running route. It was overgrown with tall grass and weeds, the purple-and-yellow merry-go-round was rusted to a standstill and the see-saw had toppled off its fulcrum, but a couple of the swings still looked functional. I seated myself on the higher of the two and rocked back and forth, gritting my teeth against the protesting squawk of the chains in their rings. The day was filthy hot and so humid that breathing felt like drinking air. The metal seat of the swing burned my butt and thighs through the light fabric of the dress. I sighed and straightened the fabric. My feet itched to dig into the earth and propel me higher into the air — to catch a hint of breeze, a moment of freedom — but I resisted the temptation.

"Tango approaching from the southeast." Fiona was calling this mission, as she had the last two M&M take-downs. "Juliet, you are good to go, we are live."

From the corner of my eye, I could see him running, fast and graceful as only a true athlete could be, down the road in my direction. Thoughts raced through my mind, even as I dragged my feet in the dirt to slow my swing to a stop. What if I missed? There were only three darts, not much room for error. What if he did have a weapon on him, or a syringe like the one they'd stuck my father with? What if some instinct told him I was dangerous before I could take him down?

Fighting the urge to shoot too soon, I slowly blew out a deep breath, wiped my right hand dry against my dress, then thrust it into the bag and grasped my weapon.

As he ran up level with the playground, the man's eyes scanned the area and rested on me. His shoulders, which had tensed as he first registered me, now relaxed. He wasn't wearing a mask, so I could see his lips curve slightly at the sight of a girl playing on a swing — such a normal, happy sight. He waved at me, and I forced myself to return the wave. Perhaps it looked off — it totally didn't feel natural — or perhaps a warning bell pinged in his brain that a lone kid playing in a plague-riddled city wasn't so normal after all, because moments after he passed by me, he turned to look back. This time he wasn't smiling, even before he registered that the swing-seat was empty, that the little girl was now standing on the sidewalk, less than six meters away, holding a weapon in a two-handed grip, firing it at him.

The dart hit him directly above the heart, and he teetered for a second or two before he collapsed. His head cracked against the sidewalk with a thud that made me wince.

I dropped the dart gun into my bag and walked away from the scene while I waited for the extract vehicle to catch up with me.

"Good job," said Fiona when I climbed in.

She must have been commending me on staying cool, because the shot itself had hardly been difficult. It would take an effort to miss at that distance.

I twisted in the car seat to stare out the tinted rear windshield. An unmarked car had pulled up beside the downed jogger, and three men who I presumed were police officers were hauling him into their vehicle.

"You okay?" Fiona said, scrutinizing me with her sharp eyes.

"I guess."

Truth be told, I wasn't sure how I was.

That didn't change over the next two weeks. I was determined, squarely committed to fighting this plague in the best way I could — even if that meant shooting people with tranquilizer darts and dissolving sleep-bullets. Images of my father, suffering and crazed, would flash into my mind at the oddest times — over lunch, or while I was brushing my teeth — and I'd feel a swell of rage surging through me, a craving for revenge. Then I'd catch Quinn's eye across the cafeteria, and doubts would kick in. Damn him. If he was so opposed to what we were doing, then what the hell was he doing working here? Waves of irritation at the pirate were almost always followed by riptides of heartache which knocked me off my precarious emotional balance. I missed his warm hands massaging my back and his soft lips closing over mine. I missed the way he laughed from his whole body and got me to do the same. I missed how whole and safe I had felt with him. I missed his good opinion.

I missed Robin, too, and felt guilty every time I remembered how he still didn't know what had really happened to our dad. I had written and rewritten a letter to him explaining what I'd discovered, but it still sat unsent in my draft email folder. It was something I had to tell him in person. Then again, perhaps he would be better off never knowing. He was such a gentle dreamer, this might crush him. One thing I was certain of, I would do anything I could to prevent him seeing that horrific footage. For the first time in my life, I understood a little what it must be like to be my mom. Huh.

Adding to my all-round un-okay-ness were the flashbacks and nightmares I got from the missions. That red shoe, walking around and around in uneven circles. The small blooms of blood on chests and necks and backs. The runner's friendly wave. The crack of his head against the sidewalk. And over and over again, that damned photo propped against the cage with the hopping, chirping canary.

That image got burned into my brain in my second terr-takedown, on an unusually cool and rainy day in early August. The setup for this one was to send me to deliver ordered groceries to the target's apartment. At least I didn't have to wear the girly getup this time. I wore jeans, the store's orange branded t-shirt and an unzipped hoodie. Sarge instructed me to cover my hair and face as I entered and exited the apartment building. As he put it, "We don't want word getting out on the street that a young blonde has been seen in the vicinity of recent hits, or they'll put two and two together and set a bounty on your head. I don't want to think about what the goblins would do to you if they got a hold of you."

Great. Something else that had been omitted from his and Roth's sales pitch.

"Sarge? There's something I wanted to ask you."

"Yeah?"

"You've shot … I mean, you were in the wars, as a sniper. What was it like for you — to shoot people?"

"I didn't shoot people. I shot tangos."

"Okay then, what did you feel when you shot tangos?"

He stared at me for a long moment then shrugged and replied, "Recoil."

There was nothing to say to that.

The apartment building was in a run-down part of the city, and the elevator groaned and creaked ominously as it lurched up to the ninth floor. I pulled my hood off my head, fluffed my hair around my face, and fitted my mask into position, staring at the girl in the speckled mirror opposite the button panel. I was on my own on this mission; my closest backup was down on street level.

"We can't have a horde of armed men marching into the lobby. I can guarantee the entrance is being watched. Their spotter would call up to the tango before you'd made the first floor, and he'd bolt to some other rat-hole before you got near."

I wasn't even wearing a comms earpiece — I'd be getting so close that wearing one might get me found out. When the elevator doors dragged themselves open, I hoisted the three sealed bags of groceries up and held them close against my chest, where the dart gun nestled in an inner pocket of my hoodie.

The door number of apartment 903 was missing its last digit, but someone had scratched a number three in ballpoint pen into the soft, cheap wood of the door. I rang the buzzer, listening hard above the thump of my heart for the sound of feet on the other side. A shadow behind the peephole told me that someone was peering out at me.

"Who is that?" called a voice.

"Grocery delivery from Bennies Best Buys," I called back.

The door opened an inch on the chain, revealing a portion of a thin face through the narrow slit. He wasn't wearing a mask. Both his mouth and eyes were tight with unmistakable suspicion. Had the word gone out among the network of terr cells that one of their own had recently been taken down and taken in for questioning? Had anyone clocked the girl with the gun? My body screamed at me to bolt back to the elevator.

"Where is the usual boy, Peter?"

This was a freaking test, must be. In the briefing on the way over, Sarge had told me that the usual delivery boy's name was Ahmed. That he had been working this route for the last two years.

"Uh, the usual guy's sick. But I think his name is Ahmed," I said.

The tight eyes relaxed a little. That bugged me, so I added in a voice thick with shock, "They think he might have the rat fever, he might be dying!"

The man swore under his breath. Yeah, take that, you bastard. How's it feel when it's someone *you* know? Still he stared at me.

"C'mon, dude," I complained, shifting the packages, "these bags aren't getting any lighter."

He closed the door to unhook the chain, then opened it and motioned me in. Every instinct in my body told me not to turn my back on him, but I had to lose the packages and extract my gun, and I couldn't do that facing him. I stepped into the apartment and moved past him, my eyes registering possible target sites. The padded khaki vest, zipped most of the way up his chest, might be hiding a protective vest. Better to target exposed flesh — a bare upper arm circled with a tattoo in an unfamiliar script, the pulsing hollow at the base of his throat, directly beneath his sharp Adam's apple.

"You can put it over there, on the counter in the kitchen."

The apartment was small and dark, the curtains drawn even at midday. Through an open doorway, I could see into another room. A mattress was pushed into a corner, three-gallon water bottles were lined up against the wall, and the rest of the floor was covered with masses of computer equipment — tower boxes, coiled cables and glowing screens.

"Hurry, please."

"Yeah, yeah." I put as much bored teen attitude as I could into the words.

The kitchen consisted of a few cupboards and a melamine counter beside a single sink. A teacup and saucer were stuck in a draining rack, and on the counter was a birdcage in which a yellow canary hopped back and forth, back and forth between two perches. Every time it landed on the left-hand perch, it gave a high chirrup. A photo was propped up against the cage. As I got closer, I could see it was a picture of a round-faced woman with long, dark hair, cradling a small baby. The baby's mouth was open in a yawn, and its one hand was reaching tiny wrinkled fingers into the air, as if trying to grasp at something.

Hop-*chirp*-hop-hop-*chirp*. I placed the bags on the counter, staring at those minute star fingers. Hop-*chirp*. Reached my right hand into my hoodie, curled my fingers around the grip of the gun.

"What's the delay?" the man said impatiently.

Hop-hop-*chirp*.

"What are you doing there? Turn around."

I did. In a single fluid motion, I spun around and fired the pistol. The dart hit him in the neck. Before he crumpled to the carpet, he had time to move his hands. One raised itself to the wound in his neck, and the suddenly slack fingers of the other lost their grip on the pistol he had been holding. Shit. He'd had a weapon. *Take before you're taken.*

I darted over to him, kicked the pistol a few feet away, just in case, and nudged him with a toe. His eyes stayed closed, and he didn't move, except for the rise and fall of his chest.

Hop-hop-*chirp*. I worried what would happen to the bird, imagined Sarge's face if I asked him and resolved not to. But at the door on my way out, I turned and ran back to the kitchenette. The photograph fluttered to the floor as I snatched up the birdcage. I would leave it in the lobby of the apartment building. Hopefully someone would rescue and take care of it.

Back on the street with my hoodie pulled up over my hair, I gave the signal that I'd completed the mission — stooping down to tie a shoelace — and then walked to the end of the city block to meet the extraction team.

"You get him?" Sarge asked.

I nodded, taking the bottle of iced water he offered and drinking thirstily. "I put him down." The water felt cold in my already unsettled stomach.

Sarge dialed a number on his phone and without greeting the person on the other side said, "Our boy is taking a nap." No doubt the team on standby to take the terr into custody would be at the apartment within minutes.

"Any problems?" Sarge asked me.

"He had a firearm." And a flipping canary. And a wife and baby somewhere. "And he had it pointed at me. D'you think they know about us? About me?"

"Nah." Sarge waved a dismissive hand in the air, as if brushing aside the very idea. "These tangos are paranoid. Have to be, I guess. Glad you kept your head, Blue."

He sat back in his seat and grinned at me.

"Cool as a fish on ice, you. Knew we'd caught ourselves something special the first time you shot me."

I said nothing. It would have been unkind to spoil his illusion. But a favorite saying of my father's was running through my mind: "The second mouse gets the cheese."

I couldn't help wondering if, in this new specialist unit, I was the first mouse.

Chapter 22

Moon Tan

"See you at the cafeteria?" said Leya, passing me on her way out of the armory.

"Yeah, just need to check this in first," I said, showing her my weapon.

"See you later," she called.

But after I'd handed the dart-gun back, I didn't go to the cafeteria. I had no appetite after this afternoon's mission, and I needed to get outside and breathe fresh evening air. Three things were clear to me. A) Even though I knew human-target missions were necessary, I still didn't enjoy them. And even though I'd completed several now, they weren't getting any easier. B) I wasn't thrilled with the idea that the bad guys regarded me more as an enemy combatant than a medication dispenser, and they *were* armed with actual guns and live ammo. C) Even though I was out in the city and suburbs on missions, I still didn't feel any more free than I had back at home.

I spent my time between the compound and missions, and I was under observation and instruction at both. My assignments were chosen for me, the type of weapon and ammo I had to use was decided for me, I was escorted to and from the shoot sites and usually ordered about via an earpiece during the mission. Nowhere, except perhaps in my small bedroom and even tinier bathroom, was I ever alone. Nowhere was I free.

I sat on one of the wooden benches at the back of the compound, staring at the gathering shadows in the trees beyond the line of fencing. Our family had often gone camping in state parks in the years before the plague. Mom had shown us how to roast marshmallows beside the fire until the outside was a crispy golden-brown skin ready to slip off the gooey heart of sweetness. I'd ignored her cautions and burned my fingers and my tongue. Robin had burned his marshmallows, watching fascinated as the balls of fire became wrinkled, black blobs. Dad had taken Robin and me on what he called "forced marches" through the forest, stopping beside each new tree to teach us its name. By the end of our week in the woods, I'd learned them all. Now I would probably only be able to recognize loblolly pines and oaks — I hadn't been for a walk in the woods since Dad died. Maybe freedom was not possible in a world where the pandemic determined almost every aspect of our lives.

I liked to come out here at this time of day. There was a brief time every evening before the compound lights fired up, when the heat of the day eased and the sun's harsh light faded. The air was soft as an embrace, and the sounds of the compound faded to a distant hum. If I sat very still and strained my ears, I could hear the breeze in the trees, maybe even make out a birdsong or two. Now, the sky paled to a dull gray behind the pink-streaked masses of cloud. That gray was the color of Quinn's eyes when he was angry. I stuffed my hands into my hoodie pockets.

Gravel crunched on the path that circled the daisy-shaped compound. I looked up, straight into the gray-sky eyes of Quinn himself.

"Oh," I said, surprised. "What are you doing here?" It was like

I'd summoned him by thinking of him.

He stopped and stared back at me. "I sometimes come out here to take a break. You?"

"I … the same."

The air between us expanded and contracted with unsaid things. In the deepening almost-darkness, I couldn't see his face clearly. Maybe it would be easier to talk to him this way.

"Quinn, I —" I began, just as he started saying, "So I guess —"

We both broke off and the silence vibrated between us again. "You first," I finally said, my voice almost a whisper.

"Your shirt," he said, gesturing to the grocery-store logo on the orange T-shirt. "You've been out undercover, shooting again."

His voice held the old disapproval, and just like that, the quiet spell between us was broken. As if to emphasize it, the security lights came on, sweeping the soft night and deep shadows away with penetrating brightness. Somewhere, behind those blinding lights, the moon was rising.

I nodded and looked away from his eyes at his faded blue T-shirt, his loose jeans, and those damned checkerboard sneakers. As black and white as his attitudes about right and wrong.

"And would I be right in guessing, since rats can't read, that you've been shooting people?"

"Taking them down, yes."

He swore and kicked at the gravel. "You and your euphemisms. Can't you even be honest about what you do?"

"Look, I know you don't approve," I said, standing up and stepping close to him.

"There's the understatement of the century."

"And I understand that," I continued. "Hell, I'm not entirely at peace with it either. I didn't want to target people, I still don't really. But for the record, when I met you, when I first started here, I didn't know that's what they were training us for. I thought it was just rats and other diseased animals."

"You expect me to believe that?" His head was tilted sideways, his eyes narrowed, his mouth twisted.

"It's the truth," I said, reaching a hand out to his arm. When he flinched and stepped back, my heart clenched into something small and hard and painful. "Sorry," I said, holding my hands up as if in surrender, and walking two steps back from him. It was like I was infected with something sick and diseased, like *I* was a plague-carrier.

"I didn't know," I repeated. "But I do now, and I'm not planning to stop."

"You —"

"Quinn, they showed me footage of my father. He died from the plague, not a heart attack. He was murdered by terrorists in one of the early attacks. They took him hostage, they injected him with the virus, and he died. He died horribly. It took days and days. It was … bad." My voice broke on the last word.

"I'm sorry. I know you loved him," said Quinn, his voice softer now, and more gentle. "But that's not —"

"I *did* love him. And I'm sure all the victims have people who love them. And no one deserves to suffer and die like that. The plague's got to be stopped, the suffering's got to be ended."

"And you truly believe that this is the right, the only way?" his voice was growing hard again.

"How else can the M&Ms be brought in safely for treatment? And the terrs need to be arrested — interviewed and brought to trial. And taking them in this way does minimize the likelihood of firefights and casualties."

"What?" said Quinn. He looked stunned. "Are you leading me on, trying to get me to talk? Or is this actually what you believe?"

"What are you on about? Why are you so angry? Please, tell me. What the hell is so bad about tranquilizing people so that they can be brought in for treatment or debriefing?"

"You're either the most naïve person I've ever met, or you're a damned good liar, perhaps even a plant, trying to get me to shoot my mouth."

"Quinn, I swear I don't understand what you're on about."

"You're serious!" He raked fingers through his hair and glanced over his shoulder. "You really don't know, do you?"

"Know what?"

"What the Academy is doing. What actually happens to the people you take down." His voice was so low I struggled to hear.

"Oh, now there's some big conspiracy? So tell me, what *actually* happens to them?"

"I can't talk about it here."

"And why's that?"

"We're being watched."

I looked around. "No one else is even out here."

Quinn flicked his gaze to the guard huts and jerked his chin in the direction of a camera mounted on the pole bearing the main electricity supply cord into the compound.

"That camera's been focused on us since we started talking."

I had to laugh. "Don't you think you're being a bit paranoid?"

"We have cameras mounted on every wall, there are microchips in our ID bracelets which can track our every move. All our communications, how much we exercise, what we weigh and eat — everything is monitored. And you're asking me if I'm *paranoid*?" he snapped.

"The cameras are for security and the rest is for our own benefit, to maximize our training regime."

"You believe everything you're told! Well, except when it comes from me. Wake up, Jinxy, see the bigger picture."

"Maybe I could — if you explained." I was so frustrated with all the hints and insinuations. "If you've got something to say, spit it out."

The sound of crunching gravel said someone was on the way, probably a routine patrol.

"Not here," said Quinn softly. "As far as I know, they haven't bugged our bedrooms. Can you be in your room after dinner tomorrow night? Alone."

"I can make a plan to be there."

"Don't tell anyone, you hear? Not *anyone*." And he was gone, and I was alone by the bench again once Bruce came strolling by.

"Trying to catch a moon tan, Blue?"

"Something like that." Something just as elusive.

The next night, I hurried through dinner, not tasting any of the food.

"Where are you off to in such a rush?" asked Leya. "There's still apple pie and ice cream for dessert."

"I've got some letters to write. My mom's been freaking out because I've sent no news in ages. She's threatening to revoke her permission and haul my ass home." This was actually true.

"No problem, I'll catch you later," said Leya.

"I'll be in the rec room until late, if you want to hang out," said Bruce.

Yeah, don't hold your breath, there, Brucey-baby.

When I heard the soft knock at the door of my quarters, I made myself count to ten before opening the door, not wanting to appear too eager.

"It'll be on the cameras that I came here tonight and probably on the ID bracelet tracking system, too. So if anyone asks, you'll have to have a story ready," Quinn said as he stepped into my room. Immediately, I was aware of his height, his faintly spicy smell, his presence which filled the space and reached out to me.

"Okay."

Quinn had been in my room many times before, and each time

he'd flung himself onto my bed like he owned it. Tonight he stood, looking awkward. His glance dipped to the shoulder straps of my tank-top, where his earring peeped out from underneath.

"You still wear this?" His fingers brushed against the ring, against my skin.

I shrugged. Would he want it back? "I didn't want it to get lonely, all by itself in the box."

The suggestion of a smile flitted across his lips and was gone. "Please, sit."

I climbed onto my bed and gestured for him to do the same. My heart shrank a little when he pulled the chair out from under the desk at the window, spun it around, and sat backwards on it.

He stared at me for a long moment with the sort of assessing look I was used to getting from Sarge and Fiona.

"You were going to explain stuff to me? About the bigger picture?" I prompted.

He folded his arms across the top of the chair back and rested his chin on them.

"Can I trust you?" he finally said, sounding like he was asking himself more than me.

"To do what?"

"Not to tell anyone what I'm about to tell you. Not to tell anyone that you heard it from me?"

"Yes!" I said. "I'm not sure what I can do to convince you, but yes, you can trust me."

"Swear it?"

"Sure."

"Say it."

What the hell was he about to tell me? "I swear that I won't spill the beans, or give you away."

Something in my eyes or voice must have convinced him, because he nodded once and then began speaking.

Chapter 23

Interrogation

"Okay, you know I'm a specialist in intel, right?" Quinn said.

"Uh-huh." I'd snagged a couple of extra sodas from the cafeteria at dinner, and now I handed him one.

"Thanks." He popped the tab and took a long swallow. "My unit is the most recent set of recruits, so we don't get to work on stuff with the highest security clearance, but we still see a lot. We get passed masses of information and we have to analyze it, look for patterns and meaning, pick up unusual activity and guess, or predict, how and where we think illegal actions might occur. Some of the data comes from spooks on the outside." He jerked a chin in the direction of the window. "But we also sift through information on cadets and specialists in here."

"That's how you know the cameras are not purely for security, and that they're checking our communications?"

"Yes. Of course, a lot of this is legit. They have to make sure that none of us is an insurgent mole. And we need intelligent information." He fiddled with the tab on the soda can, twisting it and bending it back on itself.

"But?"

"There's more. I've picked up more. They're doing —" He broke off as if unsure how to continue. He took another sip of soda then rubbed the back of one hand over his mouth. "We've been trained to see patterns and meaning in raw data. And we see what they want us to see, but also what they don't. Bottom line: I think they're getting and using the information in ways that they shouldn't. This country has changed radically, and some people have benefited from it enormously while others have really suffered."

"What do you mean?"

He downed the rest of his soda and crushed the can between his long fingers as he spoke. "Let me give you an example. I've been working on a project to track rat fever patterns in the Southern Sector, in this city in particular. And here's what I've noticed: the business of rat extermination occurs mostly in middle-class suburbia. Why would that be? It's not because most of the rats are there — if anything, there are more of them in the inner-city slum areas. I think it's because populations in poor areas are seen as more expendable. There are too many unemployed down there, too many sick, not enough useful, educated citizens. They're a drain on social funding, and they're being whittled down, or at least," he said, reacting to the skepticism I could feel on my face, "allowed to be whittled down by the pestilence."

"No! No way."

"So how many ratting expeditions have you been on in the slums?"

I considered that. "None," I admitted. How had I never registered that before?

"And how many M&Ms have you taken out in suburbia?"

Again, none. I shook my head. This was incredible, unbelievable.

"But isn't that simply because there are more ill people in the inner city?"

"Perhaps, but that would be in part because there are more rats there, not so? It happens too often, too systematically for it to be pure coincidence. To me, it looks like a kind of social engineering." He tossed the squashed can into the trashcan beside the door.

"*What?* That's absurd." It sounded like utter paranoia to me. I wanted to laugh, but nothing about this was funny.

"They're allowing rat fever to run rampant in areas with high populations of suspected illegal immigrants and the poor and unemployed. But they're making serious efforts to keep it out of middle-class suburbia — in the voting districts that support this government. And they're keeping the population segments separate."

I just shook my head.

"Answer this: did you ever go on a Fun outing with groups from another part of the city?"

"No, but that could be because it's more convenient to collect everybody from one area, surely?"

"*Convenient*? Of course it's convenient. But don't you think the government has a responsibility, even if it's *in*convenient, to make sure that different segments of the population get together?"

He ran his fingers roughly through his hair, leaving it tousled and messy. My fingers longed to smooth the tangles. I forced my mind back from his hair to his argument.

"Quinn, this sounds like some crazy conspiracy theory. Even if there was no plague, and no social program, I'd probably never mix with people from the other side of town anyway."

"Oh yes, you would. You'd go to college with people from all backgrounds, you'd mix at the workplace and on the bus or metro, or at music concerts. But the way things are now, how would a girl from your neck of the woods even meet a boy from mine?"

"We did," I pointed out.

"We're the exception. Almost everyone is only mixing with their own kind, and the status quo is getting entrenched."

I frowned in confusion, not sure what to believe. If he was

right, then it was worse than I could have imagined. He grabbed the other can of soda, popped the tab and lifted it to his lips before seeming to realize what he was doing.

"Sorry, this is yours."

"It's fine, you can have it." He looked like he needed it more than I did. "Say this is all true — and I'm not saying I believe it is — then why? Why would they do it?"

"Well, my brother, Connor, says all history is economic and we have to think about whose interest all of this serves. Who benefits from a population bound by fear of a disease that probably isn't as infectious as we've been led to believe?"

"What are you saying?"

"My brother says that there is a respected section of the medical establishment that believes the plague isn't transmitted by airborne virus or touch."

"*What*? No way!"

"Think about it. No terrorist would engineer a bioweapon that spreads too easily, because within days it would be all around the world, including in their country, killing their own people and their allies. There would be no way to confine it to your enemy."

Horribly, that made sense.

"And the same specialists say there's no way you could get it from spiked food or drinks." He took another long drink from his own. "That's just an urban legend the government allows to continue circulating. The only way you can get it is from blood and bites. And" — he tilted his head at me, his lips pursed in sympathy — "direct attacks with injections, of course."

"But we all wear masks and gloves, and stay inside, and, and everything revolves around that," I protested, even as I remembered that neither of the terrorists I'd taken down had worn gloves or masks. Neither had the perpetrators in the bank attack which killed my father.

"Everything revolves around *fear*. A fearful population is easier to control. Look at the rights we've given up, Jinxy, in practice if not officially — freedom of movement, privacy of information, freedom of association, the right to free assembly and birth control. Censorship is up, civil liberties and protections are down. Hell, you don't even need a search warrant to send a SWAT team into someone's house if you have 'reasonable suspicion' that they might be involved in insurgent activity. And that's not even to speak of covert black ops."

It occurred to me that I hadn't seen, or even been informed of, warrants for the work I'd done. Was *I* black ops?

"We've now got a massive government with all sorts of extended powers. It spies on its citizens, limits our freedoms, and labels whistle-blowers and critics as treasonous," said Quinn, passionately.

He stood up and stalked over to the window, braced his arm against the glass, and stared into the darkness outside, leaning his forehead on his arm. Beyond the window, thunder growled and wind moaned. A storm was blowing up. I wished I could run out into it, have the wind blow my doubts away, have the coming rain wash away my confusion. But Quinn was still talking, pelting me with facts like hailstones.

"We've repatriated hundreds of thousands, perhaps even millions, of foreign residents, refugees and workers. We've insulated ourselves, sealed our borders against immigrants and imports and competition. We're forced to buy local. And as a nation we've channeled billions into a defense industry that was sitting idle after the last wars fizzled out. We couldn't keep invading foreign territories, especially not when they started threatening to nuke us. What better solution than to fight a war on home ground? Connor says we needed a war to keep our economy afloat — war is big business."

"Big business? You can't think they're doing this for money?"

"Connor says that's exactly the motive."

" 'Connor says, Connor thinks' — you remind me of Bruce, only he says, 'Sarge says.' What do *you* think?"

With a crack like a rifle, lightning split the darkness beyond the window, flashing pale against Quinn's features. He sighed and then turned back to me, but I could no longer see his face in the gloom of the room. I switched on the bedside lamp, and Quinn stepped into the circle of its light. He looked sad.

"I think … I *think* that the people who made the changes to the law and set up all the surveillance and controls probably thought they were doing the right thing for the right reasons. They had good intentions, but they didn't think it through, didn't imagine the possible negative consequences. I don't think it was done in order *to* profit. But, Jinxy, people *have* profited — out of our fear and illness."

Quinn crouched down in front of me and took my hands in his. His stormy eyes were so full of cynicism that he suddenly seemed much older, and I felt like an ignorant little girl.

"Think about all those gloves, masks, disinfectants and sanitizers, the decon units and hot-boxes, new Q-bays and medical facilities and incineration plants, all the money to be made if a pharmaceutical company comes up with a vaccine, the tens of millions of copies of The Game sold every year. And that's not to mention the money that's been pumped into arms, ammunition and special training units like this."

"Are you saying the government wants us to be at war, that there isn't a threat?" I remembered Bruce telling us Sarge's opinion that nothing unites a country like a common foe.

"Of course there's a threat. We were attacked, and many victims lost their lives before we got a grip on this thing. But there are a growing number of people, like me, who think that the threat has been exaggerated because there are factions in government who want to extend its power over the individual, and there are fat cats who want to keep making obscene profits."

My head was buzzing. I pushed myself off the bed, walked to the bathroom and drank a glass of water, then splashed my face. The girl in the mirror looked like me — sixteen-year-old Jinx James. Friendly, but a bit on the shy side, likes computer games and brownies. Recently developed a love for the color gray. Even more recently got her heart broken. Could I really be a social engineering operative for a covert task team?

I returned to the room, to Quinn. Rain was driving against the window, coursing sideways in rivulets which split and forked off in different directions.

"Well?" Quinn leaned up against the desk, looking at me intently.

"I don't know what to think. It all sounds so unbelievable. And there's a part of me that thinks all's fair in — in war. What they've done, Quinn! My father ..."

"Let me be absolutely clear. I want the plague ended as much as you. I do *not* support terrorists. They are murdering criminals, and I think every last one of them should be arrested and brought to trial. But *legally*. And under the rights guaranteed by our constitution. In fighting the lowest of the low, we shouldn't become just like them."

"Your brother — what's he got to do with all this?"

"Officially, Connor's with the Civil Libs, but he's also with ... a group that's working to expose how the government is bending and breaking the law, how lobbyists have too much power and money and are corrupting our elected representatives. His group is collecting information on what's actually going on, so they can challenge it and turn things around."

"He's a ...?" I began, but I couldn't say the word. I knew what people like Sarge and Bruce and Roth would call him. "He's like a rebel?"

"We need groups like his. Too many people in this nation are too afraid to protest. Or too preoccupied with staying safe and not catching the fever. We're giving up our liberty in exchange for security."

I thought of my mother. She would happily stay in the prison of our house as long as she thought that would keep her, and us, safe. She followed the rules when it came to being a "responsible citizen", even going so far as to report our neighbors for a minor violation. We'd once been friends with the Johnsons next door. We'd swum in their pool, had them over for Thanksgiving dinner, and gone trick-or-treating together with their daughter every Halloween. Yet Mom hadn't hesitated to rat on them. She unquestioningly believed what she was told and did as she was instructed.

Had I been like that?

"And the rebels are growing in number. Connor estimates that they are about 15,000 strong in the Southern Sector alone, and they've made contact with similar groups in the Northeast and Mid-and-West sectors. They're still collecting information and trying to confirm their suspicions, but already they're planning a big campaign to reveal everything to the public. Next year on Independence Day, stay tuned to your T.V." A thin smile ghosted across his face.

"Have you been sending your brother information?" A memory of graduation day came to mind. "Sending messages via your little sister?"

He nodded.

"But, Quinn, that's not right."

"Why not? He's not a traitor!" Thunder boomed out in the night, as if to underscore his anger. "He's fighting greed and corruption and power-mongering. He wants this country to be free again, to be what it was, what it should be. Jinxy, you can love your country without loving your government."

"And if he gets caught?"

"If he gets caught, he'll be tried for treason. The only reason they wouldn't kill him on the spot is because they'd want to interrogate him. Thoroughly. Which," Quinn said, pulling his phone out of his jeans pocket, "brings me to what I wanted to show you."

"What's that?" I asked, pointing to the screen, where a video was loading.

"Proof of what they're doing, and of what you're helping them do. Proof that I'm not delusional or paranoid."

He placed the phone on its side on my bedside table, took me by the hand and pulled me to sit on the bed next to him. My eyes were glued on the screen, which showed the image of a man, gagged and blindfolded, tied to a metal chair in the middle of a small room. A man wearing a sleeveless black vest. A man with a tattoo of unfamiliar writing around his bare upper arm.

"This came in this morning. It's the recorded footage of the interrogation of a suspected terrorist who was captured in the inner city yesterday," Quinn said, shooting a quick glance at me then touching the PLAY arrow on the screen.

"How did you get this?" I asked, my voice barely above a whisper.

"This is the kind of stuff that intel goes through to analyze any information that is … extracted."

There were two men questioning the suspect. Asking the same questions over and over and over.

"I managed to download it. I erased all trace that I'd ever been in the system, I hope."

Hitting him over and over again.

"We have access to many different databases. And if you know computers, there's always a way to hack the system. Back doors that bypass the firewalls."

Doing things to him. To different parts of his body.

"This is what happens, in — what did you call it? — 'interviewing and debriefing," Quinn said, above the sound of thuds and screams and begging. "Officially, these are called *enhanced interrogation techniques.*"

It went on and on.

"Stop!" Now it was me begging. "Please, I can't watch anymore."

Quinn tapped the screen, and the image paused.

I had brought that man in. Me. He was a man who spread the plague, maybe. But he was also a man with a wife and a kid. And a canary. Was the torture justified if he was planning more death and destruction? How could an individual be both a terrorist killer and deserve to be treated with respect?

"But they've done such terrible things." My eyes were filling and my throat closing.

"Can't you see, Jinxy? It's not about them, it's about us. It's not just what we're prepared to allow happen to them, it's about what we're prepared to do, who we're prepared to become."

Then he pulled me into his arms and held me tight while I wept. The sounds and images of the video still turned my stomach. They'd be joining my collection of flashbacks for sure.

"I don't know what's right or wrong anymore!"

"Hush there, my sweet," Quinn said, cradling me against his shoulder.

He kissed my tears, and stroked my hair back from my face, held me until I was calmer. I was so tired, and so tempted just to let go and put the past behind us. I wanted to surrender to his comforting words. I wanted to forget everything I'd seen, everything I knew or feared, and just dissolve into him.

But there were things I needed to say, and it was his turn to listen.

"Don't you 'hush' me," I said, pulling away from him. "I'll cry if I want to. I have a right to be upset, given what I've just found out."

"Of course."

"What I've *just found out*, Quinn. What I never knew before. But what you just assumed I knew. How could you think that I'd be okay with helping bring in targets if I knew it would end in *that*?" I pointed to the paused video.

"That's why I was confused when I discovered you were in the sniper unit. I thought you knew what was really going on."

"You thought wrong. And you didn't make enough of an effort to check. You just dumped me."

"You dumped me, too," he protested.

I held up a hand to stop him. "I'm talking now."

"Okay," he said meekly.

"You dumped me. You jumped to conclusions and assumed the worst about me."

"Jinxy, I'm so sorry." He sounded it, too.

"You were a jerk, Quinn O'Riley!"

"I was, yes."

"And a real dick."

"That too, yes."

"You were a jerk and dick. You ignored me and gave me filthy looks and said mean things. You *took the last chocolate muffin!*"

His mouth twitched at that, but when he spoke, he sounded totally serious. "Jinxy, I was a jerk and a dick and a greedy pig. I'm so, so sorry. I felt like I had to choose between you and what I believe is right. I'm not making excuses," he said quickly when I made to interrupt, "I'm just saying that I was a *confused* dick."

I crossed my arms over my chest, not yet ready to forgive him.

"And the more I missed you, the more confused I got and the more of a jerk I became. For which I am truly sorry. Will you give me another chance?"

"Hmmm. You'll have some making up to do, buddy."

He nodded.

"And from now on, we need to agree on complete honesty between us. So if there's anything else you haven't told me …"

"There's more," he said, flicking his eyes to the phone, where the screen was still lit up with the frozen interrogation image.

"I meant anything about us. I don't want to see more of that. I've seen enough."

"I think you need to know the rest of it — some we only suspect, but some we know for sure. And I'm not sure you'll believe me unless I show you. I've been given some time off and a pass out tomorrow, and I'm going to meet up with Connor." The worry I felt must have been clear on my face, because he added, "Oh, not at home — Connor hasn't lived there for a while in case they're watching. We'll meet at our old neighborhood library. Anyway, point is, I'm hoping he'll have some evidence that will convince you."

The meeting sounded dangerous to me; I didn't want him to go. "You don't need to do that, Quinn. I don't need more proof, truly. I believe you." As I said the words, I realized they were true.

"And I believe in you, Jinxy. Hell, I'm trusting you with my life. What I've done tonight, it's enough to get me sent to GitBay. Maybe to the electric chair."

The bang on the door startled a squawk out of me.

"Jinx? It's Leya, can I come in?"

Crap! I looked an urgent question at Quinn, but Leya didn't wait for a reply. As the copper handle of the door turned, Quinn quickly pulled me down onto the bed beside him, rolled on top of me and began kissing me as passionately as he ever had, smothering any objections I might have had with his mouth. Despite how dreadful I felt, despite how mad I still was at him, my body was galvanized by instant lust. I wanted to lose myself in this, in him.

"*Well!* Sorry to interrupt. I obviously missed the relationship status update." Leya stood, hands on hips, staring down at us with undisguised amusement.

I was too breathless to speak, but Quinn was quicker-witted or perhaps just less affected by that kiss. Rolling himself a little off me, he gave Leya an apologetic grin.

"We wanted to talk things out, so we wouldn't be left with hard feelings, but then we sort of got carried away, and …"

"And now you're left with feeling hard?"

"Leya!" I said.

"Well, I'll let you lovebirds get back to what you were doing." Her eyes flicked to the bedside table. "I don't see any foil packets out — remember to play it safe, kids!" she said, and with a last laugh at us she left, pulling the door closed behind her with a bang and an "As you were, soldier!"

For one long, breathless moment, Quinn and I looked deeply into each other's eyes. He was still half on top of me, braced on his elbows, the length of his hard body pressed against mine. Long black lashes fringed the smoky gray of his eyes.

"That was quick thinking," I whispered.

"I can be quick." He looked down at me in a way that sucked the breath out of me.

"But I prefer to go slow," he said, running a hand over my ribs and down my waist, nuzzling against the soft skin of my neck. "I like to take my time, exploring every inch." He dipped his head and placed a soft kiss under the lobe of my ear. I may have whimpered. "Tasting every bit, taking all of it in." His hand ran back up my side, pressed against the curve of my breast, took my lower lip between his and gently sucked. He could brush the horror away with his caresses, drive it out of my mind with his touch, suck it out of my soul with his kisses, but still I pushed him back.

"You're right. This isn't the time or the place. Not when you still taste of tears," he said kissing each of my temples. "Not when you're still full of horror."

"And not when you've still got a bunch of making up to do before I get over your being such an ass," I said, glad to have found my pride.

He grinned. "We'll talk tomorrow, yeah? Under the secret staircase, after supper?"

"Sure. Now go, I've got things to do."

He scooped up his phone and headed for the door.

"Wait!" I said as he reached for the handle. "Throw this in the trash for me, will you?" I reached behind my neck, unhooked the clasp and tossed the hog's tooth necklace at him.

His smile was wide and free and full. He dropped the hog's tooth into the trashcan beside the door, then walked slowly back to the bed to give me a last kiss. It was deep and tender, and it left me light-headed and limp.

"Have I told you, Jinxy, that I love you?"

My mouth was still hanging open when the door closed softly behind him.

Chapter 24

The Last Tango

"Out with it, princess."

"I want to withdraw from the sniper program, Sarge." I forced myself to look him in the eye as I said it.

I was light-headed from lack of sleep. Between terrible flashbacks of the interrogation footage and debates with myself about the rights and wrongs of hurting some people to stop them hurting others, I'd spent the night alternating between floating on cloud nine with Quinn's last words echoing inside of me, and worrying about what the heck I was going to say at this meeting.

My heart kept telling me that as long as Quinn loved me — Loved! *Me.* — everything else would all work out somehow. But my head kept interrupting the blissful fantasies of happy-ever-after with inconvenient questions about what I would do once I quit. Because I had to quit — that, at least, was clear to me. I'd never been happy about shooting anything but tin and paper targets. Rats, cats and coyotes had been bad enough, but taking down people had been making me sick, peppering my days and nights with horrible images. And now that I knew what would happen to some of my take-downs, what my work was actually about, I simply couldn't go on with it.

"You want out?" Sarge's eyebrows were raised, and his grin was nowhere to be seen. "You want to quit?"

I nodded unhappily, remembering my promise to myself: *failure is not an option. I will not quit.* Was choosing not to do this work the same as failing, as quitting?

Quinn was certain about the morality of resisting the government, that torturing suspects was always wrong. I was less sure. It was really complicated. What if the information that was "extracted" wound up saving lives? Then again, if we lost our humanity while trying to save lives, what would we be left with, who would we be? It made my head spin. I was only sure that I wanted no direct part of it. I had a nasty suspicion that made me a hypocrite.

"Why?"

"Um …" I had known this part would be hard if I wasn't going to break my promise to Quinn. "It's hard to explain."

"Try." Both Sarge's lips and eyes were narrowed with irritation. And suspicion?

"Well, it's been hard for me to shoot animals. And it's been worse darting people." That much was totally true. "I know what you and Ms. Roth said about it being necessary, but I don't think I'm the right person to do it. I don't have the stomach for it, and I get flashbacks and nightmares. And I just … can't," I finished lamely.

"Even after you saw what they did to your father?"

"You need soldiers for this job, Sarge. I'm not a soldier. I'm just a girl who played a computer game really well."

Sarge stroked the stubble on his chin with his fingers, studying me until I squirmed uncomfortably.

"Has someone been talking to you, Blue?"

"No!" Damn. That came out too defensively. "No," I repeated, trying to make my voice sound reasonable. "But that last assignment — the canary and the family photo, they kind of blew my mind. I can't do it, Sarge. I haven't got the stomach for it. I think I should go home."

"Back to Momma?" he mocked.

"Back to Momma." I hoped he would mistake the dread in my voice for the shame of failure.

"I am disappointed, Blue. No getting away from that. Very disappointed. We figured you for something special, not a spineless cake-eating maggot of a quitter. We figured you for someone who wanted to use her skills to take out the people who made her daddy suffer and die a terrible death. But as I said before, no one's forcing you. Tell you what I'm going to do. I'm not going to accept your request to be discharged just yet. I'm going to give you a week to mull it over, to reconsider and maybe overcome your innate pigheadedness."

"Sir, I don't think —"

"If by this time next week you still want out, I will send you back safe and sound to your little bedroom, to contemplate the four walls."

"Yes, sir," I sighed.

"And you can go back to playing computer games."

"Yes, sir."

"While the rest of your unit — shooters not as skilled or as cool-headed as you — go back to fighting the war and saving lives."

I looked down at my feet. The smudge of spider was gone. Was I dismissed?

"In the meantime, we have an important mission this afternoon, based on fresh intel, and as you are still a part of this unit, you will be on it."

"Can't somebody else do it?"

"'Fraid not, Goldilocks. We need our little girl for this one." There was an evil smile on Sarge's face now and, unlike his usual mad grin which came and went like a flash of lightning, this one lingered on his lips.

"Get issued with your weapon at the armory. You'll take point, with Fiona in charge and Bruce providing live backup on site. Dismissed, *soldier*." His voice was acid with contempt.

I told no one of my plans to leave — they wouldn't understand, and I couldn't explain. I spent the morning exercising halfheartedly in the gym and then hung about the cafeteria in the hopes of seeing Quinn. I was out of luck. He was nowhere to be seen. After lunch, I trudged back to my quarters and put on the ridiculous pink dress, tied my hair up in the ponytail and pulled on a pair of the polka-dot gloves. The gloves that were unnecessary, if Quinn was right. I left off the mask.

I didn't want to go on this mission. I also didn't want to go home. I was no longer sure where I belonged. I'd been proud of my skill, but if the one thing that I was good at was bad, what did that make me? What exactly was I supposed to do with my life now?

Quinn had said he loved me, and I yearned for the chance to get back together with him. He planned on staying at the Academy, to feed his brother inside information. If I resigned and went home, how would I ever get to see him again? Maybe I could apply for a different job at ASTA — a cook or cleaner or cafeteria check-out person. I imagined scanning Leya and Cameron's food, or cleaning Bruce's room, and groaned. Besides, every job in this place in some way supported the unacceptable missions and methods, didn't it? Unless you were working against the system from the inside, like Quinn.

At the armory, Juan issued me with a short-range dart gun and three darts. So it would be the take-down of another terr — another man due to be interrogated like the one I'd seen in Quinn's video. Repulsion and horror made my fingers stiff on my weapon. Bruce was handed one of our usual sniper's rifles and a sidearm, plus ammo. Live ammo.

"Expecting rats?" I asked, eyeing his weapons as I dropped the dart-gun into my denim bag.

"Sarge says that according to our intel, the terrs are armed and dangerous, and may put up a fight. This could get ugly." He looked thrilled at the prospect. "And I'm there to keep you safe."

"I can keep myself safe," I snapped.

"I'm there for you, Blue, I've got your six. And we'll be in constant communication."

He handed me a small earpiece and fitted his own communication earphones and mike. In the transport — a white van this time, branded "Peak Plumbing: Only a flush away!" — Fiona was on her phone, receiving last-minute information and instructions about the operation.

"Right," she said once she hung up and we were on our way. "There will be two men. Your tango is the shorter of the two and is wearing a green shirt, according to our spotters. We'll insert you at the near end of the block, then drive past to the far end. Bruce will be talking you through, and you can call on him if things go wrong and you need backup. Insert your earpiece now so you can test it."

I inserted the earpiece and tested the equipment. Outside the van, the road was slick with puddles from the morning's storm, and the sky was low with heavy clouds that promised more rain. We passed a massive government billboard which had been defaced so that it read "Department of Homeland *In*Security: See-Say *Rats and snitches!*" A red-and-white stop sign now stated, "STOP *President Hawke*". Had there always been this much anti-government feeling, or was I only noticing it now, because of what I'd learned last night?

The van dropped me off at a rusting old bus stop in a low-end residential area. A block of small houses stretched ahead of me through a silver haze left by the rain. I walked up the sidewalk toward the two men ambling side by side in the distance. As the white van passed them, the shorter of the two men looked up and turned his head to watch it drive by. He was obviously on his guard. Would he be checking me out carefully, too? I could take him from the front or let them both pass by and then shoot him in the back. The van paused in the distance before driving around a corner and out of sight. The man glanced back again and seemed reassured. From where he was, he wouldn't be able to see Bruce, who would already be in position behind the cover of a car, or wall, or some thick shrubbery. But Bruce would see both men clearly through the magnification of his optics.

"I'm in position, Blue, with clear sightlines. Copy me?" said Bruce's voice in my ear. The volume level that I'd set in the noisy van was too loud for this quiet street, it hurt my ears, but there was no way I could fiddle with it now. That would be a dead giveaway that I was wearing an earpiece.

"Copy," I muttered.

"Your tango is the man on the left — your left — in green."

"Copy that."

The distance between me and the two men was narrowing. A shot to the neck or the exposed section of chest would be best. Then he'd be taken up by another team. *Interviewed and debriefed.* My steps slowed involuntarily. I just wanted to get this over with.

"You are good to go, Blue. We are hot."

I needed another few meters. The dart gun was most accurate at short range. At distances of more than about ten meters, the effect of drop on the dart made it too unpredictable for my liking. I walked closer, dipping my right hand into my denim bag.

A heavy dread was building inside me, drying my mouth and closing my throat. Something was wrong. I shifted my glance from the green-shirted tango to his companion. And my eyes took in what my subconscious had already registered at some level.

The man on the right, the taller man, was Quinn. And the tango at his side — I had a sudden flash of a man on a porch, holding the leads of two dogs — was his brother.

Chapter 25

Really Bad and Even Worse

Perhaps Quinn registered me at the same moment, because he stopped dead and stared back at me, the expression on his face transforming from surprise to puzzlement to anger in a second.

I stopped, too. Feet glued to the sidewalk, mere meters from them both. A trembling was moving through my body, a panic taking hold of my mind. What was I supposed to do?

"Quinn?" said Connor, looking from his brother to me, clearly puzzled. Not yet alarmed.

"You told them? About me, about him? That was what you had to do last night after I left? That was why you wanted to me to go?" Quinn hissed at me.

"I didn —" I began, my voice high and breathy, but Bruce shouted in my ear.

"Do it, Blue. Do it now. Your orders are to take the shot. Drop him!"

"Jinxy! Don't do it. It's my brother. He's not a terrorist, not a rabid," Quinn pleaded, reaching out as if to stay my hand.

I looked down at it, saw that my hand gripped the dart gun. When had I pulled it out of my bag?

"Jinxy, please. For me." Quinn.

"You'd better take the shot, Blue." Bruce.

"No." Me.

"What's going on here?" Connor.

"Because if you don't," said Bruce, his voice low and menacing. "I will."

"No!"

"I'll take him down, and I've got live ammo. And it'll be a pleasure." Only I could hear Bruce. Only I knew the real extent of the threat.

Quinn's words from the previous night were reverberating through me. *Everything revolves around fear.*

"You know what they'll do to him, Jinxy, you *know*!" Quinn was desperate.

Enhanced interrogation techniques. Tried for treason.

"But you know, Blue, I might not hit the *tango*. I'm not as good a shot as you. You know how I tend to pull to the left."

Still I hesitated.

"I might aim for the tango and take out your leprechaun by mistake. And wouldn't that be a tragedy? But at least I'd see some splash and know how to correct my aim for the next shot. Two birds with, well, not one stone, but one opportunity."

A new flash — Quinn, lying bleeding on the sidewalk. Lying dead. I couldn't let it happen. I lifted my dart-gun.

"No!" Quinn stepped in front of his brother, who thrust him aside.

My heart was thudding in my throat, my outstretched hand trembling. I didn't know what to do. If I darted Connor, they'd take him in for questioning. Quinn would hate me. I'd lose him for sure. But if I didn't, Bruce would fire. He would drop Quinn's brother and maybe even Quinn himself. Either way, I lost. And Quinn lost. It was a choice between really bad and even worse.

It's not about them, it's about us. It's not what we're prepared to allow to happen to them.

"I'm counting to three, Blue, then I'll take the shot for you. One …"

Choose, Jinxy, choose now.

"Two … I mean it!"

It's about what we're prepared to do, who we're prepared to become.

"And …"

As Bruce said, "Three", I fired.

Connor folded in on himself and crumpled to the ground, the dart sticking from his neck.

"Bitch!" said Quinn. The gray eyes blazed with hatred at my betrayal now.

Have I told you, Jinxy, that I love you?

Quinn glanced back, noted the advancing black Hummer and the white van behind it, looked down at his brother, realized that he'd never be able to carry him, and ran straight past me. I stood trembling on the spot, my knees locked to stop me collapsing, watching as Connor was hauled like a sack of potatoes into the black Hummer.

"Blue! Blue!"

I twisted around. The white van had cut off Quinn's escape. Bruce and the driver were wrestling a thrashing Quinn inside. Fiona was suddenly at my side, dragging me back by the elbow and shoving me inside the van, too. She pushed me into a seat. And then I was opposite Quinn again, just I had been on the first day we met. Straining against the plastic cable ties which bound his hands behind his back, he glared at me. His face was a rictus of rage. The van pulled off with a lurch. I stared down at his checkered sneakers, at the dart-gun in my gloved hand, lying limply in the pink satin of my lap.

"You promised you wouldn't. I trusted you!" Quinn snarled

at me.

He thought I'd ratted on him, that I'd told Sarge when and where he'd be meeting his brother.

"I didn't!"

"How would they know otherwise?"

"Shut up!" Bruce elbowed him hard in the ribs.

"Are you going to kill me too now?"

"Can be arranged," said Bruce. "Easy."

"Cool it, Bruce," said Fiona. "No one is shooting anyone."

Yet.

"You are going to be confined to your quarters, specialist," Fiona said to Quinn. "We have some questions to ask you."

They were going to interrogate Quinn. *Interview and debrief.*

"About leaving the Academy compound."

"I had permission. I was granted leave to visit my sick grandmother."

"Only you didn't visit your granny. You've been consorting with a known traitor."

"He's not a traitor!"

Quinn struggled against Bruce and kicked out savagely at Fiona and me. Fiona managed to pull her legs out of the way, but a black-and-white sneaker connected hard with my shin. Bruce twisted to face Quinn and pressed the muzzle of his sidearm against Quinn's temple.

"Sit still or I'll shoot you myself. You know I want to."

"Go to hell!" Quinn spat out. He lunged upwards, shouting at me, "You don't even know the half of it. Should I tell you what else they did?"

Fiona nodded at Bruce. His thumb moved the safety catch off.

Without a moment's hesitation, I lifted my dart gun and shot Quinn in the chest. The outrage had not yet faded from his eyes when he slumped forward. I reached out both hands, steadied him and pushed him back gently into his seat.

Bruce eased the safety back on and glared at me.

"I'm guessing there will be some questions for you, too, Blue," said Fiona.

"Yeah, what the hell was he talking about?" demanded Bruce.

I said nothing. I was doing tactical breathing to put the brakes on my rising panic. I needed to think. Hard.

I'm trusting you, Jinxy, with my life.

Chapter 26

Dirty Rat

The sun was setting, staining the sky with streaks of vermillion and violet, as we returned to the ASTA headquarters. Quinn was beginning to come around. He blinked blearily at me, shook his head and seemed to register where he was and what had happened. Who had done it. He glared at me and then made a rush to leap out of the van as soon as the door slid open. He toppled against a seat and was hauled back onto his feet by Bruce and Fiona, who half-supported and half-dragged him, tripping and stumbling, out of the van and up the ramp into the transport bay.

I followed behind, my stomach churning, my mind racing, my eyes on the ground. Leya was waiting for us in the bay with Cameron standing a little way behind her. Had they heard about our mission?

"You're back," said Leya, rubbing a finger over the tattoo on her temple. Her face wore an odd expression — somewhere between satisfaction and resignation.

"Another successful mission by our unit," said Bruce, releasing his hold on Quinn to blow the smoking barrel of an imaginary gun.

Quinn sagged against Fiona then slid to his knees.

"Pitiful." Sarge exited the armory, walked toward our little group, and stared down at Quinn with contempt etched across his features.

"Fiona, my office for a mission debrief. Bruce, haul his ass to his quarters and confine him there. Stand guard until I send further instructions."

"Yes, sir," said Bruce, yanking Quinn to his feet.

"Leya, you'd better help him with the prisoner. Then go advise Ms. Roth of developments and report to my office — we have a lot to chat about. Blue, I don't know why you're standing there like a deer in the headlights. Return your weapon to the armory and then go to your quarters. And stay there."

"Yes, sir," I said, then asked Bruce, "Do you want me to check your weapons in for you?" I didn't like the idea of him being armed while he was with Quinn.

"No. I might need them," said Bruce.

"Sir?" I appealed to Sarge, but he was already turning to leave with Fiona.

"Don't you hurt him," I whispered furiously at Bruce.

"Leya, some help here?" Bruce said.

Quinn was half a foot taller than him and still not steady on his feet.

"Coming," said Leya. Her brows drew together as she laid a hand briefly on my arm. "I decided I'd wait and see what happened first. Maybe then I wouldn't have to —" She cut herself off, then continued, "Because he's a nice guy, and I'm sorry, Jinx. I really am. But it's my job."

She moved to the other side of Quinn, and she and Bruce led him away. His right foot dragged behind him, and the sneaker slipped off and lay on the dirty concrete floor. I walked over and picked it up, still puzzling over Leya's words. Cameron came to stand next to me, and we watched them disappear through the door while he cleaned his glasses on a Kleenex. His face looked bare without the specs.

"I'm confused. What on earth did Leya mean?"

Cameron, his unfocused gaze still on Leya, spoke softly. "She knows."

I glanced up at him. For once, his face wasn't impassive. He looked sad.

"Knows what?" I asked.

"Everything." He sighed, putting his glasses back on. "She's a mole."

Those three words were a punch to the gut.

A stream of images flowed through my mind. Leya, always quizzing everyone on their politics, always fishing for their views. Leya, texting about our ratting mission — intentionally testing to see if everyone in intel could keep a secret, and later ratting on Quinn's warning? Leya, chatting with Roberta Roth down a deserted hallway, smiling and joking, "She only wanted to know how I'm getting along with the job". Leya, having no family visits — was she even a teenager? Leya, never as good a shot as the rest of us, not good enough, really, to have earned her Game score or been recruited for the unit. Had she even actually shot Juan in the simulation? Perhaps he had simply crushed a green paintball and smeared it on himself, all part of the setup. Leya, being supportive and understanding and encouraging me through all my doubts and struggles. Had it all been an act? Had she cared for me at all, or only pretended to be my friend so she could help me be the best little shooter in all of ASTA?

I clenched my teeth when I thought about how she had been all sympathetic to me after my bust-up with Quinn, all the while fishing for the reasons. And last night, coming into my room without waiting to be asked in, glancing at the side table, seeing Quinn's phone. It all clicked into place.

And Cameron. Quiet Cameron. Observant Cameron. Always shadowing Leya — listening, watching, thinking.

"Hurry," he said.

I grabbed him and kissed him on the cheek, whispered, "Thank you!" and set off, running.

Chapter 27

In Case of Emergency

I darted past the armory through the doors and decon unit, and sprinted towards the northeast wing. The sneaker and dart gun inside my denim bag bounced against my side. It was dinnertime so the hallways were mostly empty, but my little-girl getup and frantic pace still attracted one or two curious glances. I was just in time to see Leya and Bruce lead their prisoner through the entrance to his wing.

Quinn seemed steadier on his feet now. Good.

I ducked under the secret staircase and waited until Leya re-emerged and walked off in the direction of Sarge's office. No doubt the backstabbing, double-crossing sneak of a dirty rat-snitching bitch was off to raise the alarm. That gave me an idea.

It was an emergency — a good time, if ever there was one, to break some glass. I waited a few more minutes to give Leya enough time to be well away from this section of the compound, then took the dart gun out my bag and slammed its butt into the glass front panel of the fire alarm. As soon as I pulled the white T-handle down, a siren screamed through the compound. I picked the longest, sharpest shard of glass up off the floor and tucked it into Quinn's sneaker inside my bag; it never hurt to have extra weapons.

I pressed myself against the underside of the stairs as a group of people passed on their way to the nearest exit. A minute later, a couple of cadets and a trainer from the blue unit exited the northeast wing.

"Do you think it's another drill?" one asked.

"Got to be."

"Damn! I'll never get back to sleep after this. And my shift starts at midnight."

I stowed my weapon and waited a little longer, hoping that Bruce would come out and leave Quinn locked inside — that would be entirely like him. Even if he dragged Quinn out with him, I could dart Bruce and try to get Quinn away in the confusion of the evacuation. But after a few minutes with no one else emerging, I figured Bruce didn't intend to come out. Maybe he rated Sarge's orders to stay put higher than a fire drill. That figured. Bruce would rate Sarge's orders higher than a direct command from God.

I slipped out from under the staircase and entered the northeast wing, aware that my movements would be picked up by the cameras. I would need a cover story after this to account for my actions. I could say that I was checking whether my team-member had needed help with evacuating himself and his prisoner. I ran up the stairs to Quinn's first-floor room and pounded on the door.

"Bruce! It's me, Blue. Open up — there's a fire!"

The door was flung open, and I was looking into Quinn's gray eyes.

"You!" he spat out.

"Not now, okay?" I said.

"You betrayed us. You shot my brother, you shot me!"

"I darted you both, there's a difference," I said, stepping around him to where Bruce stood with his sidearm pressed against Quinn's back.

"What was that — back there?" I said to Bruce. "I thought you were on the mission as backup to protect me."

"I *was* protecting you. What do you think would have happened to you if you'd wimped out? They're already suspicious of your relationship with this one." Bruce gave Quinn a sharp poke in the back with the pistol, turning him away from the door.

I smacked his hand away. "What is it with you and guns?" I snapped.

"I'm a professional marksman," said Bruce, kicking the door closed and gesturing Quinn over to sit on the bed. "Guns is what I do."

"And are you a professional snitch, too?"

"A snitch?"

"Like Leya."

"Leya's not a snitch," Bruce said, sounding appalled.

"Oh yes, she is. She's in Sarge's office now, giving her report on her precious team members. Guess *Squad before Blood* isn't her motto."

"She wouldn't!"

"She's a plant, a mole. She's been playing us since the beginning. Running to them and telling tales about all of us."

"That is … Dude, that is so bad, I don't even have a word for it!" Bruce looked genuinely furious. His face was red, his thick brows pulled down into a single line, and the hand without the weapon was clenched in a fist. "She broke the code!"

"Hey, I guess she was only following orders," I needled.

"You think — Sarge?"

"Of course Sarge."

"No. No, man." Bruce looked like everything he'd believed in was turning out to be false, everyone he'd trusted had turned out to be undeserving. Yeah, welcome to the real world, Brucey-baby.

"You should go give Leya a piece of your mind," I urged. "If you're quick enough, you might even catch her before she reaches Sarge."

"Yeah! I will, I'll go right now!" His hand was already on the door handle when he stopped and turned back to face me, smiling ruefully and shaking his head. "Nice try, Blue. But I'm not falling for it."

Cursing wildly inside my head, I forced my face to stay neutral.

"Fine, it's no skin off my back — I haven't done anything wrong. But I thought you really valued loyalty."

"I do. Loyalty to my squad" — I made a disbelieving noise — "loyalty to my country and to the people who protect its citizens."

"Oh, please," said Quinn. "Protect its interests, maybe. But its citizens? Not so much."

"Who asked you for your opinion, you commie traitor?"

"Yeah, shut up," I added, partly because I didn't want Quinn to provoke Bruce any further, and partly to lull Bruce into thinking I was still on his side. "You haven't been out there like we have, risking our lives to shoot infected rats and take down terrorists. We've probably saved a bunch of lives, protecting and serving our government, and its people."

"Yeah!" Bruce held up his left hand for a fist-bump, and though it pained me to do it, I touched my knuckles to his.

"You are such a fool!" said Quinn. "*Protecting and serving your government.* I wonder if you'd still feel that way if you knew the truth."

What truth? Was there more to know? He'd said something last night about there being something else I needed to see.

"Don't listen to him, Blue. He's trying to mess with your head, to distract you."

It *was* distracting me.

"Should I tell you?" Quinn said.

"Ignore him, Blue, just ignore him. It's all BS." Bruce pointed a finger at Quinn. "And you, O'Riley — shut up, or I'll make you!"

I gave myself a mental shake. I could ask Quinn what he meant later, when Bruce had been dealt with. I forced my thoughts back to the present, back to the vague plan I'd devised for getting us out of here, a plan which began with getting Quinn's hands free and overpowering Bruce.

I twisted my mouth in a sneer and spoke to Quinn.

"And you look ridiculous with only one shoe. The other one's in there." I took a step closer to Quinn and tossed my bag casually onto the bed beside him. "Put it on, they'll be coming for you soon."

He glared at me, twisted his shoulders to show me the cable ties snaring his wrists. "In case you hadn't noticed, my hands are tied."

"Whatever," I said, and with my back momentarily to Bruce, I stared hard into Quinn's furious eyes, then at the bag, then back again, before slowly turning back around.

"And they're going to stay tied," Bruce snarled at Quinn.

I stepped closer to Bruce, trying to block his view of Quinn, trying to keep his attention on me.

All the while my eyes were scanning the room, noticing objects and distances and potentials. Bruce, armed with a sidearm — between me and the door, blocking my exit. Me — between Bruce and Quinn, blocking Bruce's sight-lines. Bruce's rifle — leaning up against the wall to the far side of the desk. Quinn's phone, loaded with the incriminating video and who knew what else — visible through the open door to the bathroom, lying on the slab beside the basin. The clock on the shelf beside the door, ticking away the minutes impossibly fast. Bright lights blazing through the window as the compound lights switched on in the darkening evening outside.

"Maybe I should help him put on his shoe?" I said, knowing how Bruce would respond, but playing for time.

"No you shouldn't. If he doesn't like wearing only one shoe, he can kick the other one off and go barefoot. *That* won't kill him."

How much more time would Quinn need to saw through the bindings? Had he even found the shard of glass tucked inside the shoe?

"And you don't think we should evacuate? There might be a fire or something."

"Nah, I don't reckon it's real. Wouldn't put it past you to have triggered it yourself." He waved the gun at me. "Get away from him, Blue. I don't like you so close to him — he might try something. Or you might."

"Sure," I said, holding up my hands in mock surrender and brushing my front against him as I moved to his other side. I needed to keep his attention on me. "You know, Bruce" — I moved in close, looked directly into his eyes and smiled sweetly — "for someone who's so *hot* on squad loyalty, you have some major trust issues." I tapped a finger against his chest on the last three words.

Bruce grinned. "Oh Blue-baby," he began, just as I heard a soft pop from behind him. His mouth sagged open, he slumped heavily against me and we both tumbled slowly to the carpet.

"Shit!" said Quinn, his horrified gaze moving from the dart sticking out of Bruce's back, to the gun in his own hands. He dropped the weapon as if it had stung him.

"Don't just stand there — help me!" I wheezed.

Chapter 28

Lights Out

Bruce's tranquilized body was a dead weight crushing me to the floor.

"What the hell is going on here?" Quinn said.

With a grunt and a shove, I managed to roll Bruce off me. The upper-body strength training had come in useful after all. Gasping, I snatched Bruce's handgun from where it had fallen from his nerveless hands, and placed it on the desk. I kicked aside the dart gun. It was empty of darts now — no point in hanging on to it. Then I grabbed the rifle.

"Are you going to shoot me now?"

"Don't be ridiculous," I said, pushing past him and stalking into the bathroom.

I grabbed his phone, tossed it onto the hard tile floor and smashed it to smithereens with the rifle butt.

"What are you doing?" He sounded bewildered.

"Destroying evidence," I said, kicking the flusher repeatedly with my foot as I dropped the pieces into the toilet. "Besides, you can't take it with you. They'll use it to track you. Here, take over with this."

Quinn gathered up the few remaining fragments from the floor and studied them. "That's why I didn't take my phone with me today. I left it behind. So they couldn't track where I went."

He unrolled a massive length of toilet paper, stuffed it in the toilet bowl and flushed the remaining pieces of plastic and glass, while I walked back into the bedroom and bent down to snag the Leatherman multi-tool Bruce always wore on his belt.

"Honestly, Quinn, you don't think they can use your microchipped bracelet to track you outside the compound as well as inside?"

"I wrote and inserted some code to block it on the surveillance system before I left. But maybe the hack didn't work."

"Or maybe they had a spook follow you." They might be trained on many things in Intel, but how to spot when you're being tailed obviously wasn't one of them.

"Yeah, or maybe you told them where to expect Connor and me!"

"I didn't rat on you," I said, enunciating each word, but I could tell he didn't believe me.

I flipped open the wire-cutter attachment and severed the ID bracelet. Quinn's hand felt warm, even through my latex gloves. As I tossed the thin metal band aside, I asked the question that refused to be silenced.

"What did you mean, earlier, about 'the truth'?"

He looked at me as if weighing up some decision, then said, "About how your father died."

That was unexpected.

"I already know what happened. He was killed by terrorists, in a civilian plague attack."

"Yes, but that's not how he died."

"What do you mean? I saw footage of it. Roth showed me." My fingers fiddled with the tool, opening and closing it.

"Did she show you all of it? All the way to the end? Or did she stop before the climax?"

I remembered the final freeze-frame of my father's twisted grimace. Had there been more footage? Had something happened after that moment?

"He died of the plague." I didn't know who I was trying hardest to convince — Quinn, or myself.

"He didn't. He would've, sure, but he didn't. He didn't even die inside the bank. He died outside on the sidewalk. The terrorists sent him out, as a virus bomb, and he kneeled down and started rocking back and forth, saying, 'Help me,' over and over."

My throat choked tight with grief and panic as I saw again the images of him pulling at his hair, scratching at his skin, rocking and keening, "Help me, help me."

"And then they shot him. Shot him in the street like a rabid dog. That's who they really are — the government you think is here to protect its citizens. That's what they do to a sick man. They shoot him."

"How do you know?" I demanded, my voice a low, tight rasp.

"I saw the rest of the footage. Not very reassuring, that — to see police killing sick people, innocent US civilians, at close range. I guess that's why they confiscated all the footage and banned the news stations and websites from showing it."

I was battling to catch my breath, battling to make sense of what he'd just told me. I couldn't believe it was true.

"Roth said the media embargoes were to protect public morale."

Quinn rolled his eyes at that. "I guess it's also when they came up with the idea of using snipers to take down M&Ms, so they could be removed from the scene quickly and quietly in ambulances. And also using snipers to dart suspects who could be hauled off to detention centers. And who better than snipers who look more like teens or" — he cast a contemptuous look at my girly-pink dress — "like little kids. No one would suspect them.

Plus, they're not government agents, right? Not directly. And deniability is important if word gets out. So you" — he pointed a finger at me — "are defending the people who killed your father."

If Bruce were awake, he'd say this was a lie, pure BS. But it wasn't. My shocked and sluggish brain was picking up speed again, making connections.

It was the truth. It had to be, because I'd never told Quinn that my father was killed in a bank. How could he know that if he hadn't seen the footage?

I cursed. I couldn't deal with this now. My immediate priority was to get us both out of here. I returned the multi-tool to Bruce's belt, then I snatched Quinn's sneaker off the bed and tossed it pointedly on the carpet beside his bare foot.

"We need to get moving. They know, alright? They know everything — about you, about your brother, obviously. And we're running out of time. Any minute now they'll realize the fire alarm is a hoax, and they'll come to haul your ass into lockup. And then your interrogation will begin. Then they'll want to know what I know. We've got to run, get out of here, now. You heard me tell Bruce — Leya has been spying on us the whole time."

"Are you sure it was her, and not you?"

"Quinn, there isn't time for this. Even now they'll be taking your brother to wherever it is they do those interrogations."

"Do you know where that is?" he asked, his wary eyes studying me with lie-detector intensity.

"How the hell would I know? You're more likely to have found something in your intel work."

He shook his head. "Not yet. I was still working on trying to find out. That's when I found the interrogation videos. I thought maybe you snipers would know where your victims get taken."

"All I know is that we need to get out of here before we find out firsthand. Try and help your brother. Contact his associates."

"Oh, so now you want to save Connor? Why the hell did you take him down, then? You know what they'll do to him, and you helped them capture him."

"I was trying to save your hide."

Quinn made a dismissive noise and bent over to put on his shoe. I had known, even as I sent the dart into Connor, that I was putting a lethal round into any trust or respect Quinn might have for me. But knowing it didn't stop it hurting.

"Believe what you like," I snapped. I knew that from Quinn's perspective, it must seem like I'd betrayed him, snitched on his brother, and darted them both. But there just wasn't time now to go into the details of how I'd had my hand forced, how I'd darted each of them rather than risk having them shot. Explanations would have to wait until we were out of here. "But I'm leaving. And you need to decide now: you want to wait for them to come get you, or do you want to get out of here?"

"Are we simply going to stroll out the front door?" said Quinn.

I peered out of the sealed window. There was no one in the floodlit area below — everyone would be gathered at the assembly point under the flagpole in front of the main building. I grabbed Bruce's rifle. It was a long-range, medium caliber bolt-action rifle, mounted with a telescopic scope and a silencing suppressor. Now I was pleased that Bruce had kept his weapon. I checked the small internal magazine. Five rounds were loaded.

I sent two quick rounds at an angle through the window, shattering it into pieces which rained out from the frame. A few shards bounced back into the room, and one clipped me on the cheek. Ignoring the sharp pinch of pain and Quinn's startled yelp, I bashed the dangling fragments free of the window frame with the rifle-butt, stuck my head out to scan the area and then pulled back inside.

"It's a full floor down, can you make it?"

"Of course, but what about the guards? The security floodlights and the electric fence?"

"Someone once told me that there's a weak spot, an exposed bit of flesh, on every target. You just have to find it and hit it," I said, peering out through my eyepiece.

I swept the scope slowly across the area, looking for a way, searching for a target. I had only three rounds left. I would have to make each of them count. My scope's reticles rested on a guard standing in the closest watchtowers. No, not going to happen. I wasn't killing anyone tonight. I wasn't killing anyone ever, if I could help it.

I glanced at the banks of brilliant floodlights, keeping it brief so as not to blind myself. But it was enough to tell me that shooting at them wouldn't be much help. Each floodlight consisted of several rows of dazzlingly bright rectangular globes. I had only three rounds left, and knocking out a trio of globes wouldn't give us enough darkness to make our escape. The lights were too powerful. Powerful … power … there! The main power line which connected the compound to the electricity grid was about one inch thick and about 200 meters away.

It would have been a relatively easy shot with an automatic weapon — I could easily have strafed across the line several times, sure of hitting it. With a rifle, it would be a million-dollar shot. Still, this was a sniper's rifle, and I was the best damn sniper in our unit. *Failure is not an option.*

I sat on a clear section of the sill, wedged myself against the window frame, braced the rifle against my knee, slid off the safety catch and chambered a round.

"What're you —"

"Shh!"

I had to get it right. I couldn't afford to miss. I did my best to estimate elevation and distance, and I scanned for signs of wind.

I ran through my mil-dot calculations and doped my scope. Then I locked the stock against my cheek, and eased my finger onto the trigger.

Focus. Aim. Breathe.

Squeeze.

The rifle recoiled into my shoulder with a muted crack. A small burst of sparks shot up off the power cord. One of the banks of floodlights flickered, but the compound ground remained brightly lit. I trained my scope on the power line and saw that it was fizzing and sparking at one spot. I had just nicked the top of the line.

Only two rounds left.

One of the guards lifted his binoculars to study the power line. We had mere seconds before we were discovered.

I cleared the spent casing and reloaded. Aimed a fraction lower. Fired.

This time I missed completely. I glanced at Quinn, saw my panic reflected in his eyes.

"Only one round left," I said.

I could hardly get the words past the knot in my throat. My mind was racing, my heart pounding against my ribs. My dope-scoping calculations wouldn't compute in the frantic agitation of my mind.

Stop!

Just stop and breathe. Breathe again.

Somewhere inside of me, in the muscle memory of my arms and fingers, I knew how to take this shot. I didn't need the math — I had the muscle memory of a thousand shots. This was a rat's eye, a corner of the letter on a cheerleader's vest, a small square inch of flesh on Sarge's neck.

I relaxed into the rifle. My shoulders dropped. My cheek caressed the stock. My breath sighed, paused. My finger embraced the trigger. And hugged.

A shower of sparks erupted from the cord as it split and spooled down, sparking and crackling, thrashing on the ground like a giant electric snake. All around was the sound of a hundred computers, lights and machines losing power. And then all was dark.

"Quickly! There'll be backup generators. They'll fire up soon," I urged Quinn, who was standing, still with shock.

I tossed the empty rifle aside and grabbed Bruce's sidearm. "*Go*," I said, pushing Quinn towards the window.

Quinn hesitated, clearly reluctant to turn his back on me when I was armed. I sighed. He really didn't trust me at all. I checked the safety was on, then turned the weapon around and handed it to Quinn. He took it automatically, but held it wrong and eyed it like it was a live, poisonous scorpion.

"I don't want it."

"Then ditch it somewhere as a false trail. And try not to shoot yourself."

I moved to the window and clambered over the frame, bracing first one then the other foot on the ledge outside. Then I jumped, landing hard on one knee. I'd have a bruise there to match the one on my shin. I stood up and faced Quinn, who had landed with a soft thump in the dirt beside me.

He stared at me for a long moment. In the dark, I couldn't see the expression in his eyes, but I felt his fingers gently touch the cut on my cheek, trace my lips, as if he was memorizing my face. "When you're over the fence, hit the ground running, and keep running. I'll be right behind you," I said.

"So you're coming with me?" His tone was unmistakably reluctant.

Until that very moment, I'd just assumed we'd flee together. I had nowhere else to go. I could hardly head for home, and surely his brother's secret organization must have a safe house somewhere? I wanted a chance to explain what had happened today, to make him understand, perhaps even to help rescue Connor. But it was such a lukewarm, halfhearted invitation that every fiber in my being recoiled from accepting it.

"Screw you, Quinn O'Riley!" He could take his half-assed, unenthusiastic offer and shove it up his rebel ass. "The safest place you could be is with me. You may not believe it, but you need me much more than I need you. You're going to have a posse of trained spooks and shooters on your tail, and you don't even know how to hold a gun, let alone shoot one. Good luck out there."

"I'm not helpless," he snapped.

"Right. Whatever. Just go already."

When he hesitated, I said again, "Just go!"

"How do I know you won't raise the alarm as soon as I move? And send the pack of ratters after me? Or follow me yourself so you can tell them where I am? Like you did today."

"You don't know. But you're the one holding the gun. So if you really don't trust me, shoot me now." I was out of patience.

"I guess I don't have a choice."

For a second I thought he meant he'd have to shoot me. But then, without a word, he turned and sprinted off. I watched as he ran into the night, away from the building, away from me.

I shook off my aching daze and set off after him at a different angle, so I'd hit the fence at a different spot — doubling the target, halving the odds of being hit. I was still about twenty-five meters from the fence when I heard the generators fire up. Lights flooded the compound in white brilliance. I ducked behind the inadequate protection of a slatted bench beside a potted tree.

A glance to the side confirmed that Quinn was on the other side of the fence, clinging to the mesh with the gun still held awkwardly in one hand. He'd cleared the electrified strands at the top while the power was out, but was now still about four meters off the ground, frozen in place. Clearly visible in the wash of light. At any moment, one of the guards in the security huts would see him. If Quinn moved, it would be sure to attract their attention.

The guard with the binoculars switched on a massive spotlight. I followed with my gaze as he began sweeping it slowly across the compound building, pausing on the shattered first-floor window.

I stared at the ASTA building behind me. Bright light shone from its sealed windows. Inside the security cameras would once again be rolling. Even now, Sarge and Fiona and maybe even Roth would be searching for me. Compiling questions for their Angel of Death. I could make up a story about how Quinn had overpowered Bruce, compelled me to take out the power, forced me out the window, threatened to kill me or take me as a hostage.

Maybe they'd believe me and maybe they wouldn't. If they didn't, I'd be the one tied to the chair in that room, with a sack over my head and fists pounding down on me. If they did, I'd be sent straight back to shooting. No way would they allow me to leave now. I'd have come full circle.

I turned my head to stare at the fence and allowed my gaze to reach into the darkness beyond. Freedom lay on the other side of that fence. Danger, yes, but also freedom. A chance to see my family again. And Quinn. Could I make it? In seconds, I ran through various scenarios in my head.

The current was sure to be pulsing through the strands of electric fencing again, so I'd have to figure a way around that. I didn't think my thin polka-dot pattern latex gloves would give me any protection at all. My mind raced through the options as the spotlight's bright beam slid down the wall of the building and crept across the grounds of the compound.

If I'd only thought to bring along Bruce's multitool, I might have been able to make it to the fence and use it to cause a short in the circuit of electric fencing. But there was no way to go back now without being seen.

Maybe I could try creeping across to the base of one of the guard towers, climbing up to the hut, overpowering the guard somehow and leaping to the ground beyond the fence off the back of the hut, bypassing the electrified lines that way?

But even as I weighed that possibility, the moving spotlight stole inexorably towards the fence where Quinn still clung like a paralyzed monkey. One moment more and it would find him, illuminate his outline and contrast, highlight the shine of his weapon.

Another choice that wasn't really a choice.

I stood up, thrust my hands up into the air and began shouting. The spotlight swung back to pin me in a circle of cold light.

"Help!" I screamed, as loudly and as shrilly as I could, drawing all attention to me. "Help me!" I waved my arms over my head.

A trio of armed guards stormed up to me.

"On the ground! On the ground!" they yelled. "Hands behind your head!"

I stretched out on my front in the dirt, laced my hands behind my head and turned my face so that I could fix my sniper's eye on the darkness beyond the fence. In the distance, I saw the faintest flash of motion. My pirate needed just a little more time.

Thrashing about on the ground, I struggled as if about to rise, and screamed hysterically.

A punch of pain to the side of my head. A pop of light behind my eyes. I fought the blossoming darkness, squinted at the fence. Nothing. No one. Quinn was free.

My words came out as a mumble past the smile that twisted my mouth.

"What's that you say?" a guard shouted down at me.

I lay in the dirt. Stones pressed into the softness of my cheek, and fear contracted my gut. My right hand was trapped beneath my chest, and I pushed down onto it, so that my fingers could trace the circle of Quinn's silver earring beneath the soft fabric of the awful dress.

Circles never end.

"Failure — s'not an option," I repeated. "I will not quit."

End of Book I

Jinxy's story continues in Book 2 of the series, Refuse. Check out the first chapter of Refuse at the end of this book!

Would you like to be notified of my new releases and special offers? My newsletter goes out once a month (at most) and is also a great way to get book recommendations, a behind-the-scenes look at my writing and publishing processes, as well as advance notice of giveaways and free review copies. You can sign up for my author's newsletter at my website here: www.joannemacgregor.com.

If you loved this book, please consider leaving a review on your favorite online site.

Feel free to connect with me via
my website (www.joannemacgregor.com),
Facebook or Twitter (@JoanneMacg).

ACKNOWLEDGEMENTS

I would like to thank all my wonderful beta-readers for their invaluable help and feedback, and express my special gratitude to James Bristow of Magnum Shooting Academy for his patient advice on weapons and shooting — any mistakes are on me!

REFUSE
(Book Two)

Chapter 1
Eyes Open

When I open my eyes, I am blindfolded, traveling in a vehicle, with my hands tightly bound together and lying in my lap.

I know that my hands are tied because when I try to rub at the tickle of something trickling down the side of my face, both hands move together. They must be secured to something else as well, because I can only lift them as far as my chest before some restraint kicks in. I yank hard, but it holds firm.

I know that I am in a vehicle of some kind because I hear the engine and feel my body lurch against the seatbelt when it accelerates and brakes.

I know I am blindfolded because I can feel my eyelashes brush against something as I blink, and even though my eyes are open, everything is still dark and unfathomable.

Kind of like my life.

I have never seen clearly, never fully grasped what is actually happening, even when it is happening in full view and all around me. I have been like a mushroom — kept well and truly in the dark and fed a load of crap. About my father, about ASTA, about Quinn.

The tickling sensation continues. It must be blood still oozing from the place where the guard hit my head. The fog clouding my brain begins to dissolve, only to be replaced by a throbbing headache.

"Hullo?" My voice is hoarse in my dry throat.

No answer.

I am not alone in this car or van. I can sense the presence, just about hear the breathing, of someone sitting to my left. I am totally alone, though, in my predicament. I helped Quinn escape, but it came at the price of my own capture, and I suspect that things are about to get rough.

At the thought of what I know must lie ahead, my heart kicks into a faster rhythm, and a flush of adrenalin tingles through my fingers. I am not brave, just an ace with a virtual reality gaming console and a highly skilled expert with a sniper's rifle. But I have no rifle now. No rifle, no tranquilizer dart gun, not even a freaking pea-shooter. I will need to use my brain to get through the next few hours. Or days. Weeks? I swallow hard. I am more thirsty than I can ever remember being.

"Can I have some water?"

More silence.

"Please?" It can't hurt to try the magic word.

"Shut up," says a voice to my left. It is deep, male and completely unfamiliar to me. "We'll let you know when we want you to talk."

A bubble of fear releases itself from somewhere deep in the pit of my stomach and begins to rise up into my chest. I fight against it. I need to stay calm and clearheaded, concentrating on the present moment rather than on some possibly painful near future.

And the skill of staying focused is one I have in spades. Accurate marksmanship was not the only skill that we sniping cadets were trained in by our instructors at ASTA — The Advanced Skills Training Academy of the Southern Sector. I force myself to slow my breathing, pursing my lips as I exhale to allow the air to trickle out gradually. Within a minute, my heart rate steadies.

I shift my attention to my senses, determined to register any details I can about this journey and our destination. At the Academy, the cadets in our unit were also trained to be exceptional observers, drilled to notice and memorize details. It's time to kick that aspect of my instruction into gear.

The vehicle slows, turns, moves forward more slowly — down a driveway? — turns again, and then stops. The engine is turned off. Silence. The click of a seatbelt clasp and then I am yanked forward.

"Where are we?" I ask.

"Duck," says the voice.

A hand presses against the top of my head — I guess to prevent me banging it as I stumble out. So they do not want me hurt. Not yet. All pain will be inflicted deliberately and intentionally at the right time and for the purpose of extracting maximum information from me.

I drag my thoughts back to the present, force myself to concentrate on the details of our walk. Gravel crunches underfoot, then my feet are on a smoother surface — paving? I scan my senses. I can smell the sharp scent of male aftershave or deodorant coming off my captor, but nothing beyond that. The air is cool on my face, and I don't hear birds calling, so it's probably still night then.

"Four steps up," says the man.

I make out the sound of a big car or truck somewhere not too distant. I reckon we must still be in the city, off the street, perhaps at the back entrance to some building where no one will see or wonder at the appearance of a sixteen-year-old girl with long blond hair tied up in a ponytail; wearing a pink dress, a blindfold and restraints; and being hauled, stumbling, up a set of stairs.

"Where are you taking me? Who are you?"

Aftershave says nothing, just shoves me through what must be a doorway, banging my arms against its narrow frame.

"We need to take her straight up. They're already waiting." A new voice, female.

I distinguish two sets of footsteps, apart from my own, clicking against the floor — marble or tiles, judging from the hard, smooth surface — and echoing through the open space. Are we in a foyer?

It occurs to me that we haven't passed through a decontamination unit. Then I register, belatedly, that I am not wearing a respirator and, judging from the fact that the man's voice does not sound at all muffled, neither is my escort. According to President Hawke's government, the Rat Fever virus supposedly lies in wait, patient as death, on surfaces and in the air, ready to infect and reduce its human victims to gibbering, hemorrhagic bags of pus and blood. But we are not wearing even the most basic of protective masks.

We cross the open space and wait for a few moments, and then a chime sounds the arrival of an elevator. Three paces inside. The doors swish closed behind us, and I am spun around. Going up, three soft pings for three floors.

Already I am noting our route and committing it to memory, forming a picture in my mind's eye of our course through the building. The doors open, and I am tugged forward. Left on exit, twenty-one paces, right turn, a long walk of fifty paces, another right, seventeen paces, left, thirty paces and then we halt. I use the pause to memorize the route — L21, R50, R17, L30.

I hear a door open to my left, and I am pushed inside and onto a chair. Something fastens around my waist, tying me in place. A brief tug of hair at the back of my head and the blindfold is pulled off my eyes.

"Where am I?" I demand, squinching my eyes against the sudden brightness. My only answer is the sound of a slamming door and a clicking lock.

It is several moments before my eyes grow accustomed to the light and I can look around. It takes only one swift glance for me to know where I am. I have seen a room like this before. Was it just last night that I sat beside Quinn on my bed in my quarters at ASTA — my heart full of hope about the two of us, my head full of doubts about everything he had just told me — and stared with growing horror at the illicitly obtained video footage on the screen of his phone? I watched as a man I had immobilized with a tranquilizer dart was questioned and tortured in a room just like this. Perhaps it was this very room.

Now I am the one sitting under a bright light, on a steel chair bolted to the floor, in the center of an interrogation room.

Now I am the one about to be interrogated.

The story continues in *Refuse*, Book Two of the *Recoil* trilogy